T0012246

Why, for all the ha
she find him so at

Even though his brows were drawn down into a frown above that blade of a nose and the uncompromising slash of a mouth?

A mouth that she'd kissed.

Oh! Yes, she remembered that mouth kissing hers. And the utter bliss that had spread through her. The joy. And the disbelief. Because he'd seemed like a...a god, to her.

Goodness, she'd worshipped this man, once upon a time. She remembered feeling just like this. Vulnerable, and stunned that this stranger could be so close to her, in such an intimate setting.

The difference today, she suddenly perceived, was that if, back then, he'd ever frowned at her the way he was doing now, she would have been distraught. Destroyed.

The thing was, though, that although she was starting to recover the occasional memory of that girl, and how she'd felt, she was no longer the same person. It had been a bit like meeting a stranger and getting to know them. Though she was that stranger. A stranger to herself, ludicrous though that sounded. And what she'd learned about herself was that she was rather an intelligent and capable person. A person who'd become indispensable to the troupe of traveling actors who'd taken her in. A person, moreover, who could stand up to sneering tradesmen, and even barter for good deals from hard-eyed, hard-hearted moneylenders.

A person who was absolutely not going to sit here cowering while some man berated her.

Author Note

I love reading amnesia stories and have wanted to write one for ages. But I had to make sure that the story would be right for the Regency period. At last, I came up with a heroine, and a situation, that my editor was happy to see brought to the page, and have really enjoyed imagining what it would have been like in those days and bringing the plight of my heroine to life.

I have also enjoyed returning to some research about life backstage in the Regency theater. I have often written scenes taking place in the boxes, where the privileged would sit to watch performances, but have rarely been able to write about the trials and tribulations of those who made their living by entertaining the upper classes. Even the most famous, such as Joseph Grimaldi, led a very precarious existence financially.

I hope you enjoy reading the story as much as I have enjoyed researching and writing it!

ANNIE BURROWS

The Countess's Forgotten Marriage

HARLEQUIN®
HISTORICAL™

Recycling programs
for this product may
not exist in your area.

ISBN-13: 978-1-335-59600-0

The Countess's Forgotten Marriage

Copyright © 2024 by Annie Burrows

Harlequin Enterprises ULC
22 Adelaide St. West, 41st Floor
Toronto, Ontario M5H 4E3, Canada
www.Harlequin.com

Printed in U.S.A.

Annie Burrows has been writing Regency romances for Harlequin since 2007. Her books have charmed readers worldwide, having been translated into nineteen different languages, and some have gone on to win the coveted Reviewers' Choice Award from CataRomance. For more information, or to contact her, please visit annie-burrows.co.uk, or find her on Facebook at Facebook.com/annieburrowsuk.

Chapter One

She hunched her shoulders as a squall of hail rattled against the tailor's shop door. If only she could wait here until the weather improved. But she had to leave. Jack was waiting for this suit. He needed time to get into it, and for her to make any slight alterations that might be needed before he went out.

She wanted to make sure he'd look his best for the young gentlemen. It wasn't every day that people like them invited people like Jack to join them for supper.

Besides, the tailor didn't like having her in here. She wasn't the class of customer he wanted patronizing his establishment. And he'd made it clear that he didn't want his wealthier, male clients seeing a woman like her loitering by the counter.

So she gritted her teeth, yanked open the shop door and darted out before she could think better of it. And ran full tilt into a passer-by. A man. He swore at her as she cannoned off his larger, stronger body and smacked into the railings.

'Look where you're going, you stupid woman,' he snarled as he stalked off.

This was the trouble with London. People were so…rude. So aggressive. Ever since they'd arrived here, in September, so they'd be set up by the time theatres began opening for the little season, she'd felt increasingly uncomfortable. During the summer, out in the provinces, being part of an acting troupe had been challenging, yes, but it had also been fun. Once back in London, she'd discovered there was a whole new aspect to the trade. She could see that there was bound to be a certain amount of professional rivalry between actors, since they had to compete with each other for the prize roles. But it hadn't taken her long to discover that it sometimes went further than that. As far as downright animosity, in some cases. Some actors nursed grudges for years, not only against what they considered the unfairness of theatre managers who held so much power, but also against fellow actors who'd done better than they had the previous season. And the tailors, and landlords, and, oh, just about everyone in this overcrowded, noisy, dirty city seemed to be cross about something.

She rubbed at her shoulder, which had taken the brunt of the impact with the railings. Then glanced down at the precious package containing Jack's smart new suit of evening clothes. The brown paper was intact. No sign of a tear, thank goodness. That would have been the last straw after all she'd been through to extract it from the tailor's shop. He hadn't been willing to surrender it until she'd forked over every single penny. No credit for the likes of her and Jack. She'd had to go to the Frenchman who ran his business from a pub near Sadler's Wells to arrange a loan, which had taken up far too much time. She supposed she could have accepted the exorbitant terms he'd first offered. Because, she knew, he'd thought she looked green enough to think it was a fair rate of interest, and assumed he could fleece her. To be fair, she *did* have a rather stupid-looking face. Big, pale eyes, and a sort of…helpless look about her mouth.

But she soon showed him she wasn't as stupid as she looked. That she knew exactly what he'd charged other actors in similar need of short-term loans. And then, when she'd told him that she was taking out the loan on *Jack's* behalf…well, he'd soon changed his tune. He knew how talented Jack was. He knew he'd recoup the loan, with interest. Eventually.

And speaking of Jack, he must be pacing the floor by now, wondering where on earth she was. She'd wasted enough time nursing her bruises, and wool-gathering.

She pushed herself off the railings and scurried along as fast as she could. She needed to make up for all the time she'd lost, arguing with the tailor, then going halfway across town and bartering for the loan of enough ready cash to pay the bill, then going back to the tailor again. So that a task which should have taken half an hour at most had ended up consuming half the day. And it was just typical of the sort of day she'd been having, that she hadn't gone more than a few yards before slipping on the icy pavement and pitching forward to land flat on her face. She lay sprawled for a moment, all the breath knocked from her body. The parcel she'd been clutching to her chest had broken her fall, to some extent, but her elbows and knees stung where they'd smacked into the hard paving stones. Someone nearby chuckled. A man. The same one? She wouldn't be a bit surprised.

Well, she was glad that her clumsiness was entertaining someone! Her cheeks felt hot as she got to her feet, unaided, since the man who'd laughed when she'd fallen over was nowhere to be seen. Typical. Men laughed, and hurt people, and walked off without a backwards glance. That was what they did.

How did she know that? She tried to delve into the murky mist that swirled in her brain where most people had memories, but as usual, nothing solid materialized. Apart, that was, from a surge of resentment, closely followed by a wave of grief. A wave that began to swirl faster and faster, like a whirlpool. Sucking her down.

She had to pull back, or she'd drown. She just knew it. It had happened before, when something had upset her, or someone started asking personal questions which she had no idea how to answer.

Or, if it wasn't the whirlpool that tried to drown her in an awful black misery, it would be the terror. She preferred the terror, in some ways. Because she reared back from that one, instinctively.

But the whirlpool...that one was harder to deal with.

She reached out with one gloved hand and grabbed hold of the nearest railing to steady herself. Then stood there, looking at the railing, and just breathing.

In.

She wasn't in any danger.

Out.

She was standing on a street in London.

In.

She was safe.

Out.

She wasn't alone.

In.

She had friends.

Out.

Lord, but it was cold today.

There. She'd had a sensible, relevant thought. It was amazing how well this technique of just breathing in and out, and concentrating on where she was, rather than where she might have been once, worked. She hadn't believed it would help when Jack had first urged her to try it when one of these blank, blackish episodes came over her. When that vague resentment, and grief, and pain washed over her like a tide. Or when panic threatened to take her by the throat and choke her. But because she trusted him she'd thought that there would be no harm in trying it, to please him. It could hardly make her feel any worse, could it?

Not usually, no. But today, while she was breathing in and out, striving for calm, she became aware that the shakiness of that…episode…was subtly changing into shivers of cold. And that hail was pelting down, now, in earnest. And all her bruises throbbed. And she was so *tired* of it all.

And what was she doing, standing here, striving for a better frame of mind? She ought to just go home. She *needed* to get home in time for Jack to get changed into his new clothes. And, oh, how she wanted to get out of the cold.

She hugged Jack's parcel tight and bowed her head against the stinging hail which was battering the brim of her bonnet now, until all she could see was her feet, rhythmically appearing out from the hem of her skirts, left, right, left, right, as they pounded along the slippery paving stones. She didn't want to lift her head to look out for the landmarks Jack had made her recite, over and over, until he was sure she could find her way round their little part of London. For once, she'd let her feet carry her down the second alley past the Pig and Whistle, and through the warren of streets and courts at the back of Drury Lane. She'd come this way often enough by now not to have to think, or recite the way out loud. She just needed to get back as quickly as she could. It was important. Tonight of all nights...

She didn't lift her head again until she reached the top of a set of broad front steps, where she thumped on the glossy painted door with one fist.

A glossy *painted* door? That wasn't right, was it? Shouldn't there be a dim passage, and a row of nameplates set next to it? And she had a key, in her reticule. So why had she knocked?

This was definitely not right. She didn't belong here...

She took a step back, going dizzy as finally, vague outlines started to form within the mists which, until just now, had never yielded up anything but terrifying *feelings*.

But before they could solidify into recognizable images, someone opened the door. A smartly dressed, grey-haired man who could never be mistaken for anything but a butler.

And then something really odd happened as she caught sight of what lay behind the glossy door. It wasn't that the mists totally disappeared. No, it was more like...the curtain going up on a new production, where she'd expected to see a brand-new set, but instead, recognzing every feature of the scenery, every prop, and every actor upon the stage as though she'd seen the production many, many times before.

The black-and-white tiles of the floor and the zig-zaggy pattern they formed round the edges of the hall came as no surprise to her. Nor did the imposing staircase, with the intricately worked iron balusters supporting the glossy oak banister rail. She even got the feeling that should she open that door on the left, she'd find a breakfast room. And that one on the right would lead to a study.

And that the name of the man who'd just opened the door, and who was now staring at her as though he'd seen a ghost, was Simmons.

He pulled himself together while she was still reeling. 'M-my lady,' he gasped, standing back and opening the door wider, with a slight bow to the head.

Inviting her to enter.

My lady? That wasn't right. She wasn't a lady. She was...she was...

She put her hand to her forehead. She was confused; that was what she was. But she wasn't a lady. She was a nobody. From nowhere. With no name. Jack had started calling her Perdita when they first met. Because she had looked lost. And because she had no idea who she was, or why she'd been in that little market town, that day.

But now, all of a sudden, she knew for a certainty that she was an orphan. That her parents had both died, suddenly, during some sort of epidemic. Her heart began racing as memories, real memories, flooded into her brain in an unstoppable tide. Her grief as she'd stood there, looking at the pair of shrouded bodies. The angry face of a man who'd said he was her grandfather's brother, and that she had to go with him. Her bewilderment at hearing she even had a grandfather. Her fear at having to go with this stranger, who seemed almost to hate her. Then one image after another, of houses where she'd never really belonged, and people who'd told her they were her family, but didn't behave like it. Telling her that it was their duty to feed and house her until she was old enough to go to school where she would learn how to earn her own living, as a governess, or a teacher...

But then there was an almighty crash from somewhere further down the entrance hall, which stopped the train of images which had been cantering through her brain as abruptly as if they'd run into a brick wall. She was here, on the doorstep of a grand London house, where a footman had just dropped a tray of silverware, which was bouncing and tinkling all over the polished tiles.

'Allow me,' the butler said, having cast a quelling frown in the direction of the footman, who was standing gaping at her, as though she'd grown two heads, 'to take your parcel.'

Her parcel. Perdita looked down at the brown paper package she held in her hands. At the name written on it. Jack B Nimble.

'Jack,' she whispered, her vision clouding. Jack. The man she'd been living with for the past three months. The man who had rescued her. Taken care of her. Been so patient with her clumsiness, her blank episodes, and hadn't cared that she hadn't a clue who she was, nor remembered a single thing about herself before the moment he'd scooped her up from the side of the fountain where she'd been watching him perform a comic piece for the market day crowds.

The man who *didn't* live in this house.

Chapter Two

Anthony Radcliffe, the Earl of Epping, gave the club servant an icy stare.

'I thought I told you I didn't wish to be disturbed?'

'Yes, my lord, I do beg your pardon,' he said nervously. 'But your butler said it was imperative that I give you this note.' He set the twist of paper he'd borne into the room on a silver salver, next to Anthony's hand, which lay on the polished surface of the dining table, currently being used by the committee of which he was the chair.

Anthony waited until the fellow had scuttled out of the room.

'To resume,' he said, 'where we left off.'

'Of course, my lord,' said Whittaker, whom they had voted in as secretary the last time they'd gathered about this same table. 'Now that *you* have agreed to take the chair,' he said, bobbing his head obsequiously in Anthony's direction, 'I am sure we shall have no trouble securing the support of the men on the list I gave you all at the commencement of proceedings today.'

Anthony had already cast his eye over that list. It contained the usual mix of social climbers among the genuine philanthropists. Men who, as Whittaker had implied, would be happy to open their purse strings if it meant they could claim they had access to his circle.

'And their wives, of course,' Whittaker added with a chuckle.

Yes, well, the notion that a wife would support her husband in his charitable endeavours *was* comical. Fantastical, almost.

The notion that a wife would support her husband in *any* endeavour was, to be frank, ludicrous. But he would not voice that opinion here. The important thing was to engage and retain the support of these worthies and their contacts, no matter how vulgar they probably were. To get them to dig deep, and give of their time as well as their money. Towns like London swarmed with orphans and beggars, and the formal means of caring for them fell far short in his estimation. Not like on his estates, or in the villages and towns all over the country, where people such as himself *knew* their tenants and dependants. And as winter was drawing in, the poor of London would be freezing, and starving, and dying in droves if men like him, and these comfortable, entitled fellows sitting round the table with him, didn't do something about it.

Even if it meant rubbing shoulders with the kind of people he would normally go out of his way to avoid.

It was only once they'd dealt, at tedious length, with every item on the agenda, and were calling for more port to fortify themselves against their journey home, that he deigned to pick up the note Simmons had sent, and glance at its contents. A single sentence.

But a sentence which had the same effect upon him as if an elephant had just come crashing through the ceiling and landed on the table.

Her Ladyship has come home.

He crushed the note between his fingers, icy rage surging through him and propelling him to his feet.

'If you will excuse me, gentlemen,' he managed to retain the sanity to say to the other members of the committee. 'I…'

He was not about to explain, was he? Why should he? These men were not his friends, but merely colleagues in a joint venture, that was all.

And how could he? He'd managed to keep the latest, sordid details of his private life exactly that, private. By saying nothing. Letting nobody suspect that Mary, his faithless, scheming wife…

'Of course, my lord,' came a murmur of voices round the table. They were satisfied, he could tell, from having basked in his attention for the past hour or so. They all knew he had important matters to attend to. That there were many calls upon his time. There was no need to specify what this one was.

He supposed the club servant must have helped him into his coat, and handed him his hat and gloves, because he was wearing all three when he stepped outside into a hailstorm. If he'd had any sense he would have called for a cab to take him home. But it seemed that sense has deserted him. Or that something else had taken over his brain. Besides, he would never have been able to sit still, inside a cab, and let someone else drive him back to the house on Grosvenor Square. He needed to be moving. Striding along the pavement, thrusting other pedestrians out of his way.

Hoping he'd burn off some of the anger that was surging through him before he reached her. Or he ran the serious risk of wringing her neck.

How dare she simply stroll back into his house, as though nothing had happened! Did she think he'd forgive her infidelities? He may have earned a reputation for charitable works, such as the committee he'd been chairing just now, but that didn't mean he was a sap. That he would let any woman twist him round her little finger, no matter how pretty and appealing he'd once thought she was. How vulnerable. And innocent.

Anger lengthened his stride, and quickened his pace, so that he reached his front door in what felt like next to no time. Not time enough for his anger to have abated, at any rate.

Simmons opened the door.

Anthony shrugged off his coat, scattering hailstones across the marble tiles as he did so. His hat, too, he noticed as Simmons began brushing it, had acquired a coating of ice, though he'd scarcely noticed the storm, so deeply had he been dwelling on the injustices Mary had dealt him. Which she must now be expecting him to deal with. Why else would she have come here?

'Where,' he growled at Simmons, as he draped his coat over the man's arm, 'is she?'

'In her room, my lord,' he replied, knowing exactly to whom Anthony was referring. 'But—'

He didn't pause to listen to whatever excuse the butler had been about to give him. He didn't want to hear *any* excuses. There was nothing anyone could say that would induce him to forgive her for what she'd done.

He took the stairs two at a time and went straight in without knocking.

And came to a complete standstill as he finally saw why Simmons had been trying to give him a warning with that *but*. For she was in a bath. Covered only in soapsuds. And the light from the fire, blazing in the grate just beyond where the bath sat, was casting a warm glow over her naked limbs.

Damn her to hell! How could she still make him… *want* her, after all she'd done? By merely sitting there, naked, and wet? She wasn't even looking at him! She had her eyes half-closed, as though in spirit she was miles away, as though she hadn't even noticed him come in.

He could have been anyone, standing there, watching her. And as he hadn't yet shut the door behind him, anyone happening to stroll along the upper landing might still be able to see her.

He turned and slammed it shut. Then whirled back round to confront her.

'Have you no shame, woman? Sitting there with no clothes on?'

She gave him a look that once would have made

his heart go out to her. That once *had* made his heart go out to her. A look comprised of confusion, and what he'd once thought had been complete innocence. And vulnerability. A look that had made him want to sweep her into his arms and keep her safe.

'And it's of no use looking at me like that,' he declared, folding his arms across his chest to prevent them from reaching for her and hauling her into his chest. And making a fool of himself by thanking heaven she was safe. And *here*. Before babbling out a torrent of questions he was certain he wouldn't want to hear the answers to. 'It may have worked on me once. I may have believed you vulnerable, and innocent, and in need of protection. But I know better now.'

Her brows rose.

'And if you think you can walk back into my life, and take up your position as my wife, as though nothing has happened, then you are mistaken. Do you think I'm fool enough to take you back now that your lover has grown tired of you? That I am willing to take on some other man's cast-offs? Do you take me for a complete idiot?'

She'd been sitting gazing at her toes, where they peeped contentedly at her from above the froth of rose-scented bubbles, for some time before he'd come in. Marvelling at their cleverness. Because it had been those toes, she decided, or perhaps the feet from which they grew, that had carried her here. How had they known that they could bring her to a house where there were maids to carry cans of hot water

up the stairs to fill this bath, when her mind had not?
How had they managed to remember that she had the
right to enter a house where someone would light a
fire without her having to worry about whether they
could afford the coals? She hadn't recalled it at all.
Not in all the weeks she'd been in London. Not until
she'd stumbled across the threshold, and recognized
the marble hall, and the butler.

The butler…

Whatever must he have thought of her when she'd
tottered across the hall and plumped down on the
bottom step, rather than walk gracefully up those
stairs? When she'd clung with one arm to Jack's parcel, while wrapping her other arm round the newel
post? When she'd been too dazed, too confused, to
reply to any of the questions he'd asked her?

Part of her, and she rather thought it was the part
that had wrapped its arm round the newel post, had
been telling her that she must have lived here once,
else how could she have recognized the staff, and the
furnishings? And why else would that butler have
opened the door and let her in, as though she had the
right, if she didn't?

But the part that had clung to Jack's parcel had
kept insisting she *didn't* belong here. At all.

Somehow, while she'd been sort of at war with
herself, Simmons had ushered her up the stairs, and
into this room, which he'd insisted was hers.

She hadn't felt the same sort of shock coming into
this room as she had when the door had opened onto
the hall downstairs. Because she'd been prepared
to recognize it. Which she had, the moment she'd

stepped over the threshold, though she had no real sense of belonging in here, either. Nor could she remember ever having actually *lived* in this house. Or anything that had happened to her here.

And yet, in spite of all that, her initial dizzy surprise wore off relatively quickly. After all, hadn't she had a funny, uneasy sort of feeling, ever since they'd come to London, as if someone or something was hovering, just behind her, and might tap her on the shoulder at any moment?

She'd kept on thrusting that feeling aside. And had refused to turn round and look the…spectre in the face. Because she'd been pretty certain that whatever it was that was waiting just out of sight, was not going to be pleasant. Or why did she keep having those strange, formless, terrifying dreams? And why was it that whenever she got the sense that there was something…almost there, just out of reach, she wanted to run from it? Escape from it?

Though why on earth would she have wanted to escape this house? And all this luxury? It didn't make sense.

Not until the door crashed open, that was, and the living embodiment of a thunderstorm burst into her room. A man as dark as a cloud, with a harsh, furious face. He even had hailstones in his hair. And the look on his face made her half expect him to pull a bolt of lightning out of his pocket and cast it at her.

So why, then, when she was in such a vulnerable position, and he was so angry, did she not feel so much as the flicker of fear?

Because she knew him, obviously, or *had* known him, even though he was a stranger to her now.

And why, for all the harshness of his features, did she find him so attractive, even though his brows were drawn down into a frown above that blade of a nose and the uncompromising slash of a mouth?

A mouth that she'd kissed.

Oh! Yes, she remembered that mouth kissing hers. And the utter bliss which had spread through her. The joy. And the disbelief. Because he'd seemed like a...a god, to her.

A god.

Goodness, she'd *worshipped* this man, once upon a time. She remembered feeling just like *this*. Vulnerable, and stunned that this stranger could be so close to her, in such an intimate setting.

The difference today, she suddenly perceived, was that if, back then, he'd ever frowned at her the way he was doing now, she would have been distraught. Destroyed.

And if he'd ever shouted at her the way he was doing now, the adoring, worshipful girl she could suddenly remember being would have cowered, and wept, and wanted to die.

The thing was, though, that although she was starting to recover the occasional memory of that girl, and how she'd felt, she was no longer the same person. For the past few months she'd had no idea who she was supposed to be. And so she'd had to find out, by observing how she reacted to everything, day by day. It had been a bit like meeting a stranger, and getting to know them. Though she was that stranger. A stranger to herself, ludicrous though that sounded. And what she'd learned about herself was that she was rather an intelligent and capable person. A person who'd become indispensable to the troupe of travelling actors who'd taken her in. A person, moreover, who could stand up to sneering tradesmen, and even barter for good deals from hard-eyed, hard-hearted moneylenders.

A person who was absolutely not going to sit here cowering while some man berated her.

For one thing, if this really was her room, then he had no right to walk in without knocking!

He had no right to hurl all those filthy accusations at her, either. Because, as far as she knew, she had done nothing wrong!

Slowly, she got to her feet, and reached over to gather up a towel which was warming before the fire. And had the satisfaction of shocking him into silence.

Ah, yes. The girl she'd once been had been painfully shy, hadn't she? Not only had she been hardly able to believe that a man as elevated in station as… *him* would have wanted to put a ring on her finger, but she'd almost died of embarrassment when he'd wanted to see her without clothing.

She froze in place as *that* particular memory resurfaced, her fingers just short of the towel.

This man was her *husband*.

Yes, that was right; he'd been saying, or shouting rather, something about her *position as his wife*.

She almost turned round to stare at him. The man she'd forgotten she'd married. How could she have forgotten marrying a man who owned a house like this, crammed to the rafters with servants, when she'd been trained to expect a lifetime of service in such a place?

And how on earth had they breached the barriers that should have kept them in their relative stations in life?

Only just in time did she recall the minor detail of her nudity. And, though she'd just discovered she was a married woman, and that there was no legal reason that he shouldn't look his fill at what he must have seen many times before, it would be the first time she would have *knowingly* let him see her.

She grabbed the towel and wrapped it round her torso, fumbling it into a knot over her breasts.

Goodness! It seemed that although she was no longer painfully shy, neither was she willing to flaunt herself. Well, she'd learned that on tour, hadn't she? She had never liked getting up on stage and having people look at her, not even wearing the most concealing of costumes.

So perhaps she hadn't changed so much, in essence, as all that.

'And you aren't,' said the man—no, her *husband*—'going to tempt me into taking you back by flaunting your wares.'

Oh. Well, it was just as well she hadn't bothered then, wasn't it? she mused as she finally turned to face him.

'There is only one thing I want from you,' he snarled, stalking across the room until the toes of his boots hit the opposite side of the bath from where she was standing. 'And that is to know what has become of our child!'

Chapter Three

Their child? There had been a child?

All of a sudden the spectre which had been hovering at her shoulder, all these weeks, reared up and grabbed her by the throat. His question had blasted all the mists away with the force of a hurricane. She couldn't turn away from the horror or thrust it aside any longer.

Her child.

Something like a great, dark wave of despair rushed up and sucked her under.

Her baby. Her *baby*.

She was drowning. She couldn't breathe. Blackness was sucking her under. And in her mind she was scrabbling for purchase on a wooden wall, green with slime, breaking her nails but fighting, fighting to stay above water...

She hadn't drowned.

But, oh God, her baby!

A whimper escaped her throat as the pain, the loss swamped her.

She wrapped her arms round her stomach, now empty, which had once been rounded with the fruit of her love for this man.

And wailed.

No wonder she hadn't been able to remember anything. No wonder she hadn't *wanted* to remember anything. No wonder she'd flinched from any tremulous, shimmering feelings of familiarity with her past, before Jack. Because it harboured this. This pain. This grief. This loss.

She couldn't bear it. She didn't want to bear it. Oh, where was that mist, which had shrouded it from her view? Why couldn't she sink into it, and hide in it, right now?

Anthony watched in horror as his wife crumpled over, clutching her stomach, and began sobbing. Uncontrollably.

'Epping, Epping,' she moaned.

For the briefest of moments he tried to resist that appeal for help. But found he couldn't just do nothing in the face of such distress.

So he stepped round the bath and gathered her into his arms the way he'd yearned to do from the moment he'd walked in and seen her sitting there. He had good reason, now, didn't he? Because this pain was his as well as hers. Hadn't *he* lost the child she was grieving so openly now? And he was the only person who could share the pain she was clearly feeling. Pain at the loss of his child. Her child. Their child. And he was here. And whatever else she might have done, her grief at losing his child was genuine.

Also, he felt a bit guilty. For it was definitely his fault, at least partly, he consoled himself, that she was weeping with such abandon. Because he'd deliberately lashed out. He'd been angry with her for coming back, to start with. And then even more furious when she'd stood up from her bath, magnificently unconcerned about her nudity, causing desire to lick through him like a flame when it was the last thing he wanted to feel. He'd gazed at her stunningly shapely body, hating himself for wanting her, hating her for being so brazen, so unlike the shy little bride she'd pretended to be, in those early, blissful days of their marriage, and he'd lashed out. He could see she was no longer pregnant. And any idiot could have worked out that it was far too soon for her to have given birth to a healthy child. Yet he'd still lashed out at her, demanding to know what had become of the baby.

And this was the result.

God, what a monster unrequited love could make of a man. He'd never thought of himself as being cruel. Yet what he'd just done undoubtedly had been cruel.

'Y-you came,' she sobbed.

'Well,' he admitted, uncomfortably, 'I could hardly stand there watching you sobbing like that, could I? I'm not a monster.' She smelled intoxicatingly of roses. And warm, damp woman.

She looked up at him, frowning. And shook her head.

'No…this is now…isn't it? Not then. Though it felt so real…' She raised one hand to her forehead, and speared her fingers into her hair, which was piled on top of her head in one of those complicated arrangements that somehow defied gravity.

'This is *London*,' she said, working her fingers against her scalp as though she had a pain there, and was trying to massage it away. 'It is November. Not *then*. When I really needed you,' she added, 'you weren't there. Though I called for you...' She pulled out of his embrace. 'I suppose that would have been impossible...'

'Of course it would,' he said dryly. 'I had no idea where you were.'

'No, I suppose not,' she said, sagging against his chest again. 'You couldn't help it. And at least you are here now. And this,' she sighed, 'having your arms round me, it has given me the strength to...remember it. To acknowledge it.'

Though her words didn't make complete sense, he was intelligent enough to understand the gist of them. She clearly thought that just because he'd put his arms round her, to offer her comfort over the loss of their child, and because he shared her grief, that he was ready to overlook everything else.

And he wasn't!

He may have been fooled by a pretty woman when he'd been young enough and green enough to know no better. But he was older, and harder now. He could never take a faithless woman back, no matter how much he desired her.

He stepped back, making her totter slightly as he withdrew the supporting cradle of his arms. 'Just because I was prepared to offer you comfort, it doesn't mean that I have forgiven you,' he said curtly. 'Or that I ever will.'

She looked up at him, her eyes widening in shock.

'What…what do you mean? Forgive me? What do you have to forgive me for?'

He gave a bark of bitter laughter. 'Don't think you can fool me by that display of feigned innocence. You might have been able to convince me, once, that you were purer than the driven snow. But your behaviour since has proved otherwise, hasn't it?'

'B-behaviour? What are you talking about?'

'I am talking about running off with Franklin.'

'Franklin?' She feigned a look of such bewilderment that had he not known better, he would have sworn she had no idea what he was talking about.

'Yes, Franklin. That spotty, illiterate groom.'

'Oh!' She reeled back from him, a look of shock and pain replacing the convincing show of confusion. 'His name was… Franklin. Yes.' She buried her hands in her face for a moment or two, before looking up at him. And her expression had changed again. Only this time, she looked angry as well as hurt.

'You think I…ran off, with him? With that young groom?'

'Of course I do. What else?'

Her eyes narrowed. Her mouth pulled into a tight line. 'Let me get this straight. You thought I'd run off with another man, and so…' She shook her head. A tendril of hair escaped its confines and tumbled to her neck, where it clung to the damp skin. 'Did you search for me, when I went missing?'

'Of course not,' he scoffed, tearing his eyes from

the errant lock of hair, and the creamy, silky slope of her shoulder. 'Do you think I wanted to alert everyone to the fact that my wife had proved faithless by scouring the countryside for her? For everyone to know that I only turned my back for five minutes before she played me false?'

'Five minutes? You were gone longer than five minutes! And I was ill. Didn't you take that into consideration? How could you possibly think I had the *strength*, never mind the inclination, to embark on some tawdry affair!

'Oh! Oh…' She shook her head as if trying to deny the thoughts that were tumbling into her head.

It was very skilfully done, that look of outraged innocence; he had to give her that.

'I don't suppose it ever crossed your mind,' she flung at him, 'that I might have met with an accident, did it? Let alone that I might have been in deadly peril?'

'Deadly peril?' He folded his arms across his chest. 'Don't be so melodramatic.'

'You…you…' She took a deep breath. 'You said just now you weren't a monster. But that's exactly what you are!'

'Don't you dare try to turn this round on me,' he snapped back.

'Dare? Dare! Oh, I dare all right. I dare far more now that I've had to learn to look after myself. Now that I've learned that the husband who promised to love and cherish me had no intention of doing either. You never loved me, did you? Or you wouldn't have been so quick to assume that I'd behave like a…

like a…*trollop*! Because that is what you thought, isn't it?'

He *had* loved her; that was the trouble. Fallen so swiftly and so hard that it had scared him. He, who'd sworn never to feel anything for a woman, ever again, after the travesty of his first marriage, had been so desperate to put his ring on her finger that he'd rushed her to the altar before his courage deserted him, or anyone could have the chance to talk him out of it.

He hadn't gone to that house party expecting anything more than a week of doing his duty by his extended family, and forging links with potential political allies. But then she'd run into him as she'd been scurrying to fetch something for her cantankerous employer, and, as he'd taken her by the shoulders to steady her, he'd felt…a frisson. That was all. Just an awareness of her as a woman. A woman who smelled of clean linen and soap, rather than the exotic perfume Sarah, his first wife, had favoured. And it had felt like seeing the first green shoots of spring after a bleak, harsh winter.

By the end of the house party he'd been convinced she was his only chance. His last chance of ever having anything like a normal life again.

He'd known, somehow, that he'd never find another woman like her. And that the only way to further their acquaintance would be to take the plunge. Marry her. Because it was unlikely they would ever meet again socially. Or that he'd have a chance to woo her in the conventional manner. Take the plunge… Yes, that was what it had felt like. Like diving off a cliff into freezing, surging waters fifty feet below and hoping he'd survive.

It had been a risk. A massive risk.

But on the other hand, she'd made him feel... hopeful.

And at first, oh, how glad he'd been that he'd taken the risk. He'd never known that making love to a woman could be so...rewarding. Transformative, even. She was so impressed by everything he did in bed that at times she almost made him feel like some sort of...god.

And after Sarah, who'd been unable to disguise her boredom in that regard...well, it had been heady stuff.

But how could he possibly admit to any of that? It would have been like handing her a weapon to use against him. He'd known that right from the start. That it would be the height of folly to let her know what power she could wield over him, should she choose. And if he hadn't admitted it then, when things had apparently been good between them, he most certainly was not going to do so now, when she appeared to be playing some deep, complicated game in her attempt to worm her way back into his life.

'The evidence,' he therefore said firmly, 'was unassailable. There is no arguing your way out of it now.'

'Evidence! There was no evidence,' she shouted. 'You...you... Oh, to think I *worshipped* you. You... you...' She whirled away, her shoulders heaving. 'Even if you hadn't loved me, what kind of man didn't care what became of his own baby?'

'Of course I cared what had become of my baby!' It had affected him so much, he'd just taken her in his arms even though he'd sworn he'd never fall for her charms again. So potent was her allure that it blinded him to good sense.

A horrible thought suddenly slithered into his mind like a poisonous snake. Hadn't he just been thinking about how much she enjoyed marital relations? Far more than Sarah ever had. And Sarah had made no secret of the fact that she was eager to take other lovers. And would have done so, had he not taken steps to prevent her.

And if Sarah could…then who was to say that Mary couldn't, too? *Before* she'd run off with that spotty groom!

A shaft of pain lanced through him, as bitter as a bite from a snake.

'If indeed,' he said, in bitterness, 'the baby was even mine.'

'*What* did you just say?' She whirled back round, her eyes brimming with revulsion. 'Get out of my room,' she said, her voice so cold it felt as though someone had thrown a bucket of icy water over him. 'Go on, get out,' she repeated, her eyes blazing with what looked like hatred.

How had it come to this?

He'd had such hopes, when it came to this woman. What a colossal fool he'd been.

'With pleasure,' he said, giving her an ironic bow, turning on his heel, and striding to the door.

Chapter Four

For a moment, she stood there, fists clenched, glaring at the door through which he'd just gone. Wishing there was something to hand that she could fling at it. Something that would shatter with a satisfyingly loud noise.

Well, at least now she understood why he was so angry with her. He thought she'd run off with a groom! Worse, that she might have been unfaithful from the start! How on earth could he suspect such a thing? Had she ever really understood him?

No. She didn't think she had. He'd always been a bit…aloof. Unfathomable.

Oh. That was why seeing him standing there, watching her had felt so familiar, wasn't it? Because she'd never felt as if she'd really known him all that well.

Though how on earth he could claim he had some sort of evidence to support his accusations… *Pah!* There wasn't any evidence. There couldn't be.

All she'd done was get up into the dog cart, and…

She raised her fists to her temples as a series of jumbled, horrific memories tumbled into her mind. Now that he'd smashed down the door to the very worst of them, there seemed to be nothing to prevent the rest of them from pouring through.

No wonder she'd lost her memory. Who would want to remember the things she'd been through?

No wonder she'd shied away from all those disturbing feelings that there was somebody missing from her life…

With a strangled cry, she paced across the room, not for any specific reason, but because there was too much going on in her head to cope with while she was standing still. She'd crumple to the floor if she didn't walk away from it…

No. She was *not* going to crumple. And she was not going to walk away from reality any longer. Or even try to slam the door shut on unpleasant truths. She'd spent far too long doing that already.

Anyway, it was too late to do that. First of all her feet had rebelled and brought her to this house, where they could be warm and comfortable. And then *he'd* come in and smashed through the barriers she'd erected to protect herself from all this… hurt. Pain. Grief.

No wonder she'd buried it all so deep. She'd been on her own. Naturally she hadn't wanted to break down, like she'd done just now, with strangers watching her. She hadn't had the strength, or the courage, to accept any of it…not until just now when *he'd* put his arms round her.

Even though he was a virtual stranger. And yet she'd known he was the answer to her needs, somehow.

And he had been. Before he'd hurt her all over again with his suspicions and his ridiculous accusations.

As if she didn't have enough to deal with already. She needed someone to…to help her deal with all these painful memories as they came flooding back.

Or at least, she *wanted* him to help her deal with all her troubles.

She put her hand to her forehead as she paced back across the room. When she'd called his name just now, it had transported her back to another moment when she'd done exactly the same, needing him, wanting him. She'd been lying in a cramped little bed, half out of her mind with fever. And that woman with the rough hands and the kind face had given her that bitter medicine.

'Don't think about it, dearie,' the woman had urged. 'Just drink this down and let it carry you away somewhere better. Somewhere that there ain't no more pain, nor grief.'

So she'd drunk it, unpleasant though it had tasted. And it had, indeed, carried her away into a blissful oblivion. An oblivion she'd fled back to, over and over again, rather than face up to reality. She'd become so good at *not thinking about it* that the power to recall any of it had simply shrivelled up.

But for a moment, just now, the two scenes had merged into one. It had been as if, in her mind, she'd been reliving the moments before she'd taken the medicine, when she'd been distraught, and racked with pain, while in her body here in this room she'd been stepping round her bath, and into his arms. She hadn't been entirely sure what was real, for a moment or two. Not until he'd pulled away from her, and spoken those words about not forgiving her. And she'd seen that of course, she was in London.

He might as well have slapped her, so effectively had he jolted her back to reality. A reality she'd successfully avoided while they'd travelled round the towns and villages of England. But when she'd come to London, it had begun to creep up on her. Because, she realized, she *had* been in some of the streets before. That was why they'd struck a chord. Although they hadn't been able to achieve much more than give her a funny, echoey feeling, because she'd been looking at them from a different angle, hadn't she? From street level as she walked through them, rather than from the lofty heights of a carriage as she was being driven through them. Before London, there had been nothing and nobody with the power to stir anything up, had there? *Nothing* to remind her of who she really was, or what had happened, until she'd bumped into that man on the icy pavement...

Because she hadn't been to any of those places before, or met any of those people, or done any of the sorts of things which she'd had to do to earn her bread and butter. Which hadn't bothered her anywhere near as much as it had bothered Jack.

'It must be dreadful,' he'd said sympathetically, so many times, 'not to know who you are, or how you came to be here.'

But it hadn't been all that dreadful. Not after a while. Not most of the time. Because somehow, she'd known that Perdita didn't have a care in the world, not in comparison with whoever she'd been...before.

So she'd insisted she was perfectly content to live out her life as Perdita. And she had been. Because her head hadn't wanted to remember anything from the time before she'd met Jack. And nor had her heart. Her bruised heart, she suddenly perceived, which shrank from suffering any more pain at the careless hands of the man she'd so hastily, and so recklessly, married.

It had only been her toes, in fact, that had started to grow dissatisfied with being so cold all the time.

She paused from her pacing to stare down at them. And they promptly reminded her that though this room might be grander, and warmer than what she'd been used to as Perdita, they were going to grow cold again if she didn't hurry up and get dressed.

Besides, nobody ever achieved anything by pacing about wrapped in a towel, waving their arms about, and beating their head with clenched fists. Not unless they were trying to persuade some theatre manager that they could play the part of an ancient Roman in the throes of a tragedy.

She went over to the chest of drawers by the window. Then paused to wonder why she'd done that.

Oh. Because, last time she'd been in this house, she seemed to recall she'd kept all sorts of undergarments in there. She pulled open the top drawer. It was empty. So was the one next to it, and all the ones beneath.

She reeled away.

Had her memory been playing tricks again?

Or had he thrown all her things away? Expunged her from his life?

From the things he'd said just now, she wouldn't put it past him.

On limbs that were trembling with a horribly debilitating combination of shock and indignation at his treatment of her, and creeping cold, she went over to the wardrobe which had once been full of gowns. Dozens of them. She *wasn't* imagining *them*. She'd had far more than she could possibly have worn. Gowns that Epping had bought her, in the early days of their marriage.

Strange that although it shouldn't have been an uncomfortable memory, or at least, not in comparison to the ones which had just completely shattered her illusion of contentment, thinking about those gowns provoked another tidal wave of pain. It made her hesitate before opening the door. She stood with her head bowed as, for the first time, she allowed the remembered feelings to wash over her rather than pushing them aside, fearing they'd drown her. Feelings of…awkwardness, and something not far from humiliation. And as she allowed them to flood back, another memory followed in their wake. The memory of him dismissing her feelings when she'd confessed to them, saying they were foolish.

'You have a place in society to uphold, now that you are my wife,' he'd told her. 'You cannot possibly think it is acceptable to go on wearing the same clothes you wore while you were working as a paid companion.'

'Not the same clothes, no—' she'd timidly begun to say.

'Women of my rank,' he'd cut in, making her flinch at the reminder that she was not of his rank, or anywhere near, 'change several times a day, not just a couple of times a week. You need morning dress, walking dress, carriage dress for every day, besides evening gowns. Plural,' he'd added sternly. 'And all the accessories to go with them.'

She'd known that; of course she had. Hadn't she watched women of that sort, from the sidelines, ever since Lady Marchmont had taken her on as paid companion? She shuddered. If ever there was someone she'd have been glad to forget entirely, that person was Lady Marchmont. But it was no good. She couldn't choose which memories to retrieve and which to deny. Now that she'd started remembering, it seemed they were all tumbling back, pell-mell.

But she could choose not to *dwell* on Lady Marchmont, couldn't she? And go back to what she'd been allowing to seep back to her mind, regarding the contents of this wardrobe, so that she could work out why the prospect of looking at them again should be so…unsettling.

Why had she found it so hard to have her husband buy her so many clothes?

Because, the answer came in a flash, it goaded her into looking at how little she'd brought to the marriage. Yes, one minute she'd had next to nothing, and been a nobody.

The next…

Perhaps it was no wonder she'd found it, all of it, rather…overwhelming.

But…a new thought occurred to her as she cast her mind back to the early days of her marriage. Why hadn't she been more…grateful, for all the improvements he'd brought into her life? Or at least, have tried to display the gratitude he'd expected her to feel? He'd showered her with all the things any girl could ever have dreamed of. Things she'd wished for, so often, since she'd been a very little girl. Security, first and foremost. And a choice about what she ate. And the opportunity to read a book, any book she wished, when she had the leisure to do so. And, oh, *leisure*. That most blessed, and elusive of all commodities. The luxury of not having duties to perform!

Instead, every time he'd suggested she go out shopping again, she'd protested that there was no need. She must have really annoyed him. He must have felt as if she was flinging his generosity back in his face.

Too late to do anything about it now, though.

She sighed, and on a wave of something like guilt and regret she finally made herself open the wardrobe.

The rails were empty.

As empty as her mind had been for the past few months. Nothing there, not even a wisp of silken, shimmering memory. Although the rails had once groaned under the weight of the most wonderful gowns. Sometimes, when she'd thought nobody would catch her, she'd sat on the floor and just gazed at them all. And if she'd felt her hands were clean enough she'd reach in and stroke the sumptuous fabrics, scarce able to credit the fact that they were all hers.

All that was left now was the faint, lingering scent of expensive material. The scent that always hung in the air in the shops of the haughty modiste he'd insisted she frequent.

She withdrew, slamming the door shut on the lack of clothing and her less than happy memories of buying them. Or having them bought for her, to be more accurate.

She gave a bitter laugh. What kind of woman was she? Or had been, at least? Today, if some man told her to kit herself out in silk and satin, and send all the bills to him, and not count the cost, she would skip round the room clapping her hands, not wallow in a morass of shyness and guilt.

How could she have been so…buffle headed?

As the word popped into her mind, she felt as if it applied to her behaviour right now, too. Because she was standing in this room, clad only in a towel, wallowing in memories of how many clothes she'd had, once, when what she ought to be dealing with was the far more vexing problem of what she could wear now.

Why on earth had she allowed the maid, who'd come in to help her into her bath, to remove the clothing she'd been wearing? True, she hadn't been in her right mind…and it had all been wet through, but…

Ah! She was doing it again! Wool-gathering!

Right, then. She needed to ring for the girl and

retrieve as much of it as she could. Or, if it had already gone to the laundry, then borrow some clothing from some of the female members of staff here. All their gowns, she expected, would be better than the cheap, shoddy thing she'd been wearing when she'd turned up here. The Earl of Epping made sure that all his staff looked smart. They wouldn't wear second-hand clothing cut down to fit. They'd have at least one new set of clothes each year.

And while the maid was up here, she could ask her what had become of all the expensive clothing she'd owned, when last she'd lived in this house. Surely even Epping couldn't be extravagant enough to have just thrown it all away? Without her having worn the half of it? Or ordering some servant to do it, anyway. She couldn't imagine *him* pulling gowns off the rails and packing them into trunks...

Oh. She raised her hands to her head again as another image swam into view. An image of a couple of maids, doing just what she'd been thinking of. Pulling gowns from the rails, and folding them carefully into trunks. She'd watched them do it. From that bed, over there. She'd been lying down, feeling poorly, and wishing they didn't have to set out on the journey Epping informed her he undertook every summer. To visit all his properties, and check they were in good heart.

She'd enjoy it, he'd said, chucking her under the chin.

She remembered smiling as bravely as she could, and agreeing that yes, she would, whilst silently vowing to do her utmost to appear as if she was enjoying it, anyway…

And then the memory shattered, at the sound of a knock on the door. The maid, she surmised, come in answer to her summons.

Perhaps it was as well. She'd taken just about as much as she could take, for now, of delving into her own past. A past she'd been so mercifully free from, since that awful day in August. It was her present predicament she needed to address.

When Anthony had walked out, he'd only reached the landing before stopping and clenching his fists. Because no matter what he'd felt, and no matter what either of them had said to each other, he simply could not walk away and leave her. Not when she might start weeping again. Whatever she'd done, or how faithless she'd been, or how badly she'd hurt him, her grief was genuine. Raw. Only a man with a heart of stone would be able leave a woman in that state, without any means of comfort.

And his heart wasn't made of stone, unfortunately. It still beat, and clenched, and wept, even though he'd spent months refusing to pay any attention to it. Telling himself that no woman had the power to bruise it. And yet that scene, in her room just now, and his inability to just shrug and walk away, proved how deeply he'd been deceiving himself.

But at least her reaction when he'd voiced that sudden, awful suspicion the baby she'd lost might not be his had settled one thing. She could not, surely, have been so furious, so outraged, if there had been any chance another man could have fathered it.

Could she?

He was shaking, he realized. Trembling all over so badly that he needed to turn round and brace himself with one hand on each of the door jambs.

From that position at least he could hear her, moving about inside. Which was…useful. Because if it sounded as though she needed him, he could go straight back in, and…

And what? She'd ordered him to go. After accusing him of not caring about their baby.

Of course he'd cared about their baby. Seeing that she'd lost it had hurt him so badly that coming as it did on top of everything else…

Now, yes. But to be honest, at the time he'd first heard she'd run away, it hadn't been the potential child that had been at the forefront of his mind, had it? His first reaction had been a very strong urge to track her down and drag her back by the hair if necessary. His second had been horror at the savagery of his feelings. He'd recoiled from them. Spent a long time reminding himself that he was a civilized, cultured, educated man who would never stoop to haring off on what might have proved to be a humiliating, shattering experience.

And there was absolutely no way he would have told her any of that in response to her accusation of not caring about the baby. How could he have lowered himself by admitting that it was *her* disappearance that had devastated him? That *she* was the one he'd missed, not the potential heir they'd only just learned she was carrying?

It was only now that she'd come back, oversetting all the assumptions he'd made about why she'd gone, that he'd questioned its legitimacy.

It had looked as though that accusation had been the most hurtful thing he could have said to her. But how could he explain that by the time he'd married her, he'd no longer had any hope he could father a child himself? Because he'd never managed to get his first wife with child. He'd been resigned to having one of his younger brothers inherit his title, gleefully stepping into his shoes, once his time was up. And he hadn't had the time to properly assess what her pregnancy would have meant to him, before she'd gone.

And since he wasn't prepared to tell her *any* of that, what could he say?

Nothing.

The only thing he might be able to do, should he hear her crying again, would be to hold her. She hadn't minded that, had she?

No! He shook his head fiercely, and glared at the wooden panels separating him from his wife. He did *not* want to take her in his arms again.

But he did; that was the trouble.

He bowed his head until his forehead rested against the door.

He'd been so certain, before he'd seen her, that she would never have the power to touch him again. And yet now, having spent only a few minutes talking to her, he felt as though he couldn't be certain of anything. And it wasn't just due to the physical attraction that had flared to life. No, it was her *behaviour*. And the things she'd said. Everything, everything about that encounter just now had raised more questions than answers.

Could he have got it wrong?

She hadn't done or said a single thing he'd expected. She hadn't appealed for his forgiveness, or made any excuses for what she'd done. She hadn't attempted to wheedle her way back into his favour by giving him come-hither looks. Well, if he discounted the moment she'd risen, gloriously and unashamedly naked from her bath, that was. Which had shocked him to the core. She'd always been such a shy, mousy little creature. It had been her timid nature that had first attracted his notice, if he was honest. Everyone else at that Christmas house party had been making merry in the noisiest, most ostentatious manner. But she had looked as if she wished she was invisible, shrinking into the background as much as she could. And still looking openly terrified just about all the time. Oh, how he'd longed to rescue her from the tyranny of that old witch she'd been working for as a paid companion, and give her a secure, loving home. Even when he'd begun to make approaches to her, she hadn't responded the way any other woman there would have done. She'd made no attempt to flirt with him. Instead, she'd looked as if she couldn't believe he could possibly find her interesting.

That girl, that nervous, uncertain creature, could never have argued with him, let alone yelled at him to leave her room.

But then he wouldn't have thought she could have run off with a spotty young groom, either.

He sighed. Women were a mystery to him. They made a man think she had a certain sort of character, but the moment he put a ring on her finger, she turned into something completely foreign.

For months, he'd believed he'd been a fool to hope that, because he'd rescued her from a horrid situation, she'd be so grateful that she would devote herself to him, loyally, forever. And that if he ever saw her again, he'd know exactly how to deal with her. Not for one moment had he suspected that she'd reduce him to this—to loitering outside her bedroom door, waiting for an excuse to go back in, and…

A sound, from inside the room, diverted him from what he'd been thinking. It wasn't the sound of weeping, though, but the sound of her walking back and forth, back and forth. To him, the way she was pacing sounded as though she was still angry.

Then he heard drawers sliding open, then slamming. Definitely an angry sound.

He straightened up, his mind still reeling.

He hated feeling so uncertain. He was a man who routinely held sway over hundreds of dependants. He was never unsure of how to deal with any of the problems arising on any of his estates. Or of how to act in any given situation. Yet within half an hour of her return he was…dithering; that was the only way to describe it. Doubting himself, and unsure what to do next.

The question of what to do next was answered when he heard the sound of someone coming up the stairs. There was no way he was going to let anyone catch him here, like this. So he dashed away from her door, and was halfway up the next flight of stairs to his own room by the time a maid appeared. From his vantage point, he saw her knock on his wife's bedroom door, and go in. And a few moments later, he saw her come out again, carrying a pail of soapy bath water. Just before she closed the door behind her, the girl bobbed a curtsey, and said, 'Yes, my lady. It won't take long.'

What wouldn't take long? What had she ordered his servant to do? And how dare she?

He had half a mind to go back in there and...

And what? Resume the argument they'd been having before? Demand answers to the questions that had been tormenting him ever since she'd left him? Mostly, *why*? *Why* hadn't he been enough for her? Hadn't he given her everything a woman could want?

Not that she'd ever seemed keen to spend his money, the way his first wife, Sarah, had. On the contrary, the more he bought her, the less happy she appeared. So when she'd left, he'd felt that once again, he hadn't been...enough for his wife. That perhaps he just wasn't cut out to be a husband.

But if that was the case, what did she want with him now? Why had she come back?

He'd descended two stairs on a wave of determination to demand some answers before the significance of all that drawer opening and slamming struck him. She'd been looking for something to wear. He knew for a fact that there was not one single scrap of her clothing anywhere in this house. They'd taken it all with them when they'd set out from here, to begin his annual tour of his various properties, in June. He hadn't spotted any items of luggage in her room, or cluttering up the hallway. Which meant that she could very well be naked, in there. Or at best, have only a towel draped round her.

He'd already discovered the power her semi-naked body still had over him. She'd only have to let the towel slip, a bit, and she'd render him unable to think straight, let alone form a coherent sentence. He wouldn't be able to ask her anything, or come up with a logical suggestion about how they might handle her return.

It wasn't much longer before he saw that he'd been right to stay exactly where he was. Because a procession of staff began scurrying into and out of her room, bearing bundles of clothing, and trays containing covered plates and pots.

So, that was how it was going to be, was it? She'd got back into *his* house, and was demonstrating her rights by ordering *his* staff about. Reminding everybody that she was still, legally, his wife, until he chose to do something to rectify the situation.

The word *divorce* floated into his mind, only for him to dismiss it, with a shudder of revulsion. He was not going to allow his private life to descend to the level of entertainment for the masses. He would do almost anything to keep his name, and hers, out of the scandal sheets.

He felt a pain in his hand. On looking down, he saw that he was gripping the banister rail so hard his knuckles had gone white.

He deliberately uncurled his fingers and shook them out. Forced his mind to turn to what he ought to be doing, instead of standing on the staircase, paralysed by the intensity of his feelings.

He was supposed to be dining out, at his club tonight, with some acquaintances, he seemed to recall. Though if he went, he wouldn't be able to eat a thing. The most succulent steak would taste like ashes, knowing *she* was in his house, making free with his servants.

Besides, why should he go out, leaving her in possession of the field?

On the other hand, why should he allow her to disturb him to the extent that he changed his plans?

Good God, she was doing it again! Making him stand about *dithering*.

Enough!

Better to carry on as though her return made no difference to him.

Better to carry on with his plans, as though nothing had happened.

That was the way to deal with a woman who wanted to have the upper hand in a marriage. A woman who courted scandal. By squashing her pretensions, along with any potential scandal before it could leak out.

In short, by acting in public as though nothing untoward was happening at all.

Chapter Five

It was the sound of the curtains being drawn which woke Anthony the next morning.

He opened his eyes in order to discover who it was who'd had the audacity to wake him before he had rung for attention.

'Simmons?'

The butler nodded gravely, as though admitting to his name. But before Anthony could gather himself together sufficiently to give the man a piece of his mind, he noticed Snape, his valet, bustling about the washstand with a jug of hot water and a stack of neck cloths.

'What the devil,' Anthony growled, thrusting his fingers through his hair to get it out of his eyes, 'is going on?'

'Beg pardon, my lord,' said Simmons, 'but I felt you would wish to know that Her Ladyship has left the house.'

Anthony sat bolt upright. 'She's done what?'

She'd only spent one night under his roof. And, fair enough, he hadn't exactly welcomed her home, but to just run off, without settling anything…

A cold chill shot down his spine.

He couldn't have lost her all over again! He'd barely survived the last time she'd gone.

Why hadn't he…taken the precaution of setting a guard at her door, to prevent her from running off?

Why had he gone out and left her to her own devices at all, come to that?

To prove a point, he reminded himself bitterly. The point being that she had no power to affect him, or make him alter his plans. A point whose merit he'd wondered about several times last night, while he'd been enduring the company of one of the greatest bores of his acquaintance.

'And you,' he snarled at Simmons, 'just let her go?' Even as he said it, he knew he was being unfair. It wasn't the place of Simmons, or anyone else in his household, to prevent his wife from doing whatever she wished.

Simmons cleared his throat. 'I did insist that she take Stephens with her, my lord. To carry the parcel she was so intent on delivering.'

Stephens? Oh, yes, the upper footman. Chap had served in his household for years. Why hadn't he been able to put a face to the name at once?

He was still half-asleep; that was the trouble.

'Get me some coffee,' he growled.

'I have done so, my lord,' said Simmons, indicating a silver pot on a table by the door.

'And what's all this about a parcel?' Anthony said, as Simmons went to pour out a cup.

'Her Ladyship had a parcel with her when she came home yesterday, my lord,' said Simmons. 'Brown paper it was, all tied up with string. And it did have an address on it, although nobody,' he said apologetically, 'can recall making out exactly what it was.'

Implying that several of them had tried. 'Are you saying you have no idea where she may have gone?'

So what had been the point of coming in here and waking him up? No amount of coffee was going to compensate him for hearing the news that his wife had slipped through his fingers, again.

Simmons approached the bed with a tray on which he'd placed the cup of coffee he'd just poured. 'A short while after she left,' he said, 'I sent Timothy along after her, in case, er, she may have needed anyone else to perform any errands for her, since I did not think you would wish her to be out on her own, should she send Stephens back with any further shopping.'

He had no idea who this Timothy person may be, which suggested he was fairly low down in the staff ranks, but there was one thing he did gather from all the *shoulds* and *may haves* Simmons had just spoken. The wily old bird had, in effect, made sure that not only did she have an escort, but had also arranged to have her followed.

'You did right,' said Anthony, with a feeling of immense relief, as he took the proffered cup from his butler. He was still furious with her, he reminded himself as he downed his coffee in three swift gulps, but she was still his wife. Her place was under this roof.

Until *he'd* decided how best to deal with her.

She had no right to just take off without consulting him. Or telling him what she was about.

'Thank you, my lord,' said Simmons. 'I thought you might also wish to know that Timothy returned, a short while ago, with the information that Her Ladyship, having entered a certain house, showed no signs of coming out again. And that, in his opinion, the house was in an area where he wouldn't wish, in his own words, his own mother to stray into.'

Anthony finally understood why his butler and valet had come in, and woken him, even though they knew he'd been home less than a handful of hours and would not normally have stirred from his room for several more.

They were of the opinion that he ought to go and extricate her from whatever situation she'd wandered into.

And he was of the same mind. He had no intention of letting her go back to wherever she'd been, or whoever she'd been with, all these months.

Not without facing the pair of them in their... love nest.

With something like a snarl, he flung back the covers and got out of bed.

It had taken her ages to find her way from Grosvenor Square to the warren of streets clustering round the back of Drury Lane. And it hadn't helped that she had a bewigged and liveried footman trailing along behind her, making people stare. She'd kept getting so flustered that she'd taken several wrong turns and had to retrace her steps to the landmarks Jack had made her learn so that she wouldn't get lost in what had felt to her, when they'd first come to London, like a maze.

But finally, she reached the familiar arch that led into the dank courtyard off which she and Jack, Chloe and Fenella and Toby had taken lodgings.

She gave a sigh of relief on finding her way home. Only…this wasn't home any longer, was it? It couldn't be, not now she knew she was married to an earl. Whatever that earl may think of her, personally, it would be beneath his dignity to permit his wife to consort with what he'd probably think of as vagabonds as well as actors.

But, oh, how she was going to miss them all!

And how were they going to cope without her to deal with all the…mundane aspects of their lives? Who would make sure their bills didn't exceed the amount they earned? Who would pay their rent on time, and make sure their costumes were kept in good repair, and, and, all the rest of it?

She sighed again as she began to mount the stairs. Only this time, it was through sadness at the thought of having to bid them all farewell. She paused then, and turned to confront the footman who seemed determined to follow her, even in here. For she didn't want him witnessing what was bound to be an emotional parting. There was nothing, she'd learned, that actors did more exuberantly than display their emotions.

'I think it would be for the best,' she told him, 'if you stayed outside.'

He looked as if he'd like to argue. So she lifted her chin and looked him straight in the eye, the way Chloe had taught her.

'Pretend you are a grand lady,' the actress had said. 'And that the person who is giving you cheek is so far beneath your notice that you are astonished he dares so much as to stand next to you.'

Lord, how Chloe would laugh when she found that she *was*, in truth, rather a grand lady. Or at least, that she was married to a high-ranking man. Truth be told, she'd never felt that she was anything like his equal, had she? But that probably had a lot to do with the fact that her mother had only been the daughter of a penniless vicar, and her father some sort of clerk, she'd been told, as well as having always expected to have to work for her keep.

But the footman took a step back, his head lowered. How ironic it was, she reflected as she set off up the narrow, rickety staircase alone, that it had taken an actress to teach her how to step into the role she'd struggled so hard with when she'd first married Lord Epping. She'd scarcely been able to order a cup of tea from some of his staff, so conscious had she been that only a short time before, she'd been of a similar status herself. Though possibly, she reflected, better educated than most of them, thanks to that angry old man who'd claimed to be the brother of a grandfather she'd never heard of.

But anyway, that was a consideration for another time. Right now she had to concentrate on the encounter with Jack.

Come to think of it, it would probably be better to go to her own room, first, and quickly gather together what meagre belongings she had accumulated during her short stint as a member of this acting troupe. And then, if Jack was as angry as he had every right to be, she'd be able to make a swift exit.

She pushed open the door to the attic room she'd been sharing with Fenella, ever since they'd taken up these lodgings, and peered round. She could just see the top of Fenella's tousled head peeking out from above the mound of blankets. Blankets, she couldn't help noticing, that her roommate had stripped off *her* bed. Though she could hardly blame her for having done so when it must have become obvious she wasn't going to return last night. The room was cold and damp, and she herself had never been warm once, while living there.

First thing she'd do, when she returned to Radcliffe House… Oh! That was the name of the house in Grosvenor Square, wasn't it? Funny how it had popped into her head like that, without her making any effort to think of it. Well, anyway what had she been thinking about before? Oh, yes! Buying eiderdowns. Thick ones. And a set of hot water bottles, which she'd have sent here.

Whilst making a list in her head of other items which would make these rooms less uncomfortable, she tiptoed over to her bed, opened the lid of the small trunk which sat at its foot, and then began gathering up the odds and ends of hers she'd left on such useful spaces as the windowsill, a stool, or just a corner where nobody was likely to trip over them. It didn't take long. She put Jack's parcel on top of her belongings, and then began to drag the trunk across the floor to the door. It wasn't all that heavy, but it was jolly awkward to handle. It had only been the prospect of what it would be like to try wrestling this very item back to Grosvenor Square on her own which had made her yield to that butler's pleas to allow a footman to come with her.

The trunk made more noise than she would have liked, as she dragged it across the bare boards. But Fenella didn't stir. No surprise there. For one thing, Fenella was unlikely to have gone to bed until the small hours. For another, the air in this room reeked of the fumes of whatever Fenella had been drinking the night before. It would take something like an earthquake, she mused, with a wry smile, to rouse Fenella before she'd slept it off.

When she had dragged the trunk as far as the landing, she paused, wondering whether to try and get it down at least one flight of stairs. If she went backwards, and let it slide from one step to the next, she could cushion it so that it wouldn't make *too* much of a racket. Probably. Then, when she'd reached the floor below, and knocked on Jack's door, she'd be able to show him that she was serious about leaving. The packed trunk would be proof she meant it.

But before she'd bumped it halfway down the stairs, the door to Jack's room flew open. And there stood Jack, in the process of thrusting his arms into his shirt. And, prancing round his feet, Toby. The little dog must have heard her moving round and bumping the trunk down the stairs, and alerted his master. He hadn't barked, though, so the clever little dog must have known she wasn't a burglar.

Nevertheless, as she settled the trunk on the landing, she felt her face heat as she strove to find words to explain herself.

But she need not have worried.

'Perdita,' cried Jack, flinging his arms round her while she was in the process of straightening up, and almost knocking her over, which made her glad she'd told the footman to wait outside. It was exactly this sort of behaviour that the man would have found hard to understand. She could just picture the footman's face, had he witnessed his master's wife allowing a shirtless man to embrace her!

'I was so worried about you,' Jack continued, stepping back and, to her relief, putting his second arm into his shirt, and doing up the strings. She took the opportunity to bend down, and pet Toby's soft velvet ears. She was going to miss this clever little dog, and the antics which had never failed to bring a smile to her face. 'When you didn't come home last night,' said Jack, 'I thought you'd had another, er, brainstorm, or whatever they call it. Or got lost. Or abducted. I shouldn't have allowed an innocent like you to go wandering round this big bad city on your own.'

'Oh, Jack,' she said, tears coming to her eyes. Even though she'd discovered that he was inclined to lie and cheat his way out of trouble, and even though his moral code was far more elastic than hers, she couldn't help liking him. He'd been so kind to her. So generous. So understanding.

'I am so sorry,' she said, 'that you were worried. And even more sorry that I didn't come back with your new suit.' She turned to the trunk, took his parcel off the top, and finally placed it into his hands. 'I know how much you wanted to be able to wear it when you went to supper with those young gentlemen. I tried so hard to get it to you, truly I did...'

'There, there,' he said, pulling out a scarlet handkerchief from somewhere or other, and dabbing at her cheeks. 'In the end, when we realized you wasn't going to make it, I decided to put on my motley, and go in character. And do you know what? It was the best thing I could have done. They loved having Jack B Nimble, acrobat, at their table, playing the fool and making free with his slapstick. If I'd gone as, well, me—' he grinned and spread his hands in a self-deprecating gesture '—I suspect they would have thought I was trying to ape my betters, and would have put me firmly in my place.'

'But they invited you to supper. Why would they have done that if they didn't really want you there?'

'Well, the likes of them never truly let the likes of us across the moat, do they? I mean, people invite actors to stay at their grand country houses over Christmas on occasion, but we always have to sing for our supper, don't we?'

She thought back to the early days of her marriage, when she'd been elevated from the status of paid companion to countess overnight, and the outrage it had provoked in so many quarters. His mother, above all. When Anthony had introduced her, when they'd visited his principal seat, Radley Court, he'd done so with a definite air of defiance. And rather than welcome her into the family warmly, the petite, dark-haired, elegant lady had sighed, and said that she regretted urging him to get married. The other guests at that time, all of them titled and wealthy apart from her, had also looked at her, and then at Anthony, as though they thought he'd lost his mind.

Later on, his mother had relented, and had grudgingly admitted that she supposed she could see why he'd married her, but it had been too late to make *her* feel any better.

'I know exactly what you mean,' she said sadly.

'Well, never mind me, my girl! What happened to you? Where have you been all night?'

'Oh, Jack, it was…' She shook her head. 'It is so hard to explain.' She certainly couldn't tell him about her feet suddenly developing a mind of their own and carrying her to Grosvenor Square, where they knew they'd be warm, at last. She'd sound like a complete zany! But she'd had plenty of time to ponder over the mystery of her strange inability to remember anything, and the way one look at Anthony had shattered all the defences she decided she must have built up to protect her from recalling the worst experience she'd ever had to endure. 'It was as if…a door opened.' The one to Anthony's house on Grosvenor Square, to be precise. 'And once I went through it, another door opened.' And she'd recalled snippets of what her life had been like before she'd met him.

'And then another,' she continued as, wondering how on earth she had even met someone like Anthony, she'd remembered that awful Christmas house party, and how miserable she'd been with Lady Marchmont complaining all the time. If it wasn't about the draughty rooms, it was about the food which gave her indigestion at night. And how harried she'd been, dashing about all the time for warmer shawls, or to fetch patent remedies to deal with one ailment or another, and how she'd run into him, full tilt, as she'd been rounding a corner on some errand or other. And how surprised she'd been when, instead of shouting at her, like that man on the street had yesterday, he'd steadied her, and asked her if she was all right. And as if that hadn't been enough, he'd noticed her later that day, and instead of pretending he hadn't, he'd strolled right across the room to where she'd been huddled in a corner, and struck up a conversation.

And not just that evening, no, that had only been the start. She'd lived for those precious, snatched moments when she had him all to herself. And when she didn't, she began trying to find out as much about him as she could. Which had meant listening to gossip, although she usually tried not to do so. But what choice did she have? It wasn't as if she could ask about him openly. It wasn't her place to ask impertinent questions about her betters, was it? So, little by little, she'd learned that he was a powerful man, an earl, which had depressed her. And then that he was a widower, who had buried his heart in the grave of his pretty young wife, which had filled her with compassion. No wonder he'd never smiled! No wonder he often looked so…grim.

She'd been astonished when, just before it was time for everyone to leave, he'd proposed. But she'd greedily snatched at the chance of belonging to him. Though she'd hardly known him, she'd been sure that nothing could make her happier than to have the right to see him, and talk to him every day for the rest of her life. But then he'd brought her to the house in Grosvenor Square. And made love to her, in the very bed in which she'd been trying to sleep while all the memories of those early days had been flooding back. Which had become impossible once her mind had started conjuring up images of their wedding night.

Oh, but he'd been so patient with her. Not just that first time, but every time he'd come to that bed. He'd always taken her to the heights of pleasure at least once before reaching his own satisfaction…

Not that she could possibly tell Jack about that sort of thing. She cleared her throat. 'And before I knew it,' she said, taking up the thread in a way that glossed over everything of an intimate nature, 'well, it all came back.'

'What did?'

'My memory. Not all at once. And not in any logical order. But a small thing—' if you could call her feet remembering the way home when the rest of her didn't '—which jolted another memory to surface, and then…then—' she swallowed '—a really big thing.' Losing her baby, so soon after learning that she was carrying it at all. 'The thing which, I believe, caused me to…shut the door in my mind to everything I had been, and everything I was. Oh, but never mind that. The thing is, I found my way to where I used to live.' Or at least, her feet had. 'By accident, really. Only when I got there, and all these doors began opening, it was all such a…shock that I went dizzy, and had to sit down on the bottom stair, and cling on to the newel post. I don't know why that post made me feel safe…'

'Something to cling to, in all the upheaval, I dare-say,' he said wisely. 'Speaking of which, perhaps we'd better go down into the parlour. More comfortable there.'

'Thank you, yes,' she said. The little room he called the parlour was the one room in their lodgings that boasted a fireplace, and was where they gathered to discuss rehearsals, costumes, and anything else that cropped up. It was where she had always sat to deal with bills and repair the damage to costumes.

The first thing Jack did when they went in was to go to the hearth and start raking out the ashes from the day before. She couldn't help comparing the modern efficient grate in that bedroom in Radcliffe House with this grimy excuse for a fireplace, in which Jack was busy with the shovel and brush. 'You are right about needing to cling to something,' she mused while Jack started piling up kindling. Though even when he got it going, it would only manage to take the chill from an area of about a foot in front of it. Most of the heat went straight up the chimney.

The chimney breast went up the side of the room above, and warmed it in the process. No wonder Chloe had chosen that one, even though it was so tiny, and made her and Fenella share the one above, even though it had the nicer view from the window. Who could care about views when their toes were frozen all night long?

'I was, in point of fact,' she said, taking up her tale from where she'd left off, 'shaking with…shock, I suppose. Only they must have thought it was from cold, because they kept plying me with cups of hot tea, and urging me off the staircase, and up into my old room with promises of a hot bath and a fire. And, oh, it has been so long since I've experienced such luxury that I agreed without thinking what it would mean.'

'And what,' he said, getting to his feet and brushing the ash off his breeches, 'did it mean?'

'It meant,' she said, watching Toby darting past him, circling a few times, then settling down on the hearth rug, 'that I was left in a room without a stitch on. Because the housekeeper decided all my clothing needed to go to the laundry. And then I had a…a horrible encounter with my husband…'

'Ho! What?' Jack's eyebrows shot up. A grin split his face. 'A husband?'

'Yes. Well, I always did suspect there might have been someone, didn't I?'

'Yes, you did. What a good job it is that you never agreed to marry me, then, hey?'

She swatted at him. He may have proposed to her, several times. Whenever she pulled them out of the suds, in fact. But she'd never believed he meant it. Besides which, Chloe would never have stood for it. She was the principal female in the troupe. And she was never going to allow anyone to upstage her, especially not by marrying Jack.

'Well, after all that, when I'd calmed down a bit, and remembered you would be wanting your suit, it was getting late. But when I rang and asked for some clothes, all they brought me was a nightgown. And I couldn't very well run through the streets in my nightwear, could I? But I hardly slept a wink, for worrying…'

And, to be honest, writhing in mortification, or something, as she recalled the things she'd done, in that very bed, with her husband.

'It sounds as though you have enough to worry about, on your own account,' said Jack, 'without worrying about me. Besides, like I said, it turned out for the best.'

'Yes, but after all the expense you went to,' she said, thinking of the parcel which had taken her so much time, and such ingenuity, to wrest from the hands of the tailor.

'Ah, you know me, and money,' he said, wryly. 'Never long in company.'

'Oh, Jack, if only you could learn some habits of economy…'

'Well, that was your job, wasn't it, my duck? Keeping us all afloat with your clever ways.' He sighed. 'We shall miss you. You are going back to this husband of yours, I take it? I mean, with all the talk of ringing for servants, and going into a house big enough to warrant a housekeeper, you must be tempted…'

Tempted. Yes. Anthony was temptation on legs. Everything a girl could dream of.

She looked at her feet as she remembered giving in to the temptation to say yes to his proposal, even though she'd suspected he'd made it on the spur of the moment, and probably hadn't thought things through properly. Oh, what a foolish, selfish thing it had been to do. But…but *marriage*. To a man like Anthony. A man who hadn't sneered at her, or told her she was clumsy and to get out of his way, but who'd been kind. And had then seemed interested in her, as a person, in what she'd thought, and believed. When nobody else, at least since her parents had died, had ever acted as though she had any right to her own opinions or beliefs, never mind asking her what they might be!

She sighed. Looked Jack straight in the face. 'I made vows in a church,' she said primly. Well, she wasn't about to share anything about the intimate side of her marriage, was she? Or how silly she'd been to marry a man she'd known less than a fortnight. Especially not with Jack, of all people. 'And now that I remember them, I have to at least try to keep them,' she said, cringing at how virtuous she was attempting to sound, when virtue had very little to do with it. Because last night, when she'd seen him standing there, glowering at her, she'd had exactly the same reaction as she'd had that first time they'd collided. He made her breathless. He made her want him, the kind man behind the ferocious scowl. The patient, generous lover… 'Don't you think?'

For once, his face became sombre. 'There will always be a place for you with us, if it doesn't work out.'

'Oh, Jack,' she said. And, overcome with gratitude for his kindness, she flung her arms round his neck.

It was perhaps inevitable that this was the very moment her husband chose to fling open the door, and burst in.

Chapter Six

'Unhand,' snarled her husband, 'my wife!'

Jack, who had spent his life dodging trouble in one form or another, swiftly did as he was told. And she, too, thought it would be prudent to step away from her dear friend. She had never seen her husband look so…wild. If she'd thought last night that he looked like the living embodiment of a thunderstorm, then this morning he'd become…

She shook her head at her total inability to come up with any word sufficient to describe the way Anthony looked. He hadn't shaved. And because he hadn't buttoned up his greatcoat, she was able to see that he wasn't wearing a neckcloth. He, who normally took such pains to look elegant, and aloof, had turned into a…

'Well,' said Jack archly into the smouldering silence. 'Here's a man who knows how to make an entrance.'

It was like pouring oil onto a fire. Anthony stepped

forward, his fists clenched, and took a swing at Jack. If he'd managed to land the punch, she had no doubt he would have broken Jack's nose.

But Jack hadn't acquired his stage name of Nimble without good reason. He ducked under Anthony's fist and at the same time flung himself backwards, nimbly turning the evasive manoeuvre into a somersault. Just before he landed, on his feet, on the dining table, he snatched up a swatch of material which, only the day before, she'd been planning to stitch into a costume, and swirled the length of spangled gauze round his head.

'Oh, sir,' Jack squeaked, in a falsetto voice. 'How ungallant to attack a defenceless female!' And then, the pièce de résistance, he fluttered his eyelashes.

She pressed her hand to her mouth to hide the fact that her lips were twitching with supressed laughter. Laughter which she knew would be fatal to allow Anthony to see. He would definitely *not* appreciate starring as the villain in the farcical scene that Jack had conjured out of what Anthony seemed to believe was more in the nature of a tragedy. To top it all, his look of thwarted rage had turned swiftly into one of utter astonishment when Toby, who seemed to think all this energetic activity from the humans must mean they were all rehearsing a new part, and who had been trained to shadow all the movements his master made, got up and performed his own doggy version of a somersault on the hearthrug.

She bit her lower lip hard to prevent herself from showing any amusement whatsoever as she stepped over to Anthony, and placed a restraining hand gently on his forearm before he could recover enough to pull Jack down from the table and enact the revenge he looked as though he felt cheated of.

'Epping,' she began, since that was the name he'd told her she should call him, when they were first married, except when they were alone.

'Epping!' Jack's brows rose so high they disappeared under the fringe of spangled gauze.

Jack let the gauze slip from his head as he looked down at her from his vantage point on the table. 'His name is Epping?'

She nodded. And now it was Jack's turn to see the funny side of things. But, being Jack, he made no attempt to conceal what he felt. Instead, he burst out laughing, slapping his thighs at the richness of the joke.

'I fail to see,' said her husband, icily, 'why hearing my title should cause such hilarity.'

Although it was plain to see that he imagined Jack must be mocking him, for some obscure reason.

'Title?' Jack looked her way, the gauze finally slipping from his head altogether his brows rising so high they disappeared under the fringe of spangled gauze. 'Epping is his *title*?'

'Yes,' she confessed. 'I am afraid that I have to tell you that he is Lord Epping. An earl to be precise. Though his principal seat is nowhere near Epping. I don't even know why the title is the same as the town when he has no property anywhere near it, so far as I know...'

Jack's smile vanished. He looked about as confounded as Anthony had done a moment ago, when

Toby had started doing somersaults. 'But…that makes you a countess.'

'I cannot deny it,' she said with an apologetic shrug. Even though nothing anyone had said or done had ever been able to make her *feel* like a countess. But she didn't feel that now was the time to explain anything to Jack. Not while her husband was looking so murderous.

It was more important to get him out of here before he did something he'd regret. And he would, she knew, once she'd put him in possession of the facts.

'Epping,' she said, again, 'could you send the footman upstairs to fetch my trunk down please? Now that it is packed, it is a bit heavy for me.'

'Your trunk?' Anthony, for that was the name she thought of him in her head, and in her heart, tore his eyes from Jack to scowl at her instead.

'Yes. I came here to fetch my things, you see. And to explain…well, that I wouldn't be able to work for Jack and his troupe any longer. Jack is an actor, as you may have gathered.'

'*Work* for this fellow?' Anthony shot a look of contempt at Jack, who was still standing on the table, gazing down at them with a measuring look, as though trying to work out how he ought to play the scene now he'd discovered that his audience was not what he'd first assumed.

'Yes. Unless…' Oh. She'd assumed, when he'd come striding in looking so murderous, that he'd come to drag her away from what he seemed to regard as a den of iniquity. But perhaps she'd got it wrong. Perhaps he'd just come to tell her, face to face, that this was the last straw and he was washing his hands of her. She straightened her shoulders. 'Well, if you do not want me to go back to Grosvenor Square with you, I will understand. Completely…'

Of course she could understand him not wanting her back. His lowly born, defective wife. But that didn't make it hurt any the less. To her annoyance, she found the prospect of him telling her that no, he didn't want her coming back to his house so painful that tears started to her eyes. She might just have told Jack that it was sticking to vows made in church that was important to her. And of course, it was. But how much more did it matter to her that she had a second chance to be with him? That, against all the odds, she'd found her way back to him?

'Of course you must come back to Grosvenor Square with me,' said Anthony, testily.

Oh, thank heaven!

'It is where you belong.'

Did she? Truly?

'You are,' he said, taking a deep breath, as though it pained him to have to admit it, 'my wife, after all.'

She hung her head. Yes, she was his wife. But, oh, how he must wish she wasn't. She'd sensed it before, she suddenly recalled, another one of those doors in her mind swinging open and smacking her hard in the face. Not long after they'd married. Not long before it had all come crashing down. She'd been lying there, crying, so sure had she been that he'd regretted making such an unequal match. She had been so sure that he didn't really love her…that such a sentimental thought would never enter his head.

She'd felt as though she'd been such a fool to hope that she could really be the Cinderella character to Anthony's handsome prince, and live happily ever after with him in his castle. She should have known that what had seemed too good to be true must of course be doomed to failure.

She had never, she realized, ever truly dared to believe she deserved a happy ever after. She had never, come to think of it, ever really understood why on earth he'd proposed to her. Unless it had been because he'd felt sorry for her and succumbed to some sort of…quixotic fit of chivalry.

'Come,' he said, striding to the door and holding out his hand to her in an imperious gesture that she should follow. 'The sooner you forsake this madhouse—' he turned back to shoot one last sneer at Jack '—the better.'

She followed him without hesitation. Even though she feared that all he could bring her was more hurt. Because, in her heart, she was his. His wife. For better, or worse.

She'd married him in spite of not having a clue why he'd asked her, because she'd adored him. And she'd thought she'd be the luckiest girl in the world, and the happiest, to be allowed to live with him. Because at that stage she'd had no idea just how painful unrequited love could be. That the forbearing way he appeared to tolerate her could end up with her feeling as if he was flaying the skin from her bones.

'Stephens,' Anthony said to the footman, who was waiting outside on the doorstep, 'be so good as to fetch Her Ladyship's trunk.'

'It is just on the first landing,' she put in. 'It was a bit awkward for me to move any further, or...'

She broke off as Anthony shot her an exasperated look. She had never, ever heard him explaining his orders to a servant. And it looked as if he thought she ought not to, either.

'Where,' he said to her, in a clipped tone that had her bracing herself for a reprimand, 'will we be able to get hold of a cab, in this neck of the woods?'

'A cab?' He only wanted to hire a cab? Not berate her for her conduct?

'I... I have no idea,' she admitted. Well, she'd never had the money to routinely ride about in cabs. So she hadn't ever taken any notice of where she could have caught one. 'But it won't take more than a quarter of an hour to walk to Grosvenor Square.' Provided they didn't take any wrong turns.

'If you think I'm walking through the streets like this,' he said, indicating his billowing coat, his lack of neck cloth, and his unshaven cheeks in one irritated wave, 'then you are very much mistaken. Besides, there is your trunk to consider. Do you wish Stephens to have to carry it all that way?'

'No, of course not,' she said, subsiding. Both those reasons sounded perfectly valid. Perhaps she had been wrong to assume he'd wanted to bundle her into a cab because he would be ashamed to be seen out and about with her.

Stephens came out, then, her trunk wedged under one of his massive arms, as though it weighed no more than the parcel she'd been carrying the day before. Had it only been the day before? It felt as though she'd lived half a lifetime since she'd stumbled out of the tailor's shop and slipped on the icy pavement.

With an expression of embarking on a forlorn hope, Anthony asked Stephens if he knew exactly where they could find a hackney cab stand. Stephens did, and without further ado, led them straight there. Then, most efficiently, he procured the services of one, and stowed the trunk on its floor.

Footmen, she decided as Stephens opened the door and handed her in, were jolly useful people to have at your beck and call. But as she took her seat, she heard Anthony telling him, rather abruptly, to make his way back to Grosvenor Square on foot, before slamming the door shut.

She supposed it *was* rather cramped inside with the trunk taking up most of the floor space. But also, somehow, she couldn't see Anthony *ever* sharing a cab with his footman.

But at least, since it was just the two of them, she could speak freely.

'I...' she ventured timidly, once the cab set off, 'would like to explain why Jack found your name so funny.' She hadn't said farewell to him before they left, she suddenly realized. It was as if, once Anthony had come into the room, she hadn't been able to think about anyone but him.

'I don't care,' he said frostily. 'His opinion means nothing to me.'

Oh, really? Somehow, she didn't think he'd be glaring out of the window, presenting her with such a hostile view of his hunched shoulders, if he truly didn't care.

And that revelation gave her the courage to make the explanation his mouth had told her he didn't need.

'He thought it funny you bear the name of Epping,' she said, 'because it was in the town of Epping that I first met Jack. The minister whom I was placed into the care of after—' she gulped back a wave of pain, knowing she was going to have to say it out loud, or they were never going to get anywhere '—after losing the baby, took me to Epping because, apparently, while I was delirious with fever, I kept on saying it, over and over.'

She couldn't remember it, not really. That part of things was still hazy, thank goodness. As it was, just talking about what she knew must have happened was so upsetting she felt her eyes welling up.

'I believe I was calling for you,' she said, the tears gathering and rolling down her cheeks. 'But they mustn't have understood. They must have thought it was a clue as to where I'd come from. And so they took me there.'

He said nothing. But the way he shifted in his seat told her that her words had affected him, in some way or other.

'Anthony,' she said, reaching out one hand to place it on the shoulder nearest to her, before withdrawing it before it could make contact. Because it would be just too awful if he shook her off, or flinched, or told her to keep her hands to herself, or... Oh, she could think of a million ways he could repulse her gesture. She folded her hands in her lap.

'You did say, last night,' she pointed out, though, 'that you wished to learn what became of our baby.'

'Not now,' he said in a strange tone that made her suspect he was gritting his teeth. 'Not in a cab.'

'When we get…' She was about to say *home*, but she still wasn't sure if that house was going to be her home. She certainly hadn't felt at home in it last time she'd stayed there.

'Yes, when we get home,' he said. Although she still wasn't convinced that he included her in that statement. *His* home, yes. But was it, would it ever be, hers?

They reached Grosvenor Square without saying another word. Anthony got out the moment the cab drew to a halt and went round to pay the driver.

Since he hadn't offered her his hand, she climbed out unaided. The front door opened before she'd set foot on the first doorstep, and Simmons stood there looking at her, his expression inscrutable. Although for some reason, she got the impression he was relieved she'd come back.

Or perhaps she was imagining it. Anyway, before she had a chance to think of something to say to him, Anthony joined her.

'Send one of the footmen,' he instructed Simmons, 'to fetch Her Ladyship's trunk from the cab, and put it in her room.'

Then he took her by the elbow and escorted her into the house. She wasn't sure if it was the gesture of a gentleman, or a jailer, but whichever it was, he appeared to be determined to get her inside.

'Send Snape to my room,' he said to Simmons, 'and escort Her Ladyship to the drawing room. I shall join her there once I am properly dressed.' And then, without saying one word to her, he *stomped*—yes, stomped, that was the only word for it—up the stairs.

'If,' said Simmons, his expression still so inscrutable it looked as if it would have taken thumbscrews to discover what he was thinking, 'you would follow me, my lady?'

'I think I can remember the way to the drawing room,' she said snippily. And then wished she hadn't taken out her irritation at the way Anthony was treating her, on his staff. It wasn't their fault that *he* had no manners.

'I beg your pardon,' she said to Simmons. 'Of course, you must do as His Lordship says.'

She then meekly followed him up the stairs which Anthony had just used. Only, when they reached the first landing, instead of continuing up the next flight, they turned to the left along the gallery, and along to the receiving rooms.

The drawing room was at the front of the house. From here, there was a view over the square, so that if she wished, she could have watched the comings and goings of whoever chose to take the air, or was paying visits to other residents. She had done so a fair few times during the weeks she'd lived here as a new bride, she recalled now. Half hoping someone would come to call to pay their respects, half dreading the prospect of attempting to entertain women of far higher rank. Entertain? Hah! Survive the ritual shredding from their sharp tongues had been more like it.

It had been from those callers that she'd learned so much more about Anthony's first wife. About how dazzling she'd been. How young they'd both been when they'd married. What a beautiful, stylish couple they'd made. About how tragic it was that she'd died so young, and who would have believed a cold could have gone to her lungs and carried her off so quickly? Not Epping, they'd added, looking at her to see her reaction. He had been inconsolable. Nobody had thought he'd ever marry again, though of course, he had to have an heir, they'd added, glancing at her stomach…

It was about time she shrugged off those painful memories, she decided as she made her way across the beautifully polished floor to the seat by the window which had been her favourite.

Memory was a funny thing, she pondered as she sat down. Now that she had one, that was. It was a bit like…like… Well, take the way walking into this room just now had brought the memory of how she'd felt in here, before, back to the forefront of her mind. It had been like opening a door. A door to…well, something like a wardrobe which she knew was full of all sorts of garments. She didn't have to look at them to know they were there. But only by opening the door and reaching in could she actually pull one out, and put it on. In a similar kind of way, she knew that she had a head full of memories now, which just needed a…prompt to spring into life again.

'May I,' said Simmons, from the doorway, 'fetch you some tea? Or anything to eat? I believe you went out without breaking your fast.'

She'd been too anxious about seeing Jack, and getting what she'd feared might be an unpleasant encounter over with, to have eaten a thing earlier. Which had been foolish. Because Jack had been, as he'd always been, most kind and understanding.

The trouble was that now she was even more anxious about what Anthony was going to say. Would he be kind and understanding once she'd cleared up the misunderstandings? He'd always been kind to her before, even though he'd made her feel as if that kindness had been done out of duty, rather than from any real deep affection. As though it would be beneath his dignity to be anything but kind to his poor little dab of a wife.

Only, that would mean relating the events which had led to her losing her mind.

She'd have to be brave. Braver than she'd ever been before, if she wanted to clear her name. And she did! She simply couldn't let him carry on thinking she'd been unfaithful.

But the prospect of telling him what had happened made her mouth go bone dry.

'Thank you, a pot of tea would be most welcome,' she therefore said to Simmons. And perched on the edge of her favourite chair, to try and marshal her thoughts into a logical sequence.

Chapter Seven

He didn't care what she, or anyone else, made of his decision to come upstairs, to his own room, whilst ordering his wife to the drawing room. They could all think what they liked!

'I need,' he said to Snape, who had come running up the stairs behind him, 'a shave, and a clean shirt.' As if to prove it, he pulled off the shirt he had on and tossed it aside, relishing the feeling of casting off the lingering smell of that damp and dingy boarding house. Then he went to sit at the dressing stool, while Snape, wordlessly, got busy with a bowl and a shaving brush.

He needed to look, and feel, respectably turned out before he faced her again. So it felt right that Snape should apply lather to his face just as he was thinking that. For he really did need to obliterate every last vestige of the savage he'd almost unleashed in that shabby little boarding house.

If not for that fellow's agility, and the way that ridiculous little dog had distracted him, he might have beaten the man to a pulp.

When she'd sworn she'd only been working for him.

When she'd only gone there to collect her things and come home.

He tilted his head back and closed his eyes as Snape picked up the razor. Hadn't he sworn, long ago, that he would never take action again, without taking time to consider the wisdom of what his baser self longed to do? Hadn't he learned his lesson?

Apparently not.

For there had been no need to have gone chasing after her and making a fool of himself.

Though, if he hadn't, he reflected as Snape expertly tilted his face one way or another to gain access with his razor, he would never have seen where she'd been living. Or how she'd been living. He would never have found any reason to have gone and inspected that dingy little set of rooms. Or spoken to the ugly little fellow who'd flung himself backwards onto a table with the agility of a flea.

Snape's regular swishing and rinsing was strangely soothing. By the time his valet had wiped off the last traces of soap, and was holding out a fresh shirt, Anthony felt much more capable of facing his wife.

To look her in the eyes as he demanded she explain exactly where she'd been and what she'd been doing since August.

He would have to bear in mind what little he'd learned so far. She'd certainly spent at least some of the time away from him working with actors, which meant that she'd probably learned a trick or two while she'd been with them.

She'd been able to convince him she'd been calling for him while she'd been losing their baby. Her account had been so heart-rending that, coming so soon after he'd misjudged her motives for leaving Grosvenor Square that morning, it had felt as if she was turning the knife in the wound.

He'd felt so guilty for thinking the worst of her, he'd wanted to apologize. But he hadn't been able to get any words past the lump which had formed in his throat when she'd started talking about losing the baby, and being ill, and calling for him. Calling for him while he'd been holed up in a dark room, imagining the worst of her, just as he'd done this morning.

Snape handed him a starched white neckcloth. Anthony took it, tied it, then examined his reflection in the mirror. He looked just the way he always did. Neat. Well groomed. And above all, impassive. For he never wanted anyone to be able to tell what he might be feeling. Particularly not today, when he was such a seething mass of contradictory emotions. Feelings of bitterness and betrayal warring with an almost boyish hope that she might be innocent of *all* the things he'd been so sure she'd done.

He despised that part of himself. For hoping.

And most of all, for still wanting her. Wanting to have her here, under his roof. When all evidence pointed to the fact that she shouldn't be here. She didn't belong here. For she'd betrayed him. Turned her back on all he'd offered. His hand. His title.

His heart.

And yet, last night, the moment she'd started weeping, he hadn't hesitated to take her in his arms to try to comfort her.

He eyed his neat, apparently aloof reflection with contempt. He'd *never* been able to resist her air of vulnerability, had he? The second time he'd seen her, after that surprisingly erotic encounter in the corridor, she'd been standing with her head bowed as Lady Marchmont had been telling her off for some misdemeanour or other, and he'd felt a strangely compelling surge of protectiveness for that poor, downtrodden girl. He'd wanted to sweep her up in his arms and take her somewhere safe, and shower her with all the things she lacked. Wipe away that little frown she always wore. Soothe away that anxious expression from her face by shouldering all her troubles.

He hadn't been able to understand it. Still didn't, to be honest. He'd never bothered about the feelings of a paid companion before. Society was littered with such creatures, and he'd scarcely taken notice of any of them. But he'd noticed *her*. After she'd…awoken him to the possibility of…of…

Anyway, he'd started to observe her, to try to puzzle out what it was about her that made him…care. Discreetly, of course.

Not discreetly enough, however. Because she'd noticed him watching her. Had blushed in response. Then started watching for him. Whenever he'd come into a room, her face would light up with pleasure, briefly, before she'd hang her head and try to shrink back into a corner as if to make herself invisible.

And every time she did that, Mother's words about what he ought to look for, when considering taking another wife, had rung in his ears.

This time you should choose a decent, quiet girl who has some genuine feeling for you.

Snape was still hovering behind him as he glared at himself in the mirror, waiting anxiously to hear if Anthony was satisfied with the way he'd tied his neckcloth. Anthony put him out of his suspense by nodding, as though satisfied with his effort, though to be honest, he'd rarely cared less about the intricate arrangement of folds and knots. He had a far more intricate and knotty problem occupying his thoughts. Snape set aside the remaining cloths draped over his arm, and came back with his jacket.

Even if Mother hadn't given him that piece of unsolicited advice, Anthony reflected as he thrust his arms into the sleeves, he had found Mary's shy, worshipful attitude irresistible.

That was the trouble, he reflected as he tugged his left sleeve down a quarter of an inch, more out of habit than a genuine interest in the set of his coat. He still found her almost irresistible.

She made him want things.

She made him act irrationally.

She tempted him to swear he'd do whatever she wanted if she'd promise never to leave him again.

She made him *weak*.

But he would not yield to temptation.

He would stand firm.

He lifted his chin and gave his pathetic reflection a stern look.

You must never, he reminded himself, *permit a woman to make a fool of you ever again.*

Satisfied that he looked suitably stern, he turned away from the mirror and walked to the door, which Snape darted to open for him.

He was ready. Resolute. He was as neat as a pin. Shaved and brushed and groomed to within an inch of his life. There were no more excuses for avoiding her.

Avoiding her? Was that what he'd been doing?

'No,' he muttered under his breath as he began to make his way down the stairs. He'd just been reminding himself that he needed to beware of the weapons she could wield against him. To ensure that he was not going to let her overwhelm him with either lust or that urge to protect and comfort her whenever she began to weep.

He descended the last few stairs with a scowl pleating his brows, and paused outside the drawing room door. He'd found the days without her lonely, missing the intelligence of her conversation. But the nights had been torment. He'd lain in his wide bed, sleep far from him, as he'd wondered where she was, and what she was doing.

And with whom. He'd been in such torment, imagining her being unfaithful. And deciding she'd been a worse choice for wife than even Sarah. At least Sarah had never progressed to the stage of running off with strangers. At least there had been no gossip or speculation about *that* marriage. But what was going to happen, he'd wondered, when people began to notice her absence? Or if somebody discovered her, living in sin somewhere? What would he have done? How would he have borne it?

He'd writhed in humiliation and dread, imagining facing the whispers, the contemptuous looks from all those people who'd raised their eyebrows at him marrying a woman from outside their social circle at the start. He'd cringed at how hotly he'd defended his choice to those who'd dared to say anything to his face. Her parents may only have occupied lowly positions, and she herself had to work for her living, but Mother had soon uncovered the fact that she descended from a younger son of the Earl of Comberbach on one side, and squires of impeccable lineage on the other. And she'd promised to spread that information as far as she was able.

And all for what?

It was with that bleak memory of the pointlessness of it all uppermost in his mind that he opened the drawing room door, so that the expression on his face as he looked at her was probably more than usually forbidding.

She'd been sipping a cup of tea, but at his entrance she set the cup down hastily, with fingers that trembled. And all of a sudden he remembered her asking him, with that exact look of trepidation on her face, if he wanted her to come back here.

How could she have asked such a foolish question? Of course he wanted her. All the time. Wasn't that what bothered him so much? How much easier all this would be if he didn't care one way or the other!

Although, he hadn't let her know how much he cared, had he? He hadn't welcomed her back last night. Instead, he'd shouted at her, then slammed out of the house, leaving her alone. Well, he hadn't understood why she'd come back, or what she wanted from him. Still didn't. It wasn't as if she'd ever seemed completely at ease in any of the properties to which he'd taken her, telling her she must think of them as hers, too. She'd just gazed round, wide-eyed, and carried on tiptoeing along the edges of the corridors as though fearing someone would come along and demand to know what she was doing there.

And he hadn't been all that surprised when they told him she'd run away. Shocked, hurt, and angry, yes. But deep down, hadn't he always felt as though she was poised for flight, all the time? Like some shy woodland creature that would dart away from a careless movement, or a sudden noise?

He'd never managed to make her feel at home with him anywhere, had he?

'So,' he said, forcing himself to stroll across the room and sit in the chair on the opposite side of the tea table to hers, when instinct would have had him remain in the doorway, arms folded. Because he didn't want to scare her into running off again, did he? He'd established that this morning when his stomach had plunged on hearing that she'd gone. He might not have been sure what he thought of her until that moment, and still wasn't sure of many things, but one thing he did know. His need to keep her in his sight was visceral. Defying logic and sense. It just crouched, snarling, deep inside him like some wild beast.

Which meant that he was going to have to find some way of rubbing along with her. Some way that wouldn't involve either shouting at her or taking her to bed.

Some middle ground.

Talking to her, or at least listening to what she wanted to say, seemed about as good a place to begin as any. But first of all he had an apology to make.

'I wish to beg your pardon,' he said stiffly, because apologizing was not something he'd ever done willingly. 'For my…behaviour this morning. I should not have offered violence to…that fellow, in your presence.'

He didn't know how he expected her to respond. But it was definitely not with a shrug, and her saying carelessly, 'Oh, Jack can take care of himself.'

It nettled him. He'd planned to start with that issue, then lead up to his gravest offence, that of suspecting her of running out on him again, when all she'd been doing was retrieving her luggage. But if she was going to treat such a major effort on his part with such levity, then…

Still, there were other pressing matters to discuss.

'You say you wish to tell me what became of our child?'

Her eyes filled, immediately, with tears. The cynical part of his brain warned him that she could be manufacturing them. Didn't actresses weep to order? And yet, even while that part of his brain was warning him to beware, he heard himself saying, in a voice that sounded suspiciously sympathetic, 'You need not, if you find it too upsetting.'

'No, no,' she said, lowering her gaze as she fumbled in her pockets for a handkerchief, which she used to dab at the tears which had already trickled down her cheeks. 'I think I can face it now,' she said. 'I couldn't for some time, which is why, I think…'

She blew her nose. 'I am better now,' she said, lifting her chin and looking him straight in the eye.

If that had been an act it was a damned impressive one. She looked for all the world like a bereaved mother valiantly attempting to speak of an ordeal which a gentleman would never insist she divulge.

'So?' He leaned back in his chair and crossed his legs, hoping that he looked like a man who would not be duped by the likes of her. Or any woman, no matter how appealing, how vulnerable.

'It…' She twisted the handkerchief between her fingers. A nice touch, that.

'It had been so hot,' she said, 'do you remember? Then, after you left me behind at Blanchetts, there was a thunderstorm I had thought that it might have made the air fresher. But when I went outside, the next morning, to try to get some air—because there wasn't any in the house, it was like an oven. It was like trying to breathe through a warm towel. I got as far as… Well, I'm not sure what you would call it. A little gravel walk, down by the sides of the stables. And then I found I couldn't go any further. There was a little sort of stone thing, like a boulder only with a flat top, which I sat on, to try and get my breath back.'

'A mounting block,' he put in.

'Oh?' She looked at him in a different way, then. It was as if she'd almost forgotten he'd been there, until he interrupted. As if she was casting her mind back to a scene that had happened some months ago.

Or working hard to remember her lines.

'So that explains why…' She looked away from him, to the window, although he was sure that from where she was sitting she wouldn't be able to see much outside. 'Well, anyway, this young man came along, and asked me if he could help me. First of all, I tried to tell him he need not bother, but he said he could see I was unwell, and he couldn't possibly just leave me there. He was the first person in that household,' she said, with a touch of what looked like resentment, 'who had shown any real concern for me.'

'Nonsense! I made sure that the housekeeper had strict instructions to take good care of you, since I could not do so myself.'

She turned to look at him, one eyebrow slightly raised. 'There is a world of difference between carrying out your orders to the letter and having any true sympathy for me.'

He considered that point. Mary, at that time, had still been putting on a very good appearance of being extremely timid. And Mrs Dawkins was one of those brisk, efficient women who were good at keeping a house running smoothly, but, perhaps, had not much patience for other people's weaknesses.

But before he could develop that theme, Mary was continuing.

'Anyway, when I told him that I had the headache, and had come out for some fresh air, but that it was no good, it was too hot *everywhere*, and that I would be really grateful if he would help me back indoors so that I might at least lie down again, he suggested taking me for a drive. He said that sitting in a moving open carriage would make me feel cooler, because it would feel like a breeze even though there wasn't really one. And that, besides, he'd drive me up over the…the tops, he called them, which I took to mean those hills I could see all round the property. He said it was always cooler up there. I remember saying it sounded delightful.' She stopped then, and plied her handkerchief, in a manner that would have wrung tears from anyone who wasn't steeling themselves to watch out for such ploys.

'He did have spots,' she said. 'I remember that now. That boy. What did you say his name was?'

'Franklin.'

She shook her head. 'I don't think he ever told me.' It was a few moments before she could speak again, so freely were the tears flowing.

Once more, he became irritated by not being sure how to react. If, as she was implying, the boy had been nothing to her, then why was she crying? It looked far more likely that she was mourning his loss.

Yet even so, it took every ounce of his strength to remain sitting where he was, instead of going to her and gathering her into his arms. Onto his lap.

'I beg your pardon,' she said, once she'd stemmed the flow of tears a touch. Possibly because he hadn't reacted in any way, so that it was pointless for her to keep them flowing? 'Things,' she said, 'still come back to me, even when I think I've remembered it all, and whenever another little moment pops into my head it has a tendency to overset me.'

He frowned, wondering what to make of that.

'I was just thinking it is like a wardrobe. Full of clothes,' she said. 'I know I've got a wardrobe now, at least. But I keep finding things at the back of it that I hadn't known were there when I opened the door. If you see what I mean?'

Not in the slightest. But he was not about to admit that. Let her tell her tale to the full, first, and only then would he ask his own questions.

'Please continue,' he therefore said, after giving her a nod which could have signified anything.

'Well, anyway,' she said, 'the boy said it would take him a short while to harness up the dog cart, and while I was waiting, I would be better in the shade. And he helped me a bit further along the gravel path, and over to the other side, where there was another of those boulder things, but this time in the shade of a wall.'

'The stable wall,' he said. Now, he could believe *this* part of her tale completely, since it chimed almost exactly with what Mrs Dawkins had informed him. That when she'd questioned the staff about Mary's disappearance, one of the housemaids had said that she'd been shaking some cloths out of an upper window, and had seen Franklin put his arm round Mary's waist, and take her round the back of the stables. Putting that together with their subsequent disappearance, everyone had naturally assumed the worst.

'At first,' Mary said, 'it was very pleasant, bowling along in that funny little cart thing. And once we got up into the hills, I did begin to feel better. My head didn't pound so much. And I began to feel as if I could breathe…'

She closed her eyes and shuddered.

'And then we got to this little humpback bridge. And there was a group of men blocking the way. Four or five of them.' She opened her eyes again. 'They…they said…' Tears began streaming down her face once more. And though she clutched at the handkerchief, she made no attempt to blot at them. 'One of them tried to pull me out of the seat. And *he*, Franklin, leaped down to grapple with them. He got me free, just for an instant, but there were too many of them for him to fight them all. And anyway, they had guns. He told me to run, just before they…they shot him.'

Anthony sat forward in his chair, his heart giving a peculiar lurch. 'You are telling me that you were held up by highwaymen? On *my* land? In broad daylight?'

'I don't know exactly where we were, or what they were. But, yes, they did want to rob us. Only when they found out we had nothing of value on us, they said they'd get their money's worth out of…' Her voice trailed to barely more than a whisper. 'Me.'

'I cannot believe it!' It was outrageous. It sounded

far too much like something one would read about in a novel.

She looked at him then, her face grave, and tear-stained. 'There must have been other cases of people being robbed violently, in that area. They cannot have just disappeared.'

'I will look into it.' And he would. For she was right. If there had been a gang of vagabonds, robbing travellers over the moors, there would be records of their crimes.

'Thank you,' she said, with all appearance of relief. 'They must be brought to account for killing Franklin…'

'What! Are you claiming that highway robbers killed Franklin?'

She looked up at him and frowned. 'Well, since you say he never went back to Blanchetts that can be the only explanation. Not that I saw him die, because I was too busy running away.' She grimaced. 'Oh, how cowardly that sounds. Only I was so frightened…'

He supposed this was the moment she would have expected him to reach out and take her hand, or even gather her into his arms, and tell her that she was safe now, that nobody would ever harm her again.

Only the word *actress* kept beating in his mind like a warning bell.

'So,' he said. 'What happened next?'

'One of them grabbed me by the shoulder. I think he was trying to push me to the ground,' she said in a small, fainting voice. 'Only I went over the parapet and into the river instead. And the current bore me away.'

Well, now he knew she was lying. There was no river up on the Yorkshire moors round Blanchetts which was deep enough to carry anyone anywhere. They were all, to the best of his knowledge, shallow, winding affairs whose beds were strewn with boulders.

'I cannot swim,' she continued, blithely unaware that he'd found her out in what he knew to be a lie. 'But the current was so strong that it just propelled me along, rolling me over and over. Every time my face rolled skyward I took a gulp of air. And then, all of a sudden, I was in this big, wooden enclosure. All covered in green slime. I tried to climb out, but it was too slippery.' Her fingers formed into claws as she said this, as though she was trying to portray the act of clawing at something with her fingernails. While his own hands clenched into fists. How could she carry on with this…farrago of nonsense? Did she think he was a complete idiot?

'And then,' she said, 'there was this whooshing sound, and another current caught me, and shot me through these big, black doors into a narrower body of water. And I banged into a boat. And I managed to draw enough air to scream. And the people on the boat heard me, and they got this sort of long hook thing, and pulled me out of the water and onto their boat.'

She was talking about a canal.

His blood chilled.

Because all of a sudden, her description of a fast-flowing river and a big wooden enclosure made sense. There was, just below Marwich Tor, a small reservoir, recently constructed to feed the canal. It was so far from Blanchetts that he hadn't connected it with her story. But she hadn't said how long they'd been driving for, had she? And water fed into that reservoir by means of a man-made sluice that collected run-off water from the hills. And there had been a thunderstorm the night before. So it *was* possible, *just*, that the sluice might have been brim full and fast flowing.

He got to his feet and walked to the other side of the room.

Could it all be true? *Had* she been the victim of a robbery? Had Franklin died to save her from a worse fate?

If so, then it meant that everything he'd believed about her, for the past three months, had been wrong.

She might not have been unfaithful at all! His heart leaped.

Only to plummet as he worked out that if she hadn't been unfaithful, if she was telling him the truth, then he'd failed her. Dismally.

If it was true…how would she ever be able to forgive him for abandoning her, albeit unwittingly, when she'd needed him the most?

If it was true.

'I need,' he said, going to the bell pull and yanking on it viciously, 'a brandy.'

Chapter Eight

'Brandy?' At this time of the morning?

Well, she supposed her tale must be a shock to him. Especially since he'd spent all this time assuming she'd run off with a boy half his age. And it had shocked her so much that it had caused her to blot it completely from her memory. For months.

Now it looked as though he'd like to blot it out as well. Only he was going to obliterate all the ugliness in brandy.

He went to the fireplace and laid his hands on the mantelpiece, lowering his head as he did so. He was breathing heavily.

'What,' he said, after taking a few deep breaths, 'happened next? Why didn't you make your way home?'

'I was too ill,' she told him. 'I began to lose the baby almost immediately after the barge people got me onto their boat. And they had no time to stop. They had a tight schedule to keep to, they said. They were kind enough, in their way, I suppose. The woman gave me something for the pain. And when it was all over, she told me to drink it all even though it was bitter, for it would help. And she told me not to dwell on it.' She'd forgotten some of the details, until this moment, when she was forcing herself to relive it by telling Anthony. But now she recalled the woman saying she'd lost many a child, over the years. And that she'd just had to put it out of her mind, and carry on. And so must she.

'And then I developed a fever, and the next thing I knew, I was in a white room, in a narrow bed, in the home of a Methodist family. They told me that a bargee and his wife had put me ashore, because they couldn't care for me in my illness. But the strange thing was that I couldn't remember anything before that room. I think, now, that it was as if I'd shut a door, in my mind, against all the horrible things that had happened, and was too afraid to even try to open it, for fear of what I might find there.'

'You are trying to tell me,' he said, in what sounded like disbelief, 'that you, what? Lost your memory?'

'Yes. I know it doesn't make sense but it wasn't so much that I lost it, so much as shut it away,' she mused. 'But I certainly couldn't tell those Methodists what my name was, or how I came to be in the canal. And they didn't believe me any more than you appear to,' she said, looking at the suspicious cast of his features. 'They assembled all the facts and put together a story to suit themselves. They cast me as an unmarried mother attempting to take her own life. The greatest of sinners.'

He'd taken a breath to say something when Simmons appeared in the doorway.

Anthony rounded on him with what looked like a mixture of exasperation and relief.

'Your breakfast is ready, my lord,' said the butler, relieving Anthony of the trouble of speaking. 'If you would care to proceed to the dining room?'

'Yes, thank you, Simmons,' said Anthony. Well, even though he hadn't responded to her explanation in the way she'd hoped, at least he'd thought better of starting on the brandy at this hour of the day. 'Mary?' He raised one eyebrow in her direction. 'Shall we continue while we eat?'

She wasn't sure that she could eat anything. But she didn't mind going with him to the dining room, and sitting at table with him while he ate his breakfast. He could listen, couldn't he? She could bring him up to date with the rest of it, because she really needed to clear her name. She didn't think she could bear it if he went on believing all the horrible things he'd accused her of doing.

Although she'd forgotten, until they were both sitting down, how awkward it was to have a meaningful conversation with servants about. They were all trying to ply her with the kind of food Anthony considered suitable fare for this time of day. Slices of beef, and tankards of ale, and fried eggs and all sorts of bread.

Although, to be honest, she'd been up for so long, and had done so much, that she probably could manage something more substantial than the bits of bread and cheese with which she'd grown accustomed to breaking her fast over the past few months. And there was so much food set out on the sideboard, it would be a crying shame to see it go to waste.

And she had the satisfaction of surprising Anthony when she went to the sideboard and helped herself to a substantial plate of food. When she'd been his bride, she recalled, now, she'd never been able to manage more than a mouthful of toast at breakfast. She'd been so self-conscious, after the things they'd been doing during the hours of darkness, in the privacy of her bedroom, that she could barely bring herself to raise her eyes above the level of the tablecloth. Even catching a glimpse of his hands wielding his knife and fork would bring back blistering memories of what those fingers had done to her. And how they'd made her feel.

This morning, though, she was capable of watching him slicing his steak, and raising the morsel to his mouth.

Oh, that mouth. Those lips. She could remember the feel of them, caressing her own lips. And kissing her neck, her breasts, her stomach. Oh, how long ago it all seemed. And as though it had happened to someone else. A green girl with stars in her eyes. A girl who hadn't been able to believe that a man as handsome and influential as Anthony could have chosen a nobody like her for his wife. She still didn't really understand it. Why hadn't he picked one of those pretty, cultured, capable ladies who would have known how to survive in a place like Radley Court, his principal seat?

While she was still puzzling over the inexplicable

behaviour of her enigmatic husband, he got to his feet and flung his napkin onto the table, the way he often did when he'd finished a meal.

'If you are willing,' he said, while she was still holding her fork halfway between her plate and her mouth, 'we can return to the drawing room, and continue our discussion.'

She felt her lips twitch. If *she* was willing? She hadn't been the one to create this hiatus in proceedings by demanding breakfast. Nor had it been, or would it be, a discussion. She was just going to carry on telling him what had happened, that was all, while he sat frowning at her as though he didn't believe a word of it. He'd already made her feel as though she knew exactly what a suspected felon would feel like, making his defence in court, before a magistrate who would determine his sentence.

Still, she supposed she could give him credit for being discreet in front of the servants. He could have treated her with a lot less consideration. He was, after all, giving her a chance to state her case and clear her name.

Because he was a gentleman, through and through.

She'd learned a lot about the nature of men, from Chloe and Fenella, over the past few months. The tales they'd told of the way various men had treated them had been enough to make her hair stand on end.

In oh, so many ways, Anthony really was a prince among men. He would never black her eye, or kick her down the stairs, no matter how angry he became with her.

And he *was* angry with her. Almost quivering with it.

Nevertheless, she put down her knife and fork, got to her feet, as well, laid her own napkin aside, and thanked the servants for her breakfast. Much to Anthony's surprise, she could tell. But then to him, servants were not people with feelings. They were simply there to carry out his wishes.

Oh, dear, but that wasn't fair of her. He had noticed her when she'd been a mere servant, hadn't he? He'd smiled at her, with sympathy, when Lady Marchmont had been at her most difficult. Nodded to her on the way to meals. Come to sit next to her, on the occasional evening, when she'd been stuck in a corner on her own, and embarked on conversational topics like books, and music and the like, which she was sure he would never have brought up with any of the other single ladies present. For she had known nothing about the people whose reputations everyone else was shredding with such glee. Even less of the latest fashions. He'd been so...*kind*, to notice her, and attempt to include her.

No wonder she'd fallen so desperately, hopelessly in love with him, and so quickly. He'd been the embodiment of every plain, poor spinster's dream. Lady Marchmont had laughed at her when she'd perceived the truth. Told her she was setting herself up for heartbreak if she thought Lord Epping meant anything by the attention he was giving her.

'It is more likely he is trying to snub the pretensions of one of the eligible females present, by demonstrating that he finds an impoverished, aging spinster more interesting than her,' she'd sneered. 'Or using you as a shield, perhaps, to avoid raising false hopes in any eligible female's breast.'

And she'd believed that. Oh, yes! For it made far more sense than that he could actually find her interesting. That night, she'd cried herself to sleep. And from then on had tried really, really hard not to follow him round the room, with her eyes. Or show him that, if he looked her way, it made her so happy she could have danced a jig on the spot.

She blinked as Anthony held the door open for her, which meant that somehow they'd reached the drawing room, without her noticing she'd even been walking along the corridor, so deeply had she withdrawn into her own memories.

Someone had been in, she noticed, while they'd been at breakfast, and lit a fire, so that the room now seemed far more welcoming than it had when they'd left it. Oh, how she'd missed having a fire!

She went to the chair she'd been sitting on before, and began dragging it nearer the hearth.

'Here,' said Anthony, taking it from her. 'Allow me.'

'Why, thank you,' she said. He could still surprise her with little gestures such as this. Even though he was angry with her, and clearly uncertain whether to believe her account of her adventures or not, he was still enough of a gentleman to help a female he saw struggling with a burden he considered too big for her. It was one of the ways he'd won her heart in the first place, by performing little services for her, making her feel as though she *mattered*.

While her mind flew back to that Christmas house party, and Lady Marchmont's outrage when he'd made a point of setting *her* chair closer to the fire, and sitting beside her, and talking to her, he'd gone to fetch another chair, and placed it on the other side of the hearth and sat down. Just the way he'd done when they first met.

Which brought a hopeful feeling surging through her, thrusting aside some of her anxiety. After all, he'd proposed to her, hadn't he? Even though Lady Marchmont had warned her that the on dit was he would never marry again, after the tragic loss of his first wife. But he had. He'd married her. Even if she still couldn't understand why.

It wasn't until she was comfortable, and he'd brought another chair, placed it on the other side of the hearth, and sat down too, that he spoke.

'You say,' he said, 'these Methodist people decided you were an unwed mother. Perhaps,' he said, giving her a challenging look, 'you shouldn't have left your wedding ring behind when you went out for that drive with Franklin.'

Oh! He may act the gentleman, with kind little gestures like helping her move a chair, but he was still struggling to believe a word she said.

She felt her lips tremble at the painful blow his continuing lack of trust had dealt her. But she'd already decided to do whatever it took to clear her name. She had to convince him she was telling the truth!

'For one thing,' she pointed out, as calmly as she could, 'I didn't know I was going to end up going for a drive when I went outside. For another, I hadn't been able to get my ring on for days, because my fingers were so swollen.'

He frowned. 'Mrs Dawkins never mentioned that.' His frown deepened. 'If you were unwell you should have sent for a doctor. And if you wanted to go for a drive I don't understand why you didn't summon the head groom and order him to have horses put to, rather than going sneaking off round the back of the stables with the newest groom in my employ.'

'Have you not listened to a word I've said?' Why was he so determined to believe the worst of her? 'I already told you I had no notion that going for a drive would help me to feel cool. I had no notion that driving in such a vehicle was even possible, on an estate such as Blanchetts. Do you imagine that I ever, in my life before marrying you, went for drives in carriages for pleasure? And as for summoning one of your servants and ordering them to do anything...' She shook her head in disbelief. 'It had only been a matter of weeks since I had been on their level. I didn't have the nerve to ring a bell and *ask* anyone for anything, never mind order them about! I was so sure they all resented me for...for...rising above my station that once you'd left, I just...folded in on myself. Wanted to shrink into the carpet and disappear. Can you not remember how timid I was? Why, I couldn't say boo to a goose!'

His eyes flicked sideways. Then back to her. 'I do remember you being unwell. Or at least, in a delicate condition. That was why I left you there, in one of my smaller properties.' He leaned forward, clasping his hands together. 'I sincerely believed the staff would take proper care of you, since I was unable to stay with you myself. You know I have a duty to visit all my properties, over the summer months, and speak with my bailiffs and tenants. Sort out any disputes. Show my face at public days. And I could see that it was too much for you.'

'Oh, yes, I wasn't up to snuff at all,' she said bitterly, 'was I?'

'You were wilting under the strain,' he corrected her, in an annoyingly pedantic tone of voice. 'I thought you would be better off resting somewhere quiet, while I carried on with what is always a demanding itinerary...'

'You had realized,' she retorted, reaching the end of her tether, 'by the time we left Radley Court, that you'd made a ghastly mistake, marrying me.'

At this point, yet another wave of memories burst into her mind. Of the stares, and the whispers, and of Anthony's face pokering up. Of that ghastly introduction to his mother, who'd tried to make the best of things, but who'd struggled to hide her bitter disappointment that he'd married so far beneath his station. What else could she have meant by saying that he ought to have run his decision by her, first?

'I embarrassed you by not knowing how to behave there, didn't I? By not being able to withstand the curiosity of all those grand people who came to have a look at me. By not being able to stand up to them when they kept on saying how I wasn't a patch on your first countess.'

He reared back. 'They said that? To your face? I didn't know. Believe me, I had no notion…'

What rot! He must have known. Why else had he looked so…so…pained, so very often?

'It doesn't matter now,' she said wearily, 'does it? They were right. I wasn't a patch on the dazzling creature you married the first time round. I had no birth, no breeding, and no beauty. I wasn't surprised that you grew tired of me and dumped me in that horrid, stuffy house in the dales.'

'It wasn't like that!' He frowned. 'Was that what you thought? No wonder…'

'Don't start accusing me of running off with that boy again, Anthony, or so help me I will slap you!'

His eyes widened.

But she didn't care. She was so tired of having to defend herself from his unfounded accusations. He had some things to answer for himself.

'It is clear that you didn't report me missing. That from the start, you listened to the jealous, spiteful tales poured into your ears by servants who thought I'd pushed in among my betters where I had no place to be, and wanted to see me brought down. If you'd made *any* attempt to find me, asked *anyone* in authority in the area if there were any accidents, or serious injuries to lone females with no means of identification, you would have found me within days. Instead of which…' She was by now so angry she could not sit still.

'But you just told me you had no memory of who you were,' he retorted. 'So how could any inquiries I made have found you?'

'Because, when I was delirious, or under the influence of that drink the woman on the barge gave me,' she cried, getting to her feet, 'while I was losing our baby, and while they feared I might be losing my life, I called your name. Though I had no memory of doing so, the Methodist people told me that the only clue they had to my identity was the way I had kept moaning the one word.' She looked down at him, her whole body rigid with cold fury. 'Epping,' she hissed at him. '*That* one word. *Epping*. So I know that if you had put out word that your countess had vanished, while out on a ride across the dales, it would have spread out like ripples when a boulder gets thrown into a pond. *Everyone* would have known, at once, that a woman calling for Epping, must be the missing countess. But you didn't.' She was no longer rigid with fury. She was shaking. Shaking with hurt, and anger, and the cold certainty that was creeping through her bones, making her feel as cold as the moment she'd first fallen into that swiftly flowing river.

'You didn't search for me,' she said, her stomach hollowing out as she finally faced up to the reason why he hadn't looked for her, 'because you were *glad* I'd gone! I'd solved the problem of what to do with a wife you'd repented of marrying, by vanishing!'

And with that, she could take no more. Stifling a sob, she dashed to the door, and pelted up the stairs to her room.

Chapter Nine

Anthony sat looking at the door through which she'd just slammed.

In exactly the same way Sarah would have done.

Oh, yes, a slamming door had been a very familiar punctuation to many of the *conversations* they'd had.

See? She *could* behave the way his first wife had done, even though on the surface, the two women seemed nothing alike.

Sarah wouldn't have merely threatened to slap his face, though, he mused, rubbing his jaw reflectively.

Was there something about him that turned women into…shrews?

No. Definitely not. At least, not where Sarah had been concerned. She had thrown tantrums on the slightest of pretexts. Principally, for not getting her own way.

But Mary…

He got to his feet and walked over to the window, gazing down sightlessly into the square.

She'd definitely changed. He only had to contrast her behaviour at the breakfast table, just now, to what it had been like when he'd first married her. She hadn't blushed, today, when'd he'd looked at her over the teacups. She hadn't nervously nibbled at a single slice of toast so that she made it last as long as it took for him to finish whatever it was he was having. Instead she'd helped herself to whatever she wanted, and looked irritated when he'd stood up to leave before she'd cleared it all from her plate.

Only one thing hadn't changed. The hungry little glances he'd caught her darting his way.

Or was that his vanity making him see things that weren't there? Because if even half of what she'd just told him was true, no wonder she was…disappointed in him.

If what she'd said was true, then he owed her an apology for being so suspicious. And for having acted the way he'd done.

Well, never mind all that. Couldn't he think of just one positive thing to have come out of the discussion?

He supposed at least now he knew that she'd already heard some gossip about his first wife, if people had been indiscreet enough to compare her to Sarah. Which would pave the way for him, one day, to tell Mary what Sarah had really been like. If he was to tell her what Sarah had driven him to do, then she'd more easily be able to understand why he was the man he was now.

Tell her?

He shuddered.

He'd never told anyone. The thought of owning up to his moment of deepest shame…of reliving his darkest hour…

No. He shook his head reflexively, the way a dog shakes off a shower of rain. He couldn't do it.

Except…unless…if she really had gone through what she'd just told him…then didn't she deserve he atone, in some way, for…?

And there could be no greater penance, for him, than to lay his pride in the dust by confessing to what a total, complete…imbecile he'd been when it came to his first wife.

But before he could ever consider taking such a drastic step as confiding in a woman, he had to find out if she'd been telling him the truth. Beyond a shadow of a doubt.

He turned away from the window, and paced to the fire, leaning his hands on the mantelpiece, and bowing his head.

He now had two versions of events running through his head. The one she'd just told him, and the account he'd had from the staff at Blanchetts. The upper staff, that was. He had been so shocked, so angry to hear she'd run off that he'd barricaded himself in his study and not come out for days.

But now he was looking back, in a somewhat more rational frame of mind, could he recollect a slight hint of…spite, in the words Mrs Dawkins had chosen to describe Mary's last days under her care? And a rather selective catalogue of events? She certainly hadn't said anything about Mary being unable to wear her ring for several days before her disappearance, only that she'd left it behind. She hadn't said anything about how ill and uncomfortable Mary claimed to have felt. But then she wouldn't have, would she? Or he would have demanded to know why she hadn't sent for a doctor, even if Mary hadn't been brave enough to summon one.

And hadn't there been, now he came to consider it, a slight tinge of *good riddance* about the way she'd announced Mary's mysterious disappearance?

The trouble was, it wouldn't be easy to get to the truth, so long after the event. Especially from people who were deliberately concealing their motives for saying what they had in the first place. He only had to consider his own behaviour back then. If someone were to ask him why he'd chosen to leave Blanchetts on that specific day, for instance, he'd be able to answer in at least two different ways. Three, now, according to Mary, who had just accused him of deciding he'd made a mistake about marrying her.

And if she truly believed *that*, then maybe she would have had some excuse for running off, if running off deliberately was what she'd done. Because she *had* been timid. And *had* found it hard to give orders to the servants. And some of them, he now acknowledged, on a groan, might well have despised her for it.

He had not…protected her, the way he should have done.

Yes, but, dammit, it hadn't been because he hadn't loved her! The very opposite! He'd left because he'd started to fear he cared too much. He wouldn't admit that to anyone, though, would he? He'd tell them what he'd told Mary at the time, and had repeated to her just now. That it was out of consideration for her health.

But Mary, clever, perceptive Mary hadn't believed it back then any more than she believed it now, though, had she? He'd seen the wounded look in her eyes as she'd sensed there had been more to it than that. She could see that he'd been using her health as an excuse.

And yet he'd kept on insisting it was for the best.

But then, he argued, she *had* been fading, before his very eyes, with a combination of travelling, in the heat, and facing the mockery and, yes, he now knew, hostility of people who had known Sarah. On top of that, they'd both begun to suspect she'd conceived. He'd had to think about what *that* meant. On his own. Without any distractions.

He'd hoped that while he completed his tour of his northern estates and holdings, he'd come to some conclusions about how he felt about it all. And that he'd be able to go back to her, by the end of summer, with his defences rebuilt, his armour intact, and his heart whole.

Instead…

He kicked moodily at the hearth. And cursed at the pain in his toe. And his own foolishness in standing here, questioning his behaviour. He had done what he thought best. He always did his best. Duty was ingrained in him. He owed it to his family name to uphold the highest of standards at all times…

Only, there had been times when he'd spectacularly failed, hadn't there?

He pushed himself off the mantelpiece with a muttered curse. He was getting nowhere, standing here, going over the possibility that he'd failed Mary. Considering the validity of all the versions of what might have been, as well as what had been going on, in August. What he ought to be doing was instigating a thorough investigation of all the *facts* which could be checked. Which meant he'd have to find someone who could go up to Blanchetts and ferret about until they'd dug up evidence which would either corroborate her version of events.

Or prove her a liar.

He stalked over to the door, and pulled it open with some violence. If she was a liar, then…

Well, he wasn't sure what he'd do. Send her back to the country, to live out the rest of her days in seclusion? Yes, that would work well, wouldn't it, if she had a penchant for running off and joining troupes of actors when she grew bored.

He caught himself stamping down the stairs, and deliberately slowed down to a more measured, dignified pace. That was one thing to have come out of the wreckage that had been his marriage to Sarah. The determination to behave in a measured way, no matter what turmoil might be raging within. To count to at least ten, preferably in a room somewhere on his own, before there was the slightest risk of him giving vent to the almost murderous rage she'd been able to provoke.

That was the main reason he'd shut himself away, rather than go in search of Mary. He'd been afraid that if he ran her to ground before he'd calmed down… Well, he already knew what he was capable of when he discovered his wife in another man's bed, thanks to Sarah.

He reached his study, sat down at his desk, and reached for a sheet of paper. He should, he supposed, have summoned Travers, his secretary. But some things were just too personal to dictate to a third party. So he paused after dipping his pen in the inkwell.

Was it wise to commit anything to paper at all? Who knew who might gain sight of those words, once written down? Words, once written in pen and ink, gained a kind of permanence, too. And it it turned out that his suspicions about Mary were unfounded, somehow, he would feel as if he'd blackened her name by writing them down and letting someone else read them.

He flung the pen away and leaned back in his chair.

It was all very well, thinking about banishing her to the depths of the countryside if it turned out she'd been lying. But what was he to do if he should discover she'd been telling him the truth? Even though it all sounded so unlikely?

Could she have been set upon, and witnessed the murder of a lad who'd been trying to defend her? If so, then why hadn't anyone found the body?

Because, the answer came back, the moors were vast. And nobody had been looking.

And could she have almost drowned, before losing the baby?

If all that she had told him *had* happened, it was no wonder she'd lost the baby. For Mary, the girl who'd been so timid she could barely raise her eyes to his across the breakfast table, it must all have been an appalling shock.

He could hardly bear to think about it.

He frowned. That was what she claimed, wasn't it? That it had all been so unbearable, she'd shut it out of her mind, somehow.

His gaze snagged on the pen, lying in a pool of ink, which led him to wonder if someone could really just blot away an unpleasant memory, the way he would mop up an unsightly ink stain from a badly trimmed pen.

And could it truly have all come flooding back to her when he'd held her in his arms, and she'd called out his name? The way she claimed she had done when she'd been losing their child? Or was that all too…convenient?

Didn't it have a ring of fairy tale about it? With the handsome prince waking the sleeping beauty from her enchantment with a kiss?

He was certainly starting to feel as if he was stumbling about in a thicket of thorns. No matter which way he turned, there were briars, waiting to lacerate him. If she'd been lying, then it meant she was an adulteress. If not, then she'd been through horrors too painful to contemplate.

While he'd done nothing to help her.

He glared at the pen, and the pool of ink spreading out on the sheet of otherwise blank paper. What good was a blasted pen? What he needed was a sword, or a hatchet to hack his way through this thicket of thorny issues surrounding him.

Metaphorically speaking.

Fortunately he knew of men who, for a fee, would go to places where he couldn't go, and ask questions to which Anthony would not get honest answers. He'd hired one, once before. When he'd needed to know what had become of his younger brother Benjamin. And although he hadn't liked the report that man had eventually brought him, the fellow had at least given him the plain truth. What was more, he'd kept the whole matter in strictest confidence. He must have done, else Anthony would have become a laughing stock.

He got to his feet and went to the door.

'Simmons,' he said to the butler, who appeared in the hall at precisely the right moment. 'My hat and coat, if you please.' He was going to go and root out the same fellow he'd used before. Or if not him, then one of his associates.

And, though his heart was pounding, he left the house with carefully measured steps, and kept his progress to a stroll so that no casual observer could even begin to guess at his feelings, or suspect that all was not well within doors.

An attitude he was going to have to maintain for however long it would take for his hatchet to cleave through the tangled web he needed to penetrate. Which would be several weeks, he should think. Time for the fellow to reach Yorkshire, make the necessary enquiries, and travel back to London with his report.

Once he had that report, he would know how to act.

But in the meantime…

Well, there were two things he could set right between him and his wife. Firstly, he could tell her that he had most definitely *not* been glad she'd left him. Even though he wasn't ready to explain why he hadn't searched for her.

And secondly, he could offer her a bit more sympathy over the loss of their baby. She was clearly grieving. Deeply grieving. As was he, but then men didn't admit to more than a mild disappointment, did they, when these things happened? They certainly didn't talk about it among themselves.

But apart from that, he wasn't sure how to proceed. Because he couldn't ignore the fact that though she'd gone missing in August, it was now November. Which left three months unaccounted for. Where had she been, during all that time? And what had she been doing? Even if she had been innocent of the crime his housekeeper had accused her of, even if she *had* been robbed, and lost her memory, the one fact of which he was sure was that somehow, at some stage, she'd become tangled up with that actor fellow. That rubber-faced, stringy little worm!

So, even if she had been innocent in August, could she still be innocent now?

And if not, then, depending upon what the investigator turned up, he would…well, he would just have to bear it. As he'd borne so much else as a married man.

For now, though, he'd just have to treat her as though he was giving her the benefit of the doubt. Even if he couldn't fully believe in the fantastic tale she'd told, he would have to treat her as though he was *prepared* to believe it.

He just wasn't capable of more than that. Not yet.

Chapter Ten

She looked down at her hands. They were shaking.

Well, she was shaking all over, and no wonder. She'd never shouted at anyone the way she'd just shouted at Anthony. Or at least, she'd shouted at him last night, too, hadn't she, only that had been different. Though she couldn't for the moment work out exactly why.

She tottered over to her bed and sat down.

Then sprang up almost at once. It wouldn't do any good sitting about going over and over that discussion, in her head. Especially not on that bed, which conjured up memories of things they'd done there. It wouldn't solve anything. And it would be a waste of time remembering and wishing things had turned out differently. No amount of wishing was ever going to change anything.

She went to her trunk, which someone had placed, helpfully, right next to the chest of drawers.

She opened it, and began stowing things away in

places she thought logical. Not that there were very many things. She had the gown she was wearing, one to change into, underwear and night things. Odds and ends like gloves and brushes and hairpins.

They all looked rather pathetic in the drawers that had once been full of silk and lace. And they didn't smell right, either. The garments of a countess should smell freshly laundered, or of scent, not of damp rooms and greasy chophouses. They were the garments of an impostor. And because they didn't belong in a house like this, they reinforced her feeling that she didn't, either. Although she hadn't ever felt as if she belonged in any of Anthony's houses, had she? Well, not as his wife, anyway.

But that hadn't been *all* her fault, had it? Anthony had chosen her. He'd been the one to ask her to marry him, not the other way round. If he hadn't wanted a plain, timid woman hovering about in his shadow, he should have asked one of those pretty, eligible, confident women who'd been flaunting themselves at him at the house party where they'd met.

But he hadn't.

She was his countess, whether she felt like one or not. For better or worse.

Well, she didn't think anyone could have gone through anything much worse than she had, this summer. And she'd survived.

Not just survived, but thrived, away from the depressing knowledge of how lowly she was, how grateful she ought to be for anyone who deigned to give her employment. Away from the constant worry, too, of what might happen to her should she lose that employment. For she had no family willing to take her in. No savings to fall back on.

But she hadn't needed them, had she? She'd gone out with only the clothes on her back, and look… she ran her hands over the shabby possessions she'd just been thinking didn't belong in the bedroom of a countess. She'd come back with a trunk full of stuff. Shabby stuff, compared to what Anthony and his ilk were used to, admittedly. But nevertheless, all stuff she'd earned by herself.

And it wasn't just stuff she'd acquired, either, was it?

She'd learned a great deal about herself. She'd discovered that she was far more…practical, and level-headed, and, yes, intelligent than she'd ever dreamed she could be.

She ran one hand, proudly, over the spare gown hanging up in the wardrobe. Smiled at the rather threadbare coat which hung next to it. Proof, tangible proof, that she could survive. No matter what life threw at her.

Even Anthony?

Her smile turned rueful.

She wandered over to the window. From up here she could look down over the square, though over a slightly different portion from the one she'd so often looked at from the drawing room. And her smile faded away completely as she saw Anthony strolling along the pavement, as though he had not a care in the world. Going out, carrying on with his life, without a backwards glance! Sauntering along with, with almost a spring in his step, as though he hadn't just left her up here, shaking with reaction after their argument!

She'd accused him of not loving her. He hadn't denied it. And now he was off somewhere, carrying on as though he really, truly didn't care…

She tore herself away from the window, her arms wrapped round her middle, and stalked back to the wardrobe. She glared at the clothes she'd been so proud of acquiring, only moments ago. They were nothing to be proud of, were they? They were cheap, and shoddy, and reeked of poverty.

She slammed the door shut on them and stalked back to the window, though Anthony was long gone. But on the opposite side of the square, she saw a carriage draw up. A footman leaped down from his perch to help the passengers to alight. Two ladies, she noted, swaddled in glossy furs. Ladies who looked as though they had every right to expect a footman to hand them out of their carriage, and escort them up the steps to the kind of house that stood in this exclusive square.

Whereas she…

She turned her back on the window, on the ladies, and on the square itself. Hadn't she just been congratulating herself for surviving? And if she could survive highwaymen, and Methodists, and memory loss, and all the rest of it, then surely she could survive the discovery that she was a countess. Even if her husband didn't love her, had never loved her, the way she wanted him to… Well, she gulped, many women had to put up with far worse. It was all a question of…perspective.

She dashed away a prickle of something that felt like moisture, from her cheek. And lifted her chin.

So… Anthony didn't love her.

So…she didn't feel as if she belonged in this house. But he *had* paid her the compliment of asking her to be his wife.

And she *did* live here. And would be living here for the foreseeable future. Until Anthony had made up his mind whether to believe her or not. And decided what to do with her.

So…while she was living here, she'd probably feel a great deal less awkward if she at least looked the part. Hadn't she watched Chloe and Fenella become different characters as they'd put on layers of costume and makeup?

She caught sight of herself in the mirror then, and eyed her pale, rather red-eyed reflection, and grimaced. And then imagined how shocked Anthony would be if she covered the ravages of her emotions with powder and paint! Or put on a glossy, curled wig to hide her wispy, unmanageable hair.

Not that it was her style to hide behind costumes and cosmetics, but mightn't he be just a tiny bit less disappointed in her, or might she at least feel not so obviously out of place, if she smartened herself up a bit?

After all, hadn't she been thinking, only the night before, about the way Anthony had urged her to buy fashionable gowns? And hadn't she also thought how silly she'd been to worry about the expense, believing she wasn't worthy of his generosity? That she'd done nothing to deserve it. And that if she had someone who'd buy her whatever she wanted, today, she'd just clap her hands in glee and make a list?

A smile began to spread across her face.

Making a list would pose no problem at all. She was really good at making lists. In fact she'd already started one, earlier, hadn't she? Comprised of things which would make Fenella's room more bearable. Well, now she'd start adding things that could make her own life more comfortable. To start with, she wanted a really elegant, warm coat, like those ladies across the square had. And a hood to keep her head warm and dry when it rained. And sturdy boots that wouldn't let in the rain. And thick flannel petticoats.

And for days when she didn't feel like venturing outside—and actually, why should she now she was a lady of leisure?—she might as well have some day dresses. In bright, fresh colours. And she needn't choose fabrics that would withstand laundering without fading any more, because if such a thing should happen, she could just buy another one to replace it!

And if Anthony had anything to say about her spending his money, then she would be able to say, with perfect honesty, and without apology, that she was only trying to look the part.

And why should she apologize? For anything? She yanked open her wardrobe door yet again. She had done nothing wrong. Apart from being a bit silly about, and overwhelmed by, the attentions of a handsome, powerful man. And he had no right to be angry with her. Or to go off and leave her to fend for herself when he knew she was upset.

She pulled her coat from its hook and stuffed her

arms into the sleeves. If anything, Anthony owed *her* an apology. And if he wasn't disposed to give her one, she decided, snatching her bonnet from its peg and slapping it onto her head, then she'd exact compensation from him her own way.

She got as far as the bedroom door before it struck her that it was all very well going off on a shopping spree in a fit of anger, hoping to punish Anthony for having so little faith in her, but the whole point of all the shopping was to make herself look like a countess. So that she'd fit the role. And countesses didn't go wandering about town on foot, the way she had done when she'd been Perdita. When she'd first been married, Anthony had never permitted her to walk anywhere. He'd always called for a carriage, staffed with a couple of footmen as well as the driver, and sent her out in such pomp that by the time she arrived wherever it was she'd been intending to go, she was almost shrivelled up with mortification.

What was more, just now, he'd chided her for not ordering his servants to take her for a drive, if she'd wanted to go for one.

Right. She marched over to the bell pull and gave it a determined tug. If he wanted her to order his servants about, then she jolly well would! She was ready, finally, even though it was probably too late, to step into the role of Countess of Epping, in a way she'd never dared before.

In the event, Anthony's staff gave her no trouble at all. They acted as if it was perfectly natural for her to go out shopping, while her husband was out doing whatever it was he was doing.

Her burst of defiant confidence carried her on the crest of its wave all the way to Bond Street, where it dashed into a disappointing froth of stage fright the moment she caught sight of the modiste's shop window.

She gripped her reticule tightly as one of Anthony's footmen came to open the carriage door and let down the step. She was not going to let the haughty Madame Claire intimidate her! She'd faced down a hostile tailor, hadn't she? Without the benefit of a footman and coach driver at her back! And this woman knew she had the means to pay, or at least, her husband did. What was more, she ought to value retaining the custom of a countess, considering the way she'd behaved before.

She lifted her chin and swept into the shop, determined things were going to be different this time. For one thing, after this initial visit, she was going to insist that the dressmaker came to her, rather than the other way round. She was so determined to have her own way that she sailed through the ensuing encounter with such ease that, when it was over, she had half a mind to order the carriage to take her back to the tailor's, so she could…

Well, what would she achieve by going back? It would hardly be wise to alert the man to the fact that the shabbily dressed woman he'd been so rude to was actually a countess, would it? The tale would spread like wildfire.

And Anthony would be livid. He would hate anyone knowing that his wife had been obliged to take a job with a troupe of actors, while they'd been parted. And although she had come out this morning wanting to exact a measure of revenge on him for having believed so many dreadful things about her, letting the world know exactly what *he'd* done would be taking a step too far. He would then have real cause to be angry with her.

She slumped back against the squabs. Things were bad enough between them as it was. It would be very foolish to do anything to antagonize him, unnecessarily. It would put paid to any chance of them ever patching things up.

And she did want to patch things up. Not only because she couldn't bear Anthony to keep on believing such dreadful things about her, but because she was just glad she'd been given a second chance with him. Even if he was being grumpy, and cynical. Even if he couldn't love her the way he'd loved his first wife. Well, why should he? By all accounts very few women could compete with the incomparable Sarah.

She knew he was capable of being a kind and generous husband.

She knew he could take her to paradise, in bed.

She could learn not to hope for more than he was able to give, couldn't she?

She could learn to be content with her position, her real life, and not dream about fairy-tale endings, and such childish nonsense!

However, over the next few days it began to look as if she wasn't even going to be able to reach for those lowliest of goals. Because Anthony started treating her as though she was a guest, rather than his wife. He gave no sign that he was angry with her, or that he harboured suspicions that she'd run off with a lover. Instead, he was so unfailingly polite that it set her teeth on edge.

When she saw him, that was. Which was usually only at the breakfast table. When she walked in, he would get to his feet, and bid her good morning. Then pretend not to watch as she made her selection from the buffet. Only a few moments after she'd taken her place at the table, and was drinking her first sip of tea, would he lower whatever newspaper he'd been hiding behind and announce that he was terribly sorry, but he was going to be extremely busy today.

'I do apologize,' he would say, though she didn't believe for one moment that he meant it, 'for not being at your disposal.'

'I don't expect you to dance attendance on me,' she would say, smiling through gritted teeth. After all, he hadn't done anything like it when he'd first married her, when she might have hoped it of him. There had always been people he had to see, committees to chair, and problems to solve. He'd made it crystal clear, in so many ways, that he was an important, busy man. And that the only time she could expect his undivided attention would be in her bed, where he'd visit her, after he'd finished doing all his important, lordly work.

She hadn't minded him being busy. Of course she hadn't! It was just that she hadn't known what to do with herself while he was off being important.

She'd been too used to living frugally to enjoy shopping back then. And she hadn't had any friends. Oh, plenty of society ladies had called upon her, on the pretext of paying their respects to the new countess. But they'd all come with talons bared, tongues sharpened, like so many harpies whose chief delight was ripping hapless victims to shreds.

Fortunately, she was no longer the timid, insecure girl who'd felt her only role in life was to worship at the feet of the godlike creature who'd deigned to marry her. She had far more confidence in herself after spending so much time with people who thought she was wonderful for the way she could keep track of expenses, and schedules, and props.

And far less faith in Anthony.

'I have plenty to keep me occupied,' she'd add, without going into any details. Well, if he wasn't going to tell her exactly why he was too busy to spend any time with her, or tackling the problems that were extremely important to her, then why should she tell him anything, either? They were both busy. Too busy to have time for each other—that was what it amounted to.

Too angry with each other, probably, too. At least, she was still cross with him for letting her down so badly, when she'd needed him the most, and for using the excuse that he'd believed those filthy lies his servants had told him.

And he was probably still cross with her for shouting at him, rather than flinging herself at his feet and begging his forgiveness. He'd have preferred that, she reflected, eyeing him with a touch of militance over the rim of her teacup. He could have been magnanimous, if she'd been abject.

But she was not going to beg forgiveness for something she hadn't done!

Nor was she going to make any attempt to placate him. Why should she?

And so the state of an armed truce dragged on.

After a day or so more, though, she began to look forward to the encounters at breakfast, in a strange way. And it wasn't just because it was the only time she got to see him. The only time she could hope they might break the truce, and start talking to each other, properly.

It was the bacon. And the eggs. And the fried potatoes, and sausages and toast. To start with, she'd made herself eat heartily to prove to him that she didn't have a guilty conscience. But after a while she started feeling the benefit of eating well, in other ways. Perdita had been rather a frail creature, physically, though she had been so strong in character. But then, she'd been through a lot, hadn't she? An attempted robbery, and a near drowning, and a miscarriage and a fever. That was enough to weaken anyone's constitution.

But day by day, as a result of all the good food, and leisure, and, possibly, the peace that came with finally knowing exactly who she was, and how she'd reached this point in her life, she felt her body starting to recover.

But after a few more days, as her body grew stronger her mood shifted once again. She became increasingly irritated by the state of…armed truce that Anthony was maintaining so diligently. How were they ever going to get anywhere if he kept on avoiding her when he could, and being so frigidly polite when he couldn't?

Finally, about two weeks after she'd returned, she reached the end of her tether. That was the only way to explain it. Because nothing out of the ordinary happened to provoke her. She'd sat down at the breakfast table, with her plate of bacon and eggs, mushrooms and sausage, the way she always did. And Anthony raised one eyebrow at her plate, the way he always did. Only this time, she simply couldn't just smile sweetly before tucking in.

'I suppose you think,' she said as she cut her sausage into bite-sized morsels, 'that I lack delicacy. Real ladies never eat hearty breakfasts, do they? Especially not ones who have misbehaved. Well,' she continued, spearing a piece of sausage with her fork, 'let me answer the question you keep on asking with that imperious left eyebrow of yours.'

At that, both his eyebrows drew down in obvious displeasure.

Which gave her a spurt of satisfaction.

'Hasn't it occurred to you,' she carried on, recklessly, 'that I am making the most of the bounty on offer to me, while it is still available? After all, life is an uncertain business. Who knows but that a time might come when I have to beg in the streets, not knowing where my next meal is coming from?'

His face froze. And then, without a word, he set his napkin aside, got to his feet, and stalked out of the room.

That's right, she said to herself. *Just walk away. Pretend nothing has happened.*

For that was what, she suddenly saw, he did, wasn't it? His wife makes an unguarded remark in front of the servants? Walk out of the room. She threatens to slap his face? He leaves the house. He thinks she's run away with a lover? He hushes the whole thing up.

Oh, Anthony. She sighed in compassion as her heart went out to him, just the way it had the first time she'd heard he'd buried his heart in the grave with his first wife. She might have inadvertently blotted her sufferings out of her mind, in order to survive a terrible ordeal, but he did the same, by choice, routinely.

What on earth would it take to…shake him out of his state of…indifference? To bring this awful, frozen, awkward state between them to an end?

An image sprang to her mind, then, of him trying to punch Jack. Of his untidy clothes, and his unshaven jaw and the savage look in his eyes.

So…he did care. Though he was doing such a splendid job of pretending he didn't.

He'd cared enough about her going to see Jack, without telling him, that he'd dashed off after her without paying any attention to his appearance.

She leaned back in her chair, her eggs and bacon forgotten, as she suddenly saw that he was different, now, from what he had been. Last time he thought she'd left he'd hidden away and pretended nothing was wrong. This time he'd come chasing after her at once.

It was progress, wasn't it?

He clearly wasn't sure how to handle her, now he'd got her back under his roof, though.

Hmm…

Perhaps it was time she stopped waiting for him to make the first move, and came up with a way to just…smash through his rigid barriers herself? Or they might carry on like this indefinitely.

And she had a pretty good notion of what might just do the trick!

Chapter Eleven

Anthony was struggling to make sense of the convoluted language of the latest parliamentary bill he was supposed to be studying. The most annoying thing about it was that normally he would have had no trouble getting to the nub of the matter. But ever since Mary had come back he seemed to have lost his ability to concentrate. Even though he went to all the meetings he had promised to attend, and read all the necessary paperwork, his mind kept straying to Blanchetts, and what the investigator might have discovered there. And to Mary, and what she might be doing. Or thinking. Or planning.

Because she was definitely planning something. He could see it on her face, every morning, at breakfast.

He raised his head with relief from the words which wouldn't make any sense when a knock sounded on the study door.

It was Simmons.

'Beg pardon, my lord,' said his butler, 'but I thought you would wish to know that Her Ladyship has ordered the carriage.'

Anthony let the document slip through fingers that had gone numb.

'The carriage?' She'd gone out a few times during the day, in the carriage he'd bought for her use when they'd first married. Which was fair enough. She always took at least one footman with her, so he always knew where she'd gone, because they reported back to Simmons the moment she came in. And Simmons reported back to him. Besides, he had no objection to her visiting modistes, and milliners and the like. It certainly explained that peculiar statement she'd made about a wardrobe the other day. She needed to fill it; of course she did. Hadn't he encouraged her to do so, right from the start?

But never mind her wardrobe. What on earth could she want the carriage for, *in the evening*?

'Do you happen to know,' Anthony asked, 'where she is going?' She hadn't received any invitations to go anywhere. She couldn't have done. Because she hadn't received any post at all. Simmons brought all the post to him. Always had. When they'd first been married, Anthony had passed on any invitations that had been addressed to her. After vetting them to make sure they were to events she might enjoy, that was.

Besides which, nobody of note knew she'd come back. Or even that she'd been missing in the first place. For if they had, those of the *ton* who were in London would have added her name to the invitations they sent him, in the hopes of discovering where she'd been, and what she'd been doing, and why.

'She mentioned an intention to go to the theatre, my lord,' said Simmons. 'Though I was not able to ascertain which one.'

The theatre.

Anthony's blood ran cold.

If she planned to visit the theatre, without informing him, it could only mean one thing.

She was going to watch *him*.

That stringy, rubber-jointed weasel he'd caught her embracing.

'Thank you, Simmons,' he said, getting to his feet. 'Send Snape to my room to prepare my evening clothes, would you?'

'He is already doing so, my lord,' said Simmons with what looked suspiciously like a smug expression.

Thank goodness he had such loyal staff, Anthony reflected as he ran up the stairs two at a time. They'd kept him informed of all her movements, without his having to give a direct order to that effect. Even if he'd been otherwise engaged tonight, he was sure that Simmons would have sent him a message, just as he'd done when Mary first showed up on the doorstep. In which case, he would already have been in evening dress. So he could have just gone straight to whatever theatre Mary planned to visit, and catch her out in whatever she was planning to do.

She had a nerve, going to the theatre without running it by him first. Apart from anything else, had she no idea what gossip it would cause, for her to make her first public appearance in London, after her long absence, alone?

Possibly not, he realized as he swiftly donned his evening wear. She hadn't been brought up in the same social sphere as he'd inhabited all his life. She'd floundered, rather badly, at most of the social occasions he'd taken her to, as his bride. That had been one of the reasons he'd left her at Blanchetts. The strain had been getting too much for her. He'd been able to see it in the shadows under her eyes, the way she only picked at her food, even though she wouldn't admit how unhappy she was becoming.

Well, she certainly didn't pick at her food now! It was as if she was determined to prove she had no worries at all, any longer. That she didn't care what he, or anyone else thought of her. From being a girl who was too timid to say boo to a goose, he had a feeling that nowadays, if a goose crossed her path, she'd be fully prepared to kick it down the stairs.

Perhaps going to the theatre tonight, on her own, was another way of showing him that she'd changed. Of proving to the polite world that she could hold her head up now, among them, no matter what they might whisper about her.

Or perhaps, he thought, his mood swerving from grudging admiration of her bravery to a dark suspicion of this apparent change in character, she was bored of him and wanted to see her acrobatic actor friend again.

Well, thanks to the loyalty of his staff she wasn't going to get away with it. They might appear to obey her orders by agreeing to ready the carriage for her, but they'd made damned sure *he* knew what she was up to, so that he could put a stop to it should he see fit.

He paused, his hand on the latch of his bedroom door. Had his staff acted like this when they'd first been married? Or was this extra watchfulness due to the tension they must be noticing between them? And their own suspicions about her unexplained absence. And the dramatic way she'd reappeared on the doorstep, clutching a brown paper parcel, rather than sending notice, so that the housekeeper could prepare a room, and then sweeping up in a carriage laden with luggage.

Had they *always* checked to make sure he approved of whatever orders she'd given them? He didn't think the London staff had. But then he couldn't actually remember her attempting to give them any orders back then. *He'd* organized her trips to the shops. And her outings to breakfasts, and ridottos and the like.

And she claimed she'd been too timid to attempt to make any of her wishes known to the staff at Blanchetts.

His staff, she'd called them.

He felt a frown pleating his brow. A moment ago he'd been pleased by the loyalty Simmons, and the others, were showing him by keeping him informed of her movements, and subtly running all her orders past him to make sure he approved. But now he wondered what effect such loyalty might have had on her.

His staff. She'd always referred to them in that way. He'd always insisted they were her servants, too, now that she'd married him.

But they hadn't been, had they? And they still weren't.

Under normal circumstances, he'd suggest she choose and hire a maid, but…

He shook his head and shelved that particular train of thought as he left his bedroom, ran down the stairs, and reached the front door, which stood open, just in time to see Stephens letting down the carriage steps for her.

'Oh,' she said, as he strode across the pavement to her side. 'Are you on your way out?'

'Yes,' he said, as he handed her into the carriage, climbed in, and took the facing seat. 'I am going to the theatre with my wife.'

She tilted her head to one side, giving him a quizzical look. 'How interesting,' she said. 'I wonder why it is that this is the first I have heard of it.'

'Possibly because until a few moments ago, I had no idea you were planning to go out. Alone. Good God, woman,' he said as the carriage lurched into motion, 'have you no idea what gossip it would have caused had you shown your face at the theatre, unaccompanied, when nobody of note is aware you are in London at all?'

She gave him a level look. 'Keeping my return quiet, are you, so that it will be easier to dispose of me without giving rise to talk?'

'No such thing!' Though to begin with, the thought had crossed his mind. If, for example, it proved impossible to repair the tattered shreds of their marriage, then, depending on what he discovered about those missing months, he could either send her to one of his properties in the country, where she could live out her days in seclusion…

Or…

He recoiled from the prospect of going through a divorce. No matter what she'd done, the scandal…

Likewise, the thought of consulting a doctor about her claims to have lost her memory made him feel distinctly queasy. Though if that memory loss *had* been genuine, then he ought to make her see a medical man. She might need treatment. Although what anyone could do about it…

Besides, once somebody pronounced her not of sound mind, that stigma would stay hanging round her for the rest of her life. And would affect the future prospects of any children they might have. *Madness in the family*, the matchmaking mothers would say when considering the possibility of a marriage with any children she might have. He couldn't just think of himself, and her, in this situation. He had to consider the effect of anything they did would have on future generations.

However, there was one matter he could deal with. One he'd been looking for an opportunity to broach. And what she'd just said gave him the perfect opening.

'You are completely mistaken in accusing me of wishing to dispose of you,' he began. 'And of thinking I was glad you left me in the first place. I was not. Nor did I think I had made a mistake in marrying you.' There, he'd set the record straight.

She tilted her head to one side as she gave him a searching look. He could see questions bubbling

up in her mind. But he wasn't ready to answer any
of the things she might possibly ask. So he'd better
steer the conversation away from any topic he was
not ready to be completely honest with her about.

'I don't,' he said, deciding to deal with present
practicalities, 'have a box at any of the theatres, you
know. I hadn't been planning to spend my evenings
in such a fashion.'

She gave him another look. This time it was
more…resigned, if anything.

'It is just as well,' she then said, with a touch of
what sounded like smugness, 'that I have friends at
the theatre then, isn't it? And that they have arranged
for a box for my private use.'

They? Who was she talking about?

'Apparently,' she continued, completely ignoring
the scowl he was sure she must be able to see, 'not
many people of your rank have booked boxes so far
this season. Harry believes that things will pick up
in the New Year once the new pantomimes begin.
But in the meantime he has said that I could have
my pick of the private boxes.'

'Harry? Who is he?'

'The theatre manager.'

'And what is your relationship with him? And
how,' he asked, since his staff hadn't reported her
visiting any theatres, or receiving any male visitors,
'have you been communicating with him?'

One side of her mouth curved upward, making it
look as though she wanted to laugh, and was struggling not to.

'Chloe, the principal lady of the troupe that took

me in, has been slipping in and out of the house whenever the dressmakers have been coming for fittings. She spoke to Harry about coming to see this performance. And organized everything for me.'

He sat back, winded. Although the staff had kept him abreast of the flurry of fittings she'd had, not one of them had noticed that one of the seamstresses was not, in fact, a seamstress at all.

'I dislike the way you have resorted to subterfuge,' he growled. It put him in mind, far too much, of the behaviour of his first wife.

'Well, do you know, we neither of us thought you'd want people's attention drawn to my association with *the likes of her*, as she put it, now that I've discovered I am a countess. Would you,' she asked, sweetly, 'have preferred it if Chloe had walked up to the front door, dressed as she usually is for social occasions, rather than in a demure costume as what she fancies a seamstress would wear? So that everyone would know, because, as you have pointed out, people of your class generally have nothing better to do than watch each other for excuses to gossip, that your wife is openly receiving an actress to tea?'

She had him there, he had to admit. He *didn't* want anyone knowing she'd been… Well, he still didn't know exactly what she'd been doing with those actor people. He hadn't been in the right frame of mind to question her about it.

'Or,' she added, 'should I have gone to the theatre, during their rehearsals, whenever I wanted to speak to them?'

'No,' he admitted, grudgingly. 'That would have been worse.'

'That is just what I thought,' she said, with a nod. 'I assumed that you would rather the *haut ton* did not know too much about my involvement with actors. Which is the only reason I asked Chloe to be discreet. For myself,' she added, with a touch of defiance, 'I don't care *who* knows that she is my friend.'

He mulled over what she'd told him. If what she said was true, then she had only engaged in the deception for his sake. To spare his blushes, if you like.

That was *not* the kind of deception in which Sarah had engaged. She had done the things she'd done with only her self-interest in mind.

'Ah, we're here,' said Mary, as the carriage drew to a halt. 'That didn't take long, did it?'

Stephens was letting down the steps as he opened the door, ready to hand Mary out. As the light from the flambeaux caught her, he noted the expression on her face. One of excitement, as though she was expecting a treat. He'd never seen her look so happy. Which cut him to the quick. For *he'd* never managed to put such a look on her face.

He held out his arm for her to take, and she laid her gloved hand on his sleeve. New gloves, he noted, of the palest blue.

A young lad bounded up to her, a huge grin splitting his pimply face.

'Evening, Perdita,' said the lad. 'I'm to lead you to your box.'

'Thank you, Pat,' she said, and followed the lad serenely, without pausing to bother making any introductions. Not that he wanted to make the acquaintance of this lad. Or, heaven forbid, for the lad to discover precisely who he was. Not yet, anyway.

'I suppose I should be grateful,' Anthony said grudgingly as she drew the curtains of the box to which the lad had taken them, granting them privacy from anyone who might be strolling along the corridors, 'that you clearly haven't spent much time in this theatre, or you would have known your way round better.'

She blinked. Turned away from him, and went to the edge of the balcony, from where she took a good long look at the action already taking place on the stage. He dimly registered some singing, and various people in improbable costumes dancing about and waving their arms like windmills. But it was Mary who held his attention. She looked so pretty, tonight.

'I *have* attended a few rehearsals, as an observer,' she said, darting him a look over her shoulder. 'But I have never actually acted, upon that stage, if that is what is worrying you.'

Hearing her say so did take a weight off his mind. It was no good her being all discreet about her continuing friendship with an actress, if there was still a risk that anyone he knew might recognize her from a performance in which she'd acted.

'I may as well tell you,' said Mary, undoing the strings of her cloak, and flinging it aside, 'that it didn't take long for everyone to discover that I have no talent for acting.' The gown she had on was the most stunning thing he'd ever seen her wearing. Or at least, she looked stunning in it. She'd chosen a material of pale blue, and had it adorned with darker blue ribbons, and tiny pearls swirled round the neckline and hem in an intricate pattern that shimmered as she moved away from the balcony.

'And never appeared in any production, anywhere,' she continued without pausing to notice that she'd, momentarily, taken his breath away, 'unless I was disguised as a tree, or a duck, or something of the sort. Which was how,' she added, arranging her skirts as she took her seat, 'I managed to remain friends with Chloe. She would have hated me if I'd ever upstaged her, in any way.' She'd twined strings of pearls in her hair, too. Where on earth had she got them from? He supposed he'd find out, when the bills started arriving.

He'd never thought she had it in her to be expensive.

He'd never thought she had it in her to be so... independent.

But then he'd never thought she had it in her to run off and vanish for several months, either.

'But because I was so clearly her inferior,' Mary continued, 'and was never going to get top billing, she was prepared to tolerate me joining the troupe. Now that she knows I'm a countess, of course, I think she will regard me as her very *best* friend...'

'You believe she will attempt to impose upon you?' He put the brakes on his reflection of his wife's capacity to surprise him, and went to sit next to her. 'I will soon deal with her,' he vowed, 'if she tries it.'

'Oh, for heaven's sake,' she said, darting him a look of impatience. 'I owe her and Jack and Fenella so much that I will feel as if I will be in their debt for the rest of my life. Now that I'm in a position to do them a favour or two, naturally I shall do so. And I won't consider it an *imposition*. Why, if Jack hadn't come to my rescue, the way he did, I shudder to think what might have become of me.'

Jack.

'I…'

'Oh, hush,' she said, impatiently, turning her face from him as the dancers began to vacate the stage. 'The pantomime is about to begin. That's what I've come to watch. And I don't want to miss a second. Jack is going to attempt something totally new and original tonight, and I want to see how the audience receives it.'

Jack, Jack, Jack. He was sick of hearing about the man. Especially since she was speaking of Jack as if he was some kind of hero, implying that he, her husband, was not.

He'd much preferred the days, he reflected sourly, when she'd acted as though *he* was the centre of her universe. Though perhaps he had forfeited her regard, if he'd somehow made her believe he'd regretted marrying her.

'Oh, here they come,' she suddenly cried, reaching out to clutch at his sleeve, as a young man and a young woman came running onto the stage from opposite sides, and embraced with an air of desperation.

He looked down at the little hand which had shot out and taken hold of him as though it was the most natural thing in the world. But it wasn't. For she had never, before this moment, reached out to touch him of her own volition. Oh, she'd never recoiled from him. Had always responded sweetly to his advances. But had never...dared to initiate, well, anything. Not even such an innocent gesture as this.

If only she'd been bold enough to have done something like this before things had gone wrong. Might he have then had the courage to tell her what she was starting to mean to him? Would that have made a difference?

Or would he have just made a mull of it in some other way?

'That's Chloe,' she said, pointing with her free hand to the brunette who had flung back her dark head and begun to warble a song about how her father would never allow the young man to marry her. 'And the harlequin is Connor. I hadn't met him before we came to London, because he was touring in Ireland. But he regularly performs as Harlequin to Chloe's Columbine,' she explained, as the young man launched into a song about the nobility of his love overcoming the lowliness of his birth.

He reminded himself that she'd intended to come here on her own. That she didn't really care whether he was here or not. That he had no business feeling... touched...at the confiding way she was explaining the action taking place on the stage, or her relationship to the actors.

And yet he couldn't help thinking that if she didn't care about him at all, she would just be sitting there tolerating his presence. Giving him the cold shoulder, rather than reaching out to touch him, and chattering away like this. He knew only too well what that sort of treatment felt like. Sarah had been extremely skilful at letting him know he was not in her good books on public outings such as this.

All of a sudden, the words of the song began to filter through his ears to his mind. The pair of star-crossed lovers were both belting out the hope that heaven would come to their aid in overcoming all the obstacles preventing them from marrying each other. For once, he realized with some surprise, it didn't sound like sentimental drivel. On the contrary, he felt as if he could understand the way they felt, *and* why they were wailing about it at the top of their voices. Because he wasn't far off crying out to some higher power for guidance in dealing with his own marriage.

'And here comes Jack,' Mary said, the grip of her hand on his sleeve growing tighter.

Jack.

He felt his mouth flatten into a tight, angry line. Felt his nostrils flare with distaste.

He said nothing, of course. But he placed his hand over his wife's where her fingers were creasing the material of his sleeve.

Which would remind anyone who cared to look that she was *his* wife.

His.

Chapter Twelve

Anthony had been bracing himself to see the acrobat somersault onto the stage to an admiring burst of applause and cheering.

So it came as a surprise to see the bulky form of Mother Goose hesitating in the wings, peering with apparent timidity at the audience. The hopeful young couple on the stage began to make impatient signals to the nervous goose, and someone in the pit shouted out, drunkenly, 'Get on with it!'

Then an unseen somebody in the wings gave Mother Goose a hefty shove. Mother Goose should, at that point, he dimly remembered from attending other, similar performances, have sung her own song about granting the couple their wish, providing they could prove that it was true love by overcoming a series of tasks. But instead of singing anything, the goose froze, as if paralysed by stage fright, by the brightness of the lights, and the rowdy behaviour of the crowd. With a look of supressed panic, the awkward creature began to sidle back to the safety of the curtain in the wings.

Mary raised her free hand to her mouth to stifle her laughter.

'What,' said Anthony, who didn't see the joke, 'is so funny?'

'It's me,' she said, her shoulders shaking with laughter. 'That was exactly what I was like every time they tried to get me to perform. Even when they put me in costume. And, oh, how clever it is of Jack to manage to convey my shyness, my reluctance to perform in public, when you can't see anything of him under that bulky costume apart from his legs.'

He grudgingly conceded that it must take a good deal of skill to convey both timidity, and surprise, whilst hampered by the confines of a papier mâché head and a pair of cardboard wings.

'Jack warned me,' Mary continued, her eyes riveted to the stage, 'that he was going to put in every single thing I did, in this routine, that made audiences laugh so much all the way through Essex.'

That comment made him watch the antics of the bashful goose with keener interest over the next half hour than he'd ever paid to anything he'd seen performed on stage in his life. Throughout the course of a ridiculously complicated plot, involving Harlequin and Columbine engaging with ballet dancers, jugglers, and a monkey riding a donkey, Mother Goose kept on coming on stage, and bumbling clumsily about, barging into the dancers, and knocking over scenery.

Eventually, Columbine, who'd been growing increasingly annoyed by the way the clumsy goose kept making her a figure of fun, lost her patience completely, and gave the goose such a hefty shove that it fell off the stage and into the orchestra pit. The woodwind section rose, en masse, to repel the intruder, the flautist leading the way by beating the hapless bird about the head with his instrument.

The audience in the pit began to boo the flautist, and the other woodwind players, calling them bullies, and urging the goose to fight back. The atmosphere in the pit reminded him very forcefully of bare-knuckle fights he'd attended as a youth. Eventually, the goose managed to seize the flute in its beak, and run off with it, emitting a series of toots and squeaks that no flute he'd ever heard could possibly make. The theatregoers in the pit parted to make way for the goose, cheering wildly as the flute player chased after it through the auditorium.

'Ladies and gentlemen,' cried a tall, harassed-looking man who'd just dashed onto the stage. 'Please,' he shouted above the hubbub, stretching out his hands in appeal, 'return to your seats! And you,' he added, pointing to the goose and the flute player, with menace, 'if you don't return to your positions, and carry on with the performance, you won't be playing in this, or any other theatre for the rest of your lives!'

Many people in the audience booed him for attempting to spoil their sport, and called him a variety of rude names.

Anthony was on the verge of feeling rather pleased that he'd been here to witness this Jack character lose his employment, when he noticed that Mary was not looking the slightest bit worried.

The flute player snatched his instrument from the beak of the chastened-looking goose, gave it one last, lingering look of resentment, and stalked back to the orchestra pit. The goose then began to make a series of clumsy, and unsuccessful attempts to get back onto the stage, hampered by the fact that the actor's hands were encased inside the costume. As each failed attempt was greeted by fresh gales of laughter, Anthony realized what was going on.

'This is all part of the...something different you told me Jack was going to try tonight,' he said to Mary, 'isn't it?'

'Yes!' Mary turned to him, her face glowing. 'When Chloe said I was so useless on stage I'd be more use taking the hat round, I was so clumsy and awkward that people thought it was all part of the show. And they loved thinking they were being included when I bumped into someone and spilled his drink, or stepped back into a cart of cabbages knocking them everywhere. And it's the same tonight, isn't it? Harry was worried that letting one of the actors go out among the audience might provoke a riot, but Jack suggested that he only need take a few precautions, such as having a few stagehands dotted about the pit, to ward off any really nasty attempts to harm him.'

'He appears to think of everything,' said Anthony, with a touch of resentment.

'Well, you cannot pull off an act like this without planning it in meticulous detail, and rehearsing it thoroughly,' she replied.

At that moment, the goose acted out suddenly remembering it had wings.

Mary sighed in admiration. 'How he manages to convey thoughts, and feelings, while he's wearing a costume that is three parts feather bed, covering his hands, and face, by just the tiniest movements of the head piece, or a tilt of the neck, or a despondent flap of the wings, is a marvel.'

Anthony wrestled with himself for a moment, but only a moment. Only a callow youth, in the first flushes of a love affair, would be foolish enough to declare that he despised his rival, and everything about him. And he was no longer a callow youth who would rise to such bait. Besides, hadn't he thought much the same thing himself, earlier on?

'He is certainly a very skilful acrobat,' he said, albeit grudgingly.

As if to prove the point, the goose backed up the aisle, then ran forward, flapping those tiny, cardboard wings, faster and faster, before suddenly leaping into the air and landing on the stage, where, unsurprisingly, it managed to knock over two ballet dancers and Harlequin. The audience gave a rousing cheer.

Anthony was less impressed. He'd seen the fellow somersault from standing to land on a table, but nobody, surely, could have jumped that high? He must have placed a springboard in a strategic location, to give the impression of taking flight.

'They love it,' said Mary, turning to look at him

with shining eyes, 'don't they? The way Jack went right in among them. Harry said that Jack would never get out alive, but he pulled it off, didn't he?'

Had it only been an hour or so ago that he'd been thinking that if she met a goose, she'd be prepared to kick the creature down the stairs? Hah. For now it was *he* who very much wanted to kick a goose. One specific goose, anyway. Right out of her life.

'It is time,' he said sternly, 'to leave.'

'Oh, no. Really?'

'Yes,' he said, picking up her cloak and draping it round her shoulders. 'You have witnessed your friend's triumph. And I can sense the action winding up to a conclusion. And I really think it would be wise to make our escape before the final curtain falls.' He allowed her to see him running his eyes over the people sitting in the boxes over the way.

'You may not have noticed, but several people in the boxes opposite have been training their opera glasses our way. And looking far more interested in us, than what has been happening on the stage.' And many of them were notorious gossips and muckrakers. They would be dying to be the first to find out why Mary was back in London, and, more importantly, why there had been no word of her for so long.

He had also recognized several of the men in the pit. Some of them were just the sort to come swarming up to the box the minute the final curtain fell, and ambush him with their lethal brand of bonhomie. Which would give the tabbies he'd spotted, opposite, time to make their way over here and sink their claws into his wife.

Her face fell. But she went, meekly enough, to the curtains at the rear of the box.

They'd made it halfway down the stairs before anyone did accost them. Fortunately, it was only the younger brother of his secretary, Travers. Unfortunately, he took up a position directly in their path, preventing them from descending any further.

'Leaving,' said the young man, 'so soon?'

'Yes,' Anthony replied, ruthlessly pushing him to one side.

'I say, no need to be like that,' Travers junior objected. 'Was only hoping to pay my respects to your countess.'

'Noted,' said Anthony, continuing down the stairs.

Travers put him in mind of a spaniel puppy who would not be deterred from frolicking all over his master's slippers, when he turned and fell into step beside Mary.

'Take it that this was a bit much for your first trip out, my lady, since your return to Town?'

How the devil had the fellow come by such information? Had his older brother been indiscreet? If so...

'It was tremendous fun, though,' Travers was persisting. 'Wasn't it?'

'Well, I thought so,' Mary replied. 'Though we only came in to watch the pantomime. Um. Which bit, in particular, did you enjoy most?'

'Of the pantomime? Oh, well, I can't make up my mind between the bit where the buxom Columbine pushed the goose off the stage, or its attempts to climb back up.'

Mary's pace slowed. Short of picking her up and throwing her over his shoulder, there was not a lot he could do to hasten their departure.

'And what about,' she said, across him, to Travers, 'the fight with the flautist? Didn't you find that funny?'

'Oh, yes,' Travers agreed, as they reached the foyer. 'But it didn't take me long to wonder if it was all just a touch…smoky. I mean to say, you wouldn't really expect a musician to use his instrument as a weapon, would you? I mean, that is his livelihood. If he damages it, I daresay it would be terribly expensive to buy a new one. And then,' he chuckled, 'the noises that goose pretended to make with it as it ran off were clearly made by a trumpet. Or possibly a trombone. I mean, any idiot knows how hard it is to get any kind of tune out of a flute, let alone when held in the beak of a goose!' He chuckled.

'And you are clearly,' said Mary, 'not an idiot of any kind.'

Travers blushed. 'Oh, I don't know. Some chaps do say I am a bit of a downy one, but…' He petered out, probably because he finally noticed Anthony scowling at him.

'But not, perhaps,' Anthony suggested silkily, 'terribly tactful.'

'What? Ah. Oh,' he said, as Anthony kept on steering Mary in the direction of the exit. 'Of course. Don't want Her Ladyship to overdo things, too soon. That is, heard you were indisposed, and, er, well, lovely to have met you,' he finished, executing a swift, face-saving bow before scuttling off.

Anthony shot his retreating form a dark glance. How the devil could he, or anyone, have heard that Mary had been indisposed, or know that this was her first appearance in public since returning to London? Or that she had returned to London, come to that? He'd been so careful to prevent news of her reappearance leaking out.

He'd believed he could trust his staff to say nothing.

He turned to look at Mary. Who hadn't seemed at all surprised by Travers saying he knew more about her comings and goings than he had any right to know.

He took her firmly by the elbow.

'I think,' she observed, as they left the building, and stood on the pavement where he hoped the coach would be waiting, 'that you may be overreacting.'

Overreacting? He'd just discovered that word of her return to London had circulated in spite of his attempts to keep it quiet. And that after spending hours, or at least what felt like hours, watching his wife admiring the antics of another man, while the hoi polloi cheered and applauded.

'On the contrary,' he said as he bundled her unceremoniously into the carriage, which had, fortunately, arrived precisely when he needed it. 'I think I have been exercising a praiseworthy amount of restraint. To start with, I did not utter one word of censure about your foolish decision to attend the theatre tonight.' Well, that wasn't exactly true. But he hadn't said half as much about it as he'd liked to have done. 'Instead, I came with you, to give you countenance.'

'Now, just a minute,' she began.

'Then,' he continued, as though she hadn't spoken, 'I sat and listened to you admitting that you have been deceiving me, by smuggling undesirable people into my house. People,' he said, holding up his hand to silence her when she took a breath to object, 'that you knew I would not approve of you mingling with, or you wouldn't have had them coming in, wearing disguises.'

'It was only Chloe,' she protested. 'You make it sound as though I had legions of disreputable people swarming through the house. And I explained why I did it...'

He ignored that point. Particularly since he'd seen the sense of it when she'd made it, and he had no intention of allowing her to calm him down, or put him off course.

'But worst of all was learning that you have been performing on stage, dressed in such a way that every man who cares to can ogle your legs.'

Jack's legs, enclosed though they had been by thick white tights, were very muscly, and clearly not the legs of a female. But had it been a woman in the goose costume, every man in the place would have known. And reacted accordingly.

Her mouth dropped open. 'My legs,' she finally managed to say. 'You have the gall to sit there, looking down your nose at me, and say you object to people looking at my legs?'

'Of course I do!'

'Let me get this straight. You are criticising me for doing what I had to do, to survive, while you were sitting about trying to ignore the fact that I might be in danger?'

'That is not how it was!'

'Oh, that is exactly how it was. Don't you remember, when I first came home, I told you how I called for you when I was at my lowest point? By *name*?'

'What does that have to do with you flaunting your legs for the world to see?'

'Because I worked out that even if you had believed I'd run off with a groom, if you'd even bothered to set Bow Street Runners after me, to apprehend me and make me pay, they would have found me not five miles from Blanchetts. But you didn't, did you?'

He'd been thinking, for some time now, that he ought to explain exactly why he'd been so reluctant to raise a hue and cry over her disappearing act.

'I… Look, when you disappeared,' he began, in a roundabout way, 'you crushed me. My pride was in the dust. I…'

'That is clearly not the case,' she replied with some asperity. 'Since it was still robust enough to take precedence over admitting your wife had gone missing and organizing any kind of search for her.' She frowned and shook her head. 'For *me*. So you have no right, now, to complain about anything I had to do while I was out there, *on my own*.'

'Any man would object to hearing that his wife had been displaying her legs in public…'

'If you cared so much about my legs you would have taken better care of them, not washed your hands of them the minute they were out of your sight!'

'Are you not the least bit ashamed of…of flaunting them?' She sounded so much like Sarah in that moment, who, when taxed with rumours of her misdeeds, would try to throw the blame back on him, that he just *might* have overreacted. And yet somehow he could not stop himself. 'Are you not in the slightest bit sorry?'

'Only,' she said, viciously, as the carriage juddered to a halt outside his house, 'of putting you on a pedestal, in the first place. Of making a…a god of you! Well, there, idolatry has its reward, doesn't it? I worshipped a false god, and now I discover he has feet of clay. No, actually, not just your feet,' she said, looking down at them with dislike. 'You are clay all the way through. Just gilded with a veneer made up of rank and wealth.'

He had to get her to stop talking. Stephens was opening the carriage door. The man would hear. Because she was not talking in her normally soft, pleasing tones, but in a strident voice that people could probably hear clear across the square.

'That's enough,' he began, urgently.

'Yes, quite enough,' she shouted back at him. 'Because,' she said as the door swung open, 'not only did you never love me back, but you have proved completely unworthy of any feelings I ever had for you.'

And with that, she tumbled out of the carriage, and went flying up the steps to the front door.

Chapter Thirteen

Well, he'd been right about her having the courage to kick a goose down the stairs, he mused as she dashed through the front door. It was just that he'd never imagined *he* would be the proverbial goose she'd want to kick.

Stephens put on a particularly wooden expression as Anthony got out of the carriage in a deliberately leisurely fashion. But then he must have overheard most of the latter part of Mary's complaint. About him being nothing more than a cipher. A facsimile of a man who would be nothing were it not for the title and the wealth.

Was that truly what she thought? Or was she, he pondered as he entered the house, just lashing out in an attempt to hurt him?

It had certainly stung, he reflected, as he handed over his hat, gloves, and coat to Simmons, to hear her say that she no longer worshipped him. Which should not be the case. After all, he'd assumed, from the moment he'd heard she'd run off with a groom, that the love he'd believed she'd borne for him had been a figment of his imagination. That he'd conjured up the worshipful look in her eyes when she gazed at him, because it had been what he'd wanted to see.

But she'd just told him that she *had* worshipped him. Which implied that she'd returned his feelings for her.

That was why he had been willing to listen to her wild story of murderous highwaymen and lost memory, wasn't it? Because if it was true, perhaps it meant she hadn't left him voluntarily after all.

Was he the greatest fool in London when it came to matters of the heart? Was he so desperate to be loved that he'd swallow any old cock and bull story?

But on the other hand, if her account of why she'd gone missing was true, then it meant that he had let her down. And he *was* no longer worthy of her admiration.

And he had made *her* pay for Sarah's crimes.

He turned blankly away from Simmons, who was maintaining an expression as wooden as only a really good upper servant could manufacture. He must have heard Mary shouting at him. He'd certainly seen her go dashing into the house and up the stairs.

But then he was used to witnessing scenes of marital discord, wasn't he?

The fellow's next words confirmed it.

'There is a fire in your study, my lord. And a decanter of brandy.'

'Thank you,' said Anthony tonelessly, before making for the refuge he'd so often sought in that room, with a liberal application of the identical remedy.

He unstoppered the decanter and poured a measure of the liquid comfort into a glass. Was it time, he wondered, as he began swirling the brandy round, to warm it, to tell Mary about his first wife? About Sarah?

Oh, not *literally*. Not this very minute, he reflected with a grimace as he raised the glass to his mouth and took a sip. He knew only too well how it went when he barged into the bedroom of a furious woman, demanding they settle a matter. It would start with her shouting at him, slapping him, him taking her by the wrists to prevent further assault. Her panting, looking up at him with excited, wild eyes. Daring him to do his worst. Then…conflagration. He'd take her to bed, where they'd slake their mutual lust without really resolving anything.

No. He slapped the glass down on his desk. No, that was *not* how it would be with Mary! She wasn't Sarah. The worst that would happen, if he continued their argument tonight, while her temper was still frayed, was that they might both say things they could never take back.

But he didn't want to run that risk with Mary, did he?

He knew from bitter experience what could happen when he allowed his temper to get the better of him. So he needed to wait until he could speak to Mary calmly. Rationally. Explain it all, or at least enough to make her understand. And forgive him, if forgiveness was necessary. Or tell her that he was willing to forgive her if…

He picked up his brandy and took a gulp. *Could* he forgive her if she'd been unfaithful? Could *she* forgive *him* for thinking she had, if she hadn't?

He sat down heavily in the chair behind his desk, the brandy glass dangling loosely from one hand.

Tomorrow, after breakfast, he would invite her to join him in here, he decided, glancing round at the book-filled shelves, the ledgers and papers strewn across the desk. No risk of passion taking over in a room as businesslike as this. He would sit on one side of the desk, and she on the other, so there would be no risk of physical contact to distract either of them from having a civilized conversation. He would explain about Sarah, and how she'd left him so wrung out that he had trouble trusting anyone, once she'd gone, male or female. Then, if Mary's story was true, she would hopefully be more willing to forgive him, if his actions required forgiveness.

In any case, once he'd made a clean breast of things, he would have more right to expect her to give him a full account of what she'd been doing during the missing months. To explain how she'd gone from the home of a Methodist family somewhere that was, from what she'd let slip this evening, less than five miles from Blanchetts, to the lodgings of a troupe of actors in the warren of slums at the back of Drury Lane.

Having made that decision, he finished his brandy, set the empty glass down on his desk, and was just about to leave the room when there came a soft knock on the door. Before he could say anything, it opened, and Mary peeped round the edge.

'I could not let the evening end this way,' she said, sidling into the room and shutting the door behind her.

He froze, the images of scenes with his former wife playing out in his mind.

Though Sarah wouldn't have knocked, would she? She would have just stormed in and started throwing things.

'I just had to come,' said Mary, 'and say I was sorry for losing my temper with you like that. And saying all those horrid things.'

This was new territory. An angry woman, admitting she might be in the wrong? Apologizing for the things she'd said?

She stepped away from the door and hesitated, her hands clasped at her waist. 'I didn't mean them. You aren't made of clay. That is to say—' she paused, looking a touch awkward '—there *is* more to you than a title and all that.'

'It is generous of you to say so,' he began, stunned, yet again, by how surprising Mary could be. 'But I am only human. I make mistakes. I made a lot of them with you, didn't I?'

She flinched.

'Oh, not in marrying you, I didn't mean that,' he said, coming out from behind his desk to go and take her hands, and reassure her. To thank her for being the one to come and smooth things over. 'But in not looking after you properly. In allowing you to feel that I didn't care about you. And tonight, I know

I provoked you into that outburst. By complaining about you showing your legs to the world. But you have to know that it was from jealousy, surely?'

'Jealousy?' She looked up at him as though he'd said something outrageous.

'Yes. You have such lovely legs. So shapely and slender. As your husband, naturally I don't want any other man to see them.'

'My legs,' she repeated, searching his face as though suspecting him of making a May game of her.

'Instead of finding fault with the things you may have done while I wasn't looking after you,' he said ruefully, 'I would have done better to tell you how pretty you looked tonight. And then you might not have been so cross with me by the end of the evening.'

'Really?' She gazed up at him in a shy, uncertain way that put him in mind so forcibly of how she'd been when he first met her that the feelings he'd had back then all came surging back.

'Did I never even tell you how pretty you are?'

She shook her head, her eyes widening in disbelief.

And all of a sudden all he wanted to do was kiss her.

'I've been such a fool,' he groaned, hauling her into his arms and pressing his lips to her mouth.

'Mmm,' she said against his mouth, briefly, before flinging her arms about his neck and kissing him back.

For a moment or two there was nothing but the

bliss of having her in his arms again, passion, mutual passion consuming all else with its devouring heat.

Never had he had an argument end this way before...

Or at least, not exactly.

He ended the kiss, closed his eyes, and rested his forehead against hers.

'This can go no further,' he said, to himself as much as her.

'What,' she asked breathlessly, 'do you mean?'

'I mean that giving way to physical urges never really solves anything.'

'What do you mean?' Her face darkened. 'What are you implying?'

'Go up to your room, Mary,' he said resolutely. 'Before this gets out of hand.'

She drew back from him. The hurt and confusion on her face smote him.

'I am not accusing you of doing anything wrong,' he said, suddenly seeing that it was what she'd thought he meant. 'On the contrary it was sweet of you to come and apologize for your part in our quarrel. But now is not the time for...this.' He made a gesture between the two of them, hoping she'd understand what he meant. 'And this is not the place.' He glanced round his study. Had he really thought that there would be no risk of passion flaring in such a businesslike atmosphere? Hah! He'd totally overlooked Mary's allure, hadn't he? She'd probably be able to get him interested in making love in just about any setting.

But he was absolutely not going to allow her to

make him lose control anywhere inappropriate. It wasn't his style.

'We will speak again, in the morning,' he assured her.

She didn't look all that happy about his decision. But she didn't argue. She just backed to the door, never taking her eyes off him.

'I understand,' she said sadly as she slipped out of the room.

Did she? Well, that was more than he did!

The next morning, when Mary came into the breakfast room, his heart did a funny sort of skip. He hadn't been looking forward to seeing her, because it was going to mean broaching topics he'd never thought he'd have to share with anyone. Yet, when she didn't appear at her usual time, he'd started to worry she wasn't going to grant him the opportunity to…to…clear the air. But here she was at last, looking a bit pale as she marched defiantly over to the sideboard, where she heaped her plate with a mound of food. He couldn't help smiling at the way she marched back to the table, sat down, and picked up her knife and fork without sparing him a single glance. Or wondering why he'd ever thought she could behave like Sarah, in any situation. Sarah would have waited with her ear to her door and ambushed him last night if he hadn't gone to her room. Would have thrown a selection of breakables down the stairs at him, the more expensive the better. She would most definitely not have come to apologize for having lost her temper.

Mary always behaved with studied dignity, no matter the provocation, didn't she? For all that she lacked the bloodlines of his first wife, she was far more a lady than Sarah had ever been.

'Mary,' he began, 'you know we need to discuss a few things. After breakfast, would you do me the honour of joining me in my study?' Would it be safe? He'd thought that it would be impossible to give way to passion in such a workaday room, but last night he realized he was wrong.

She blushed, as though thinking along the same lines, but kept right on cutting up her bacon, and putting food into her mouth for a minute or two, as though thinking it over. Then, having made him wait for her answer, she shrugged one shoulder.

'I suppose it is about time,' she said.

'Good,' he said, although he couldn't say that he felt anything like pleasure. He was going to have to reveal things he'd kept private from the whole world. And also hear, from her own lips, an account of things he would in all likelihood much rather not have to hear as well.

'Then,' he said grimly, getting to his feet and laying his napkin aside, 'I shall await your arrival. Whenever,' he added, looking at the amount of scrambled eggs she still had to finish, 'you are ready.'

The moment he left the room, Mary felt her shoulders droop. Even though the footmen were still bustling about, clearing his plate and tankard, and whisking up his crumbs.

She wished it was easier to understand him. Last

night she'd begun to hope that at least they could re-kindle the passion which they'd shared in the early days of their marriage. But he'd brought it to a halt before it could get further than a kiss or two. Warning her that it wouldn't solve anything.

What had he meant? It felt as if whenever she managed to get one step closer to him, he'd take two steps back. Later on, as she'd come up with and discarded one answer after another to that question, she'd sunk to the level of wondering if it had suddenly occurred to him that if they'd made love, it might have made it harder for him to get a divorce, if he eventually decided that a divorce was what he really wanted.

Although, surely he wouldn't go to such lengths as divorcing her, would he? It would mean letting the whole world know he'd made a mistake of such catastrophic proportions that there was no hiding it any longer. No, no, she had to cling to what he'd said earlier on. He'd told her, categorically, that he didn't think he had made a mistake in marrying her.

Besides, if there was one thing Anthony hated, it was people talking about him. That was the one thing she'd known, for certain, that she'd had in her favour, to start with. He'd told her, she mused as she reached for her teacup, that he liked the fact that she was willing to live a quiet life, and knowing that she would flee from notoriety. He'd liked the fact that she was timid, and shy.

The trouble was, Perdita had never been timid, or shy. Not knowing she had any reason to be, Perdita had just done whatever she wanted. And, although she remembered now that she'd been Mary once, and knew she had to live Mary's life again, Perdita had survived, and would not…lie down and be quiet. She frowned down into her teacup. It was so confusing, all this thinking about herself as two separate people. And worrying, too. People, normal people at least, didn't forget who they were one minute, then decide they were two people inhabiting the same body, the next.

And that peculiarity of hers would give Anthony a jolly good reason for putting her aside, never mind the fact that he didn't want a wife who sneaked actresses into his house, and who was determined to stay friends with actresses, and who shouted at him, and told him he was worthless. No man could possibly want a wife who'd become…unstable. No matter what he might have thought of her to start with.

She lifted her chin as she set her teacup back on its saucer, trying not to let her lower lip start to quiver. She was *not* going to cry. Not here in the dining room over a plate of bacon and eggs. She'd done enough crying last night, in the privacy of her own room.

She'd hoped, oh, how she'd hoped, during these days while Anthony had been mulling over whether to believe her or not, that he'd decide, in spite of everything, to take her back.

But how likely was that? She'd never been good enough for him. She never would be.

This really could be the end.

Chapter Fourteen

Anthony's feet already felt heavy as he made his way to his study. But they became impossible to move when he noticed, loitering in the hallway, twirling his hat between his hands, a neatly dressed and all too familiar young man.

Baxter. The man he'd hired to go north, and ferret out the truth.

'I do beg your pardon, my lord,' said Simmons, appearing as if out of nowhere. 'I did tell this person that you were at breakfast, but he insisted on waiting. He said it was important.'

Important. Yes, if he'd discovered something about Mary's movements while she'd been missing, it was important all right. And he must have done, or he would not have come. Not in such a relatively short time.

Baxter had done well to convince Simmons that he had an important matter to impart. If he hadn't done so, Simmons would have thrown him out, not permitted him to wait. But then, Baxter did have the air of a man who'd come here to impart news of the utmost urgency.

'Tell Her Ladyship,' Anthony said to Simmons, 'that I have received a visitor of some importance… someone I, er, forgot might be coming today. And that I will have to rearrange our own…discussion, until later.' By which time he would be in possession of the facts. Which would, hopefully, help him to find his way forward with Mary. So that he would be able to make better judgements about their future.

'Very good, my lord,' said Simmons, melting away.

'You had better come to my study,' said Anthony to Baxter, extending his arm to point the way across the hall.

'Thank you for agreeing to receive me, my lord,' said Baxter, the moment Anthony had closed the study door behind them. 'I could have called back whenever it was more convenient,' he said, his expression turning a touch apologetic. 'Only, you did specify you didn't want anything in writing, that you wanted me to tell you what I'd found out, face-to-face…'

'Yes, yes,' said Anthony, impatiently making a chopping motion with his hand to halt the flow of excuses. 'Take a seat,' he said, indicating the chair in front of his desk, while he went round to take the chair behind it. 'And tell me what you have found out.'

Baxter cleared his throat. Looked Anthony straight in the eyes. 'Well, to start with, I didn't think I was going to have any success at all. I began my investigations at Blanchetts, as you suggested, but found the staff there remarkably close-mouthed. Normally,' he said, with a conspiratorial grin, 'I can manage to find a bored housemaid who is willing to flirt, and part with the family secrets in return for a bit of flattery…'

Anthony had no trouble picturing the fellow doing just that. Baxter had an engaging grin. And the kind of looks he would guess a young woman would find attractive.

'But in this case…' Baxter spread his hands wide and gave a shrug.

Anthony was simultaneously gratified, and annoyed to hear that even the lowliest of his servants were so loyal. It would have been useful to have heard something of what had gone on, inside Blanchetts, while Mary had been there on her own.

'Likewise, in the local taverns, people wouldn't say anything about your, er, current wife…' Baxter broke off, his eyes shifting sideways.

Anthony leaned back and eyed the investigator more thoroughly. It wasn't hard to imagine him visiting the local taverns, in the guise of a sporting young gentleman, getting friendly with the locals over tankards of home-brewed ale. Funny, when he'd first had the notion of hiring a private investigator, he'd assumed such men would be ferrety-faced, shifty-looking chaps wearing rather greasy clothes. Instead of which Baxter was, well, frankly ordinary looking. Medium height. Mid-brown hair. Light-coloured eyes. Neatly dressed.

Five minutes after meeting him, Baxter had confided, at that first interview, all those years ago, people wouldn't be able to give a description of him that wouldn't apply to hundreds of other men. That he was, to all intents and purposes, invisible.

'I suspect,' Anthony ventured, 'you heard plenty about the first Lady Epping, though. She made herself odious in those parts.'

'Indeed I did,' said Baxter, looking relieved that he hadn't had to say any more about that. 'Well, after that, I thought it might be worthwhile looking into the story of the Methodist family who lived near the canal you thought might be the one in question.' He paused.

'Yes?'

'Found 'em,' he said, with an air of triumph. 'With no trouble at all! They go by the name of Hapcott. Got very agitated when I enquired after a young lady who had been fished out of the canal. Apparently, she hurt them badly by being so ungrateful for all they'd done for her...'

'Then it was true, they did nurse Mary—that is, my wife—back to health?'

'They nursed *someone* back to health, my lord,' said Baxter, adopting a more cautious tone. 'A young woman who fits Her Ladyship's description.'

'Ungrateful, you say? How ungrateful?'

'Well, in that she refused to confide in them, and maintained the fiction that she did not know her own name. Which they felt must be a lie. Even so, they arranged for her to go to the town where, for some reason, they thought she must come from. I must say, they did seem like a remarkably charitable sort of couple. And seemed genuinely sorry to have their suspicions about her confirmed by hearing the news that she gave her escort the slip.'

Baxter said a lot more about the Hapcotts, and the time and effort they'd expended on the ungrateful, sinful woman who fit Mary's description. But Anthony only heard a few words, here and there.

Even though the Hapcotts had nursed a half-drowned woman back to health, it didn't necessarily mean that woman was Mary, he cautioned himself. She hadn't given them her name.

He had to consider the possibility that Mary could have heard about a woman undergoing such a fate, and told him the story, pretending that she was the woman in question, rather than grasping at this account of events as evidence of her innocence.

He had to ask himself if she had it in her to tell him such a barefaced lie.

And how she could have heard of such a story.

But no matter how much he cautioned himself, it seemed far more likely, taking all things into consideration, that she'd simply been telling him the truth.

'And then, deciding I'd found out as much as I could from them,' Baxter was saying, 'I went on to investigate the account of the highwaymen. Now,' he said, sitting forward in his chair, 'I had to do a good bit of travelling, on their account.' Which would no doubt be reflected in the expense sheet the man would present, Anthony reflected cynically. 'Because,' Baxter continued, 'they don't have a fixed territory, like most highwaymen. They seem to travel from place to place, or at least, there has been a series of crimes, similar to the one Her Ladyship described, getting steadily further north. The last one I found out about took place in Haltwhistle, a little place almost in the borders. By that point I didn't think it worth following their trail any longer as it looks to me as if they'll be terrorising villages and hamlets in Scotland by now.'

'You speak of them as though they really exist. These...highwaymen.'

'Oh, they exist, all right,' said Baxter grimly. 'A nasty lot. Four of them. Armed. They set upon travellers on quiet roads, in broad daylight. People are always unprepared for them, because they only strike the once in any area, before moving on. The only reason I can tell it is the same gang is by what they do.'

'Which is?'

Baxter looked down at his hat briefly, before raising his eyes. 'They threaten to shoot the men, but, without fail, they rough them up. And if there is a woman, then they assault her, in, well, the worst way. All of them. One after the other.'

Dear God.

'One of their victims,' said Baxter, darkly, 'hanged herself, after. And it is largely on account of the outrage her death caused in her village that I was able to follow the progress of the villains as far as I did. Her family set up a hue and cry.'

Dear God.

She *had* been telling the truth. About all of it.

For how could she have known about such a set of villains, if they moved on from the scene of one crime to another, heading steadily north, when she'd come south, unless she'd been one of their victims? Potential victim, he hastily assured himself. She'd escaped, hadn't she? Fallen into the canal in the process, but hadn't suffered the worst indignity of all...

'Someone will catch them, my lord,' Baxter was saying, as though from the other end of a long, dark tunnel. 'Bound to. Ruffians like that, well, they always make a mistake sooner or later. Drink too much and start boasting of their misdeeds in the wrong tavern. Hold up what they think is a helpless-looking couple who turn out to both be heavily armed. That sort of thing.'

Anthony realized he must be looking as green about the gills as he felt, for Baxter to be attempting to offer him consolation.

It was time to pull himself together.

'Is there anything else I need to know?'

'Ah, no, my lord.'

'You didn't,' he said, with a troubled frown, 'make any attempt to try and locate the young groom's body? It seems logical to deduce that they killed him after what you have told me, and given the fact that he has disappeared. I am sure it would bring comfort to his family to know what has become of him, and lay him to rest.' And it would be far better to send Baxter to look for Franklin, rather than sending his tenants out searching ditches and beating their way across the moors. 'Do you think you can do it?'

'Oh, yes, my lord,' replied Baxter, with a confident smile. 'I know of a man with a dog that has a remarkable nose.'

'I see,' said Anthony, foreseeing yet another hefty bill for expenses. And speaking of which…

'I may as well settle with you for the work you have done to date,' he said. 'If you can render me an account.'

Baxter reached into his breast pocket and drew out a folded sheet of paper which he lay on the desk.

After giving it a brief perusal, and noting that it wasn't as steep as it might have been, Anthony drew out some banknotes which he'd been keeping locked in the top drawer of his desk, against this eventuality.

'Always a pleasure doing business with you, my lord,' said Baxter, pocketing the cash, and going straight out.

Anthony sat there, his eyes open, but seeing nothing. Not of what was round him at present. His mind was too full of what Baxter had said, which confirmed everything Mary had told him.

What she must have endured!

And when she'd found her way back to him, what had he done? He'd shouted at her. Accused her of all sorts of crimes.

How on earth was he ever going to be able to face her again?

He was going to have to do more than ask her forgiveness, he realized. He was going to have to beg for it. Grovel.

No. He could not grovel. Not to any woman.

But nothing else would suffice. He'd wronged her. Neglected her, then vilified her.

He could not grovel. The very thought of it made him feel sick to his stomach.

But she deserved it. Deserved that he abase himself...

He didn't know how long he'd been sitting there, alternately telling himself he had to find a way to make amends to Mary, then baulking at what that might involve, when a knock sounded on the door.

'What?' He was not ready to face anyone. Whoever it was could…

Simmons poked his head round the door.

'Begging your pardon, my lord, but I thought you would wish to know that while you were engaged with your business, a visitor arrived for Her Ladyship.'

'A visitor? At this hour?' It was far too early for any respectable person to go calling on a countess. No wonder Simmons had alerted him.

'Exactly so, my lord. I put her in the drawing room, and served her tea.'

'Her?' It was not, then, that acrobat whose name he couldn't bear to so much as allow to flit through his mind, come to gloat about last night's performance.

'Lady Dalrympole,' said Simmons, gravely.

'Good God!' What on earth could the woman be thinking, to come here at such an unsocial hour? Nothing good, knowing her.

He got to his feet, his dilemma regarding how to face Mary, now that he knew what he knew, pushed aside for the moment.

'Thank you, Simmons,' he said, rounding the desk and heading for the door.

He may have made mistakes in the past, but from now on he was going to be a better husband. And good husbands, he was sure, did not leave their wives to face dragons like Lady Dalrympole alone.

Chapter Fifteen

Mary lingered at the breakfast table for as long as she could. But there was only so much bacon even she could consume. And she'd drunk so much tea she felt as though she was awash with it.

She laid her napkin aside with reluctance, and went with heavy feet to the door, feeling like a prisoner about to hear what sentence the judge would mete out.

The moment she reached the hall, however, Simmons came as near to bustling over as she'd ever seen the dignified man move.

'Beg pardon, my lady,' he said in hushed tones. 'But His Lordship has received an unexpected visitor. He sends his apologies and begs to inform you that he will rearrange your own discussion for a more propitious time.'

She would warrant he hadn't said anything of the sort. That was all put in the diplomatic tones Simmons always used. Anthony simply didn't want to face his bothersome wife this morning; that was what it amounted to. Someone more important had come to call. Well, probably *anyone* would be more important to him than her.

Fine!

'Thank you, Simmons,' she said, hoping he wouldn't be able to detect how hurt she felt by the way Anthony had brushed her aside. And went, in what she hoped was a steady, dignified way, up the stairs to her room.

She flung herself on her back onto her bed and glared up at the blue pleated canopy. It was exhausting her, the way he kept giving her glimmers of hope, then dashing it away like this. Saying he didn't want to dispose of her, that he hadn't been glad she'd disappeared from Blanchetts, and then refusing to give way to the passion he clearly felt for her. Showing her how unimportant she was in the scheme of things, by seeing some other person who'd turned up at the house, when she'd been waiting, on tenterhooks, all night for the discussion he'd said they were going to have!

And it was so unfair that he had all the say, and she had none. When she'd done nothing wrong! Well, not really wrong. She could see why he wasn't pleased to hear that she'd acted on the stage, a few times. But then what else could she have done? Far worse things, that's what. Things that really *were* wrong. She'd take great pleasure in informing him of some of the dangers she might have had to face, if Jack hadn't seen what was going on, and stepped up to intervene. Yes, Anthony ought to be grateful that becoming an actress was the worst that he could say of her!

She wasn't sure how long she lay there, planning what to say to him, and how she would say it, when he eventually deigned to have the private discussion he'd told her he intended to have, when she heard someone knocking on her door.

She sat up and ran her hands over her hair, before calling out permission to enter, hoping she didn't look too disreputable.

'Beg pardon, my lady,' said the housemaid who stood there, bobbing a curtsey. Her name was Jane, and she was the one most likely to come up here when Mary rang for a servant. 'But Mr Simmons sent me to inform you that you have a visitor. An important one, must be, because he's taken her, himself, to the drawing room, and has ordered tea.'

Not Chloe, then, was her first thought. Nor the dressmaker. Simmons would have sent either of them up here, after one of the staff had come up to enquire whether it was convenient for her to receive them.

Which meant it was a proper visitor.

She gulped, recalling the few times she'd received visitors, in that parlour, when she'd been a timid new bride.

'Who is it?'

'Lady Dally something,' said Jane, and blushed. 'Sorry, I didn't quite catch the name.'

'Lady Dalrymple?'

'Yes,' said Jane, brightening up. 'That was it!'

Oh, no.

For once, her memory did not fail her. She remembered Lady Dalrymple only too well from her last, brief foray into society. She was the sharpest clawed of the tabbies who'd done their best to rip her to pieces when she'd had the temerity to marry a man so far above her station.

'How do I look?' She ran over to the mirror, to check her outfit for grease spots or egg stains. Should she change into something a little more...?

A little more what? For heaven's sake! What did it matter what she looked like? Or indeed what Lady Dalrympole would think of her? It couldn't be any worse than she'd thought last time. Besides, later on today, or perhaps tomorrow if he was too busy to bother with her today, Anthony might very well give her her marching orders. She had to face up to the fact that not even the desire he still had for her was able to completely obliterate his doubts and suspicions about what she might have done while she'd been away from him. And there was nothing she could do to make him change his mind.

But rather than plunging her into despair, she found that thought surprisingly liberating. Because if nothing she did, or said, could make any difference, then she might as well say exactly what she liked.

'You look very fine, my lady,' said the housemaid, rather untruthfully. She didn't look the slightest bit fine. She looked as though she'd just got out of bed, with ends of her hair straggling out from where she'd dislodged pins, and creases in her gown from when she'd been lying down.

'Perhaps,' suggested Jane, diplomatically, 'it might be an idea just to run a brush through your hair?'

Well, that might make her *hair* look better. But she'd have to change into a fresh gown if she wanted

to look neat. And there was nothing she could do
about the shadows under her eyes, which a night of
poor, disturbed sleep had caused, short of slapping
half an inch of stage makeup over them. All of which
would take ages.

'No,' she said, making for the door. 'There is no
need to keep my visitor waiting.' Lady Dalrympole
wouldn't like being kept waiting, anyway. Ladies of
her stamp expected everyone to hop to it when they
clicked their fingers. Hadn't she spent years working for a lady cut from just the same cloth as Lady
Dalrympole? And she would never have dared keep
her waiting for an answer to a summons.

She'd run halfway down the stairs before a voice,
which sounded very much like Perdita's, asked her
rather tartly why on earth she'd just dashed out of
her room like a startled hare. Lady Dalrympole was
not her employer, was she?

She paused then, resting one hand on the banister for balance as the Perdita part of her asked why
she'd suddenly become so scared of offending Lady
Dalrympole by keeping her waiting.

Was it because Mary had been in the habit of
rushing to answer any summons from her employer?

Or was it because of the experiences she'd been
remembering when she'd been a young bride? Of
encounters with ladies such as the one waiting in
the drawing room.

Well, whichever it was, she didn't want to bring
any of Mary's silly habits and fears into the room
that morning. She would do far better to summon
up the Perdita side of herself. Perdita, who could

deal with moneylenders and landlords and theatre managers and jealous actresses calmly, tactfully, and with courage.

Having decided that, she set off down the stairs at a more measured pace, and reached the landing just in time to see Simmons himself going into the front parlour with the tea tray.

She followed him in, to see him reverently depositing it on a low table by the window. And noted that Lady Dalrympole was sitting in *her* favourite chair. As though to demonstrate her intention to dominate. As if she'd chosen that chair deliberately, knowing it was Mary's favourite.

'That will do,' said Lady Dalrympole to Simmons, who was still fussing with the arrangement of cups, spoons, sugar bowls, and the like. 'Lady Epping can pour for me. And make sure you don't hover outside the door when you leave,' she added. 'We don't need you listening in on our conversation.'

So, it was to be like that, was it?

She sat down in the chair opposite Lady Dalrympole as Simmons made his stately way out of the room, giving no hint that he'd so much as heard the reprimand, let alone taken offence at the implication he was the kind of man who would listen at keyholes. And as she did so, she realized that she really had left timid Mary upstairs. It was definitely Perdita who was eyeing up her adversary and assessing her behaviour.

'Milk?' She was rather proud of the fact that her hand was steady as she picked up the jug. Last time she'd had an encounter with Lady Dalrympole, she'd come away so shattered she'd thought she'd never be able to see her again without bursting into tears. But that timid young bride was no more. Perdita had taken her place this morning. And the practical Perdita could not think of a single reason why she should be afraid of this elderly, conceited, unpleasant woman sitting opposite.

'Thank you, just a splash.'

'And sugar, naturally,' she couldn't help saying, dropping three lumps into the cup before Lady Dalrympole indicated that was enough. Well, if anyone needed sweetening up, it was her!

'Most surprised to see you at the theatre last night,' said Lady Dalrympole, as she stirred her tea. 'I had no idea you were back in town.'

'Why should you?'

Lady Dalrympole raised one eyebrow. 'I make it my business to know what's going on.'

'Ah, yes,' said Mary, pouring herself a cup of tea now she'd served one to her visitor. Even though she didn't really want one. 'Of course you do.'

Lady Dalrympole took a sip of tea. Set her cup down in the saucer. Looked at her from the top of her dishevelled head to the crumpled state of her gown.

'You are wondering, I dare say, why I have chosen to call upon you at such an unsociable hour.'

Not exactly. She only wondered why Lady Dalrympole had come calling at all.

'As I said,' Lady Dalrympole continued in the absence of any response, 'I like to be the first to know what is going on in Polite Society. In your case,' she said, her eyes gleaming, 'I believe I am the first to know of your return to London. Is that so?'

Second, after Anthony. Or third, if you counted young Travers, or maybe fourth, taking Madame Claire into account, but she didn't see the point of quibbling, so she just nodded.

'In which case, I may be able to be of use to you.'

'You?' She couldn't conceal her astonishment. But Lady Dalrympole's eyes, far from expressing affront, twinkled with what looked like amusement.

'You still don't look all that well,' said Lady Dalrympole. 'You should, perhaps, have stayed in the country for a while longer. But there,' she added, with a sly smile, 'we could all see how head over heels you were for Epping. And knowing how many others were on the catch for him, I daresay you didn't dare leave him to his own devices for much longer.'

Mary sat back in her chair. And said nothing. She no longer felt obliged to fill a silence with some form of response. Besides, her visitor hadn't actually asked her a question which demanded an answer. She'd just ventured an opinion in the form of a taunt.

'I assume,' said Lady Dalrympole, 'since Epping has not informed anyone of your arrival in town, that he does not think you are ready yet to enter the fray.'

She could assume what she liked.

'But I have to warn you,' Lady Dalrympole continued, 'that word of your presence at the theatre last night is bound to spread. People are going to start calling upon you on the flimsiest of pretexts, or including you in their invitations to Epping. There was, you know, intense speculation about the reason why

Epping's bride did not accompany him when he came to town for the opening of parliament.'

For the first time, she saw that inevitably, people would have gossiped about her. The kind of people who had nothing better to do, that was.

'I have it in my power, you know,' Lady Dalrympole continued, rather haughtily, 'to ease your return to society considerably. I could spare you a good deal of irritation if I were to put it about, for example, that you are not yet up to balls, or anything too rackety. Because you are clearly not, are you?'

She had no idea what game Lady Dalrympole was playing, but she had no intention of deliberately antagonizing her. That would amount to committing social suicide.

'You are,' she therefore said, 'correct.' And then sighed, for good effect, marvelling, as she did so, how much she'd learned from Chloe.

Now it was Lady Dalrympole's turn to say nothing. Instead, she spent a few moments examining her, making her very conscious of her unkempt hair, her creased gown, and, when she lingered for some time over her features, of the pallor of her cheeks and the shadows under her eyes.

Then she set down her teacup with a decisive snap.

'Even an outing to the theatre has tired you, I perceive. Though I noticed that it put you in good spirits, for a while at least.'

'Yes,' she said. Then couldn't help smiling at the success she'd seen Jack achieve with his act. 'The pantomime,' she said, remembering how important it was that Jack should gain the favour of people of Lady Dalrympole's status, 'was very original, wasn't it? Most amusing.'

'It was kind of Epping to take you to such an event,' Lady Dalrympole replied, ignoring her attempt to turn the conversation to a discussion of the performance. Like a dog with a bone, she went straight back to the subject that held *her* interest. 'Kind of him to allow you to stay in the country until you had recovered, too. I did wonder if you would ever return to town. We could all tell, when you first married, that you were not going to flourish in the rarefied atmosphere of the *haut ton*. That you would never, for example, be a leader of fashion.'

'No,' she readily agreed. 'But then, as you so astutely pointed out, that was not why I married Epping, was it?'

Lady Dalrympole's mouth relaxed into something that almost looked like a smile. And then she leaned over, as far as her creaking stays would permit, and said, in a tone of one uttering something in the strictest confidence, 'A little bird hinted that you'd suffered a…disappointment.' Her eyes flickered to Mary's stomach. Then returned to her face. 'Went through the same sort of thing myself, several times, when I was younger. Came to offer my sympathy. Because you do not have a mother to steer you through these sorts of trials. And I cannot think that Epping was able to do much for you in that regard. Men are useless,' she continued, scornfully, 'at such times. They have no idea what to say, so end up either saying nothing, or something silly and offensive. So you did the best thing to stay in the country, on your own, in my opinion, until you felt ready to start, um, resuming marital relations.'

She took a sip of tea.

'That is what,' she continued, in a confiding sort of tone, 'my own doctor advised me, after my second disappointment. And Lord Dalrympole, too. Rather sternly,' she said with a decisive nod. 'I can give you his name if you like. I am sure he would see you if *I* recommend you to him, though he is very exclusive.'

And probably ancient, too, if he'd counselled Lady Dalrympole when she was still of childbearing age.

But before she had to come up with an excuse for not consulting this venerable doctor, Lady Dalrympole was speaking again.

'I meant to offer you some advice, too. Although now I have seen you, I don't think you need it.'

'Oh?'

'I was going to advise you not to brood over it. To keep your chin up. To be frank—' and when, Mary wondered, wasn't she? '—I wasn't impressed with you when Epping first married you. Thought he'd made a fool of himself. I understood why he wanted someone as unlike his first countess as possible, of course, but still thought he could have done far better than a nobody with no countenance. Although Epping's mother has since informed me that you are not quite nobody, are you?'

Wasn't she? That was news to her.

'Your branch of the family,' Lady Dalrympole explained, 'may have fallen upon hard times, but you can boast of an earl on the distaff side, even though it is several generations back.'

Was that so? All that she'd known was that her mother's grandmother had defied her family to marry someone they hadn't thought suitable. Was that where that angry man who claimed to be a brother of her grandfather came in?

'To be frank,' Lady Dalrympole was saying, preventing her from probing too far into the murky mists of her lineage, or what little she knew of it, 'I thought you vulgar, the way you wore your heart on your sleeve. However,' she added, extending one pudgy hand to pat Mary's across the table, 'after seeing you at the theatre last night, began to wonder if first impressions were mistaken. The way you behaved last night, as though nothing was wrong, was just the thing. You are clearly still grieving, but you only do it in private. You appear to have got over your tendency to let the world and his wife know exactly what you are thinking, or suffering. In short, you appear to have developed a backbone.'

Before she had a chance to make any response to that astonishing statement, a sort of choking noise, from the doorway, alerted them both to the fact that Anthony was standing there.

'Lady Dalrympole,' he said, in the same way a man might remark on finding a scorpion in his shoe, just as he was about to put his foot into it. 'What an unexpected honour.'

Lady Dalrympole straightened up and gave him an amused glance. 'Breathing fire and smoke, Epping? Come to protect your little wife from the *ton*'s most lethal dragon?'

'Surely, he should be bearing a sword and shield,' put in Perdita, who'd grown to dislike the mangling of metaphors since her stint poring over scripts and plot lines, 'not breathing fire and smoke? Unless it is a duel between two dragons?'

Lady Dalrympole let out a hoot of laughter, to Anthony's evident surprise. 'As you see, Epping,' she said, getting to her feet, 'your little wife has no need of your protection. Chivalrous though it is,' she added patronizingly, 'of you to offer it. She has backbone. Has come through a fiery trial and is stronger for it. Well done, my dear,' she said, turning one last time to Perdita, before waddling across the room and out of the door.

'"Well done"?' Anthony remained by the door watching, she supposed, Lady Dalrympole's progress down the stairs as though to make sure she was really leaving. 'Did my ears,' he said, turning to Perdita, 'deceive me? Did the old besom actually congratulate you on your behaviour? I have never heard her say anything complimentary about anyone in my life. Never mind to their face. "Well done"?'

How much had he heard? She had to know that before she could give him an answer. He was already cross enough with her, about so many things...

Oh. If she was reacting so timidly, it must mean that Mary had come back.

'H-how much did you hear?'

'I heard her talking about grieving in private.'

But not about what a poor replacement for his first wife everyone thought she was?

'Yes,' she said. 'She appears to think I am being brave to go out and give the appearance of enjoying myself, when she understands what I must be feeling.'

'Understands how you must be feeling? About what?'

'I imagine, since she spoke of going through a similar experience when she was younger, that she is referring to my loss of our baby.'

Anthony flinched. 'And how the devil,' he snarled, shutting the door, and stalking over to the tea table, 'did she find out about that? And how much,' he added, glaring down at her, '*exactly*, do you think she knows?'

Chapter Sixteen

'I, er, I suppose I had better explain,' she said, her heart beating fast. With nerves. Oh, why did Mary have to come to the fore just when she could do with a dose of Perdita's nonchalance? Why couldn't she summon Perdita at will?

Although she couldn't imagine ever feeling...or wanting to feel...nonchalant about Anthony.

Was that why she had been able to handle that visit from Lady Dalrym, le with nonchalance? Because she didn't really care about the woman, or what she might think of her. Whereas she *did* care about Anthony. Very much. And what he thought of her. Or she wouldn't still be here trying to persuade him she hadn't done any of the things he'd suspected. She could have gone back to Jack's troupe. They'd have welcomed her with open arms.

Actually, there were probably loads of ways she could earn her own keep.

Not that Mary had thought so. Mary had clung

on to that post as Lady Marchmont's companion because the woman had kept insisting that she'd only taken her on as a favour to an old family friend. That she was far too silly for anyone else to put up with.

But that hadn't been true, had it? Or not completely. She had often been so sick with nerves that she'd become tongue-tied. Or clumsy. That was how she'd come to run full tilt into Anthony, wasn't it?

'Explain?' He took the seat Lady Dalrympole had just vacated. 'Yes. Explanations are long overdue, aren't they?' And then, though his expression remained grim, he ran his fingers through his hair, just as though he felt some discomfort on his own account.

As well he might! Oh. Thank goodness. Perdita had returned.

Was it because all of a sudden he looked less sure of himself? Had that reminded her that *he* was the one who was very much in the wrong, and who ought to be apologizing for letting *her* down, not the other way round? Just as the sight of him looking angry had made timid Mary take centre stage.

But anyway, his attitude to her offer of an explanation made Mary slink off into the wings.

'If that is your way of saying,' she said tartly, 'that you want to know how I managed to prevent my mysterious disappearance, and unexplained return to London, from turning into a scandal that would ruin your reputation as well as my own, then I shall tell you.'

'*You*…managed?' He blinked. 'I had assumed one of the servants must have been speaking out of turn.

That was what worried me. I thought I was going to have to find out which one could have been capable of such disloyalty!'

'Oh, no. It was all my doing. I thought it for the best.'

'The best?' He leaned back, crossing one elegantly trousered leg over the other. 'In that case, you had better enlighten me.'

She really ought not to allow him to distract her with the elegance of his legs. She was supposed to be cross with him. But when he had such wonderfully muscled thighs, what woman would be able to think straight?

With a wrench, she tore her eyes from the muscles straining through the fabric, and looked him straight in the eyes. Which was almost as bad. He had such beautiful eyes. Such finely arched brows. Not bushy and unkempt, like those of so many men...

He cleared his throat. Reminding her that he was still waiting for her explanation.

'Yes. Well,' she said, feeling her cheeks heating at the suspicion he knew she'd been ogling him. As well he might, after last night and the way she'd flung herself at him. 'It was perfectly simple. I just told the dressmaker, in the *strictest* confidence, the bare bones about...' she gulped. It was so hard to speak of it, even now. Although at least it took her mind off the way she'd humiliated herself last night, in her attempt to remind him of just how good they could be together. 'Losing my baby,' she managed to say, in a voice so quiet even she could hardly hear it. She cleared her own throat. 'And being very ill after. And how I was only just well enough to join you. Which,' she said, 'has the benefit of being the truth, even if not the whole of it.'

A look of confusion flickered across his face. 'How was that supposed to achieve anything?'

'Oh, come on,' she said, pursing her lips. 'You must know that the reason Madame Claire is so popular has as much to do with what snippets of gossip she can pass on, as her skill with the needle. Why on earth do you think I chose to patronize her? After the way she...' She broke off, then, and began fiddling with the cups and saucers.

'The way,' Anthony said, 'she...what?'

She put Lady Dalrympole's used cup on the tray that Simmons had set to one side. Then the milk jug. Then the teapot.

'Well, if you must know,' she finally admitted, since he was going to have to hear about this sort of thing if there was any hope of getting him to understand, 'when you recommended I go to her for my gowns, when you first married me, she got me to confide in her, by being all...caressing, and motherly, I suppose you would call it. I told her a few things about...well, how nervous I was, and how I hoped I wouldn't let you down.'

She glanced up at him to see how he was taking her tale. Those fine brows of his were drawn down so far that they had almost achieved a straight line. Matching the grim slash of his mouth. Oh, well. That was only to be expected.

'And,' she continued, on a sigh of resignation, 'she repeated them to the very worst ladies she could have chosen. All those ones who were livid that you'd picked me and overlooked them. She handed them the weapons with which to wound me.'

'So why on earth should you ever give her custom again?'

She gave him a level look. 'Because I have the measure of her now. I know that I cannot trust her with true confidences. She was not, and never will be, my friend. But if there is anything I wish to spread through the *ton* like wildfire, I have only to whisper it to her, in the *strictest* confidence, and...' She spread her hands. 'Voila.'

'I see. Yes, I see. But,' he added, in a voice to match the grimness of his expression, 'what was all that about ladies using weapons to wound you? Who were they? What did they say?'

She felt her eyes widen in surprise. 'You want to know about *them*? *Now?* Isn't it rather...beside the point?'

'I agree,' he returned, irritably, 'that it might have been better had you shared your troubles with me when I might have been able to do something about them!'

Do something? What could he have done? She picked up her half-finished cup of tea. Set it down on the tray with such force that much of it slopped over into the saucer. 'You could not have fought my battles for me.'

'I still want to know,' he said, 'what was said to wound you.'

She sighed. Rubbed at her forehead. 'It all seems so long ago now.' And almost as if it had happened to someone else. To Mary. Which, actually, would make it easier to talk about. She didn't have the same feelings about it all now, as she'd had at the time. Or if she did, they'd been blunted by all that had happened since. Of all she'd learned about herself. Or by becoming Perdita, or whatever it was.

'Well, look' she began. 'First off, I admitted that I didn't feel worthy of your notice. And then I explained, to Madame Claire, because she appeared *so* interested, so sympathetic, and so understanding, about my background, first how I had to live on the fringes of various distantly related families who took me in out of charity after my parents died, and then how the only person willing to give me any sort of position was Lady Marchmont, and how horrid it had been to be at her beck and call, but how I dared not leave because I had no savings, and no family to fall back on, because they'd made it crystal clear that they'd done their duty by me, and that they'd expected me to earn my own living once I achieved a certain age, and not be a drain on their finances any longer. But the…ladies to whom she repeated those facts, repeated them in such a way as to make me sound like a homeless vagabond, who'd set my cap at you to escape the awful drudgery of my employment. They made me sound like an opportunist, like a scheming witch who'd got her claws into you…'

She flung her head up, then. And gave a brittle little laugh. 'Well, it just goes to show, doesn't it?'

'Show what? I mean, I had no idea that people were saying such things behind your back. Or worse, to your face, since you say you heard them mangle what you'd confided to that dressmaker.'

She shook her head at his inability to grasp what she was trying to show him. 'It shows how wrong people can be. And how stupid. And how unkind.'

'Stupid, yes. To believe that of you. If indeed they did believe it. But definitely unkind.' He got, abruptly, to his feet. Walked a couple of steps away from the table. 'I should have looked after you better. Protected you.'

She watched him make his way to the far side of the room, where he turned, and walked back again. He seemed very…agitated. And the way he'd said he ought to have looked after her better sounded positively repentant.

Had he begun to revise the opinion he'd held, all this time, about her being faithless?

Or was he just speaking of the early days of their marriage, before he'd left her to her own devices at Blanchetts?

'I know,' he said, with bitterness, 'what many of the so-called ladies who inhabit the *ton* are like.' He came to a halt, with his back to the window, and clasped his hands behind his back, as though bracing himself. 'My first wife was one of them. If anyone could be described as a scheming witch, who sank her claws into me, it was her. Never you.'

It was a good job she was already sitting down. Or her legs might have given way beneath her. As it was, she felt her jaw drop open.

'But,' she said, 'your first wife was perfect for you. Everyone kept telling me so. That she was a dazzling creature, with eyes that sparkled like emeralds, and bushels of glossy black hair, and that when she died you were devastated. They told me how you sat at her funeral, with your head in your hands, and were inconsolable, for days. Weeks. That you shunned society and shut yourself away for months.'

He squeezed his eyes shut, as though he couldn't bear to face memories too painful to endure.

She knew just how he felt. Hadn't she done the same? Though in her case, she'd gone to extremes. Had shut her eyes so tightly against her pain that she hadn't been able to open them again whether she'd wanted to or not.

'They were right,' he said, his voice bleak, as he opened his eyes, and gazed at her, sadly, 'to describe her as dazzling.'

Her heart sank. She knew it! She knew he'd buried his heart in the grave with his first wife, and that he had little emotion left to give to her. And to begin with, that had been enough. When she'd worshipped him, it had been more than enough to know that he'd chosen her, out of all the women he could have picked, to provide comfort.

'But consider, if you will,' he added, 'the meaning of the word *dazzle*,' he added. 'When something is dazzling, it blinds you by being so bright and sparkling. Bright and sparkling,' he repeated, bitterly. 'That sums her up, to perfection. She was so beautiful, so captivating, so witty, that I was blind to other aspects of her character.'

What? His first wife was *not* the perfect paragon that everyone had held up to her, like a mirror, to prove just how lacking in all the qualities she'd been to bear the title of Countess of Epping?

'And it is true,' he added, his eyes boring into her in a kind of desperation, 'that I could not hold my head up at her funeral. That I shut myself away for a long time after she'd gone. But it wasn't because my heart was broken. It was because I felt...' He paused, took a deep breath, then blurted out, 're-lieved. Relieved it was all over. And guilty for feel-ing relieved, because what sort of man can feel such a thing when his wife has died?' He whirled round and strode back to the far side of the room. 'I spent the next few weeks...crippled by the knowledge of how stupid I'd been about her.' He turned and paced the floor again, his head down. 'How gullible.' He turned and paced away again. 'I, who prided myself on being so *clever*.' His face, like his voice, was an-guished. 'I'd let that woman wreck my family, and rob me of any hope of ever siring my own heir. Be-cause after her, I could never imagine ever trusting any woman, ever again.'

He stopped pacing, and just stood still, by the window, his face turned to the street below, although she was pretty sure he wasn't really looking at any-thing outside. He just stood there, breathing deeply, as though he'd just run all the way up three flights of stairs.

She'd never seen him looking so uncertain. So torn. Before she knew it, she'd risen to her feet, and had crossed the room to stand beside him. Shyly, she laid one hand upon his sleeve. He placed his own hand on top of hers, as though to anchor it in place.

'You do not need to tell me any more, if it pains you so much,' she said.

'On the contrary,' he said, grasping her hand more tightly. 'I do need to tell you. I owe it to you, to tell you everything. Every last damned humiliating, shameful secret of my first marriage. Otherwise, I fear you may never understand why I have treated you the appalling way I have. That you will never forgive me.'

Her heart began to pound in her chest. For it sounded as though, far from wanting to broach the topic of divorce, or separating in some other way, he'd been steeling himself to make an apology.

And if he was speaking of *her* forgiving *him*, then it must mean that he'd finally decided to believe that she'd been telling the truth.

She turned her hand over in his. And with their hands linked, she drew him over to a sofa. Sat down beside him. Because she had a strong suspicion that he'd find it easier to tell her whatever it was he had to tell her, if he didn't need to look her in the face while doing so.

'I was very young when I first met Sarah,' he began, gazing across the room in the direction of the window, and yet probably looking inward, down the years, into his own past.

'My father had died while I was still up at Oxford. And my mother, well, she became so anxious about the succession that she urged me not to delay the important business of choosing a wife. So when the period of mourning was over, and I went up to London to make my debut as the Earl of Epping, I was not, like most men of my age, just there to enjoy myself. I was actively looking for a wife.

'And there was Sarah,' he said gloomily. 'The undisputed belle of the season, favouring me out of all the men clustering round her. I could hardly believe it when she accepted my proposal, out of the dozens of offers she must have had. I thought I was the luckiest man alive.

'And at first, it all seemed pretty marvellous,' he said bitterly, hunching his shoulders. 'I was actually flattered when she said what a perfect match we made, as we stood side by side looking into a mirror.' He ran the fingers of his free hand through his hair. 'In hindsight, I should have heard alarm bells ringing. And then, when I took *her* to Radley Court to meet Mother, I couldn't believe it when she asked why on earth I hadn't consulted her before taking the plunge. I was so offended that she didn't appear to approve of my choice. I thought she should have been thrilled. After all, I'd done as she'd asked, hadn't I? Well, you know my temper,' he said. 'Especially when she said that it was too late, and the damage had been done and that she hoped I wouldn't live to regret it.'

'Your mother didn't like Sarah, either?'

He blinked at her as though he hadn't understood the question. Or perhaps had forgotten she was even there.

'Either? What do you mean?'

'Well, your mother wasn't exactly taken with me, was she? Saying so grudgingly she *supposed* she could see why you'd picked me. Long after saying how much she wished she hadn't urged you to get married in the first place.'

'You misunderstood,' he put in hastily. 'She regards you as a vast improvement on Sarah. It was just that, after my first wedding, and the argument we had, there had been a distinct…coolness, shall we say, between us. It was only after Sarah died that Mother attempted any form of reconciliation. And at that meeting, she said that if I wanted her advice, if I was ever to consider marrying again, I should pick a girl who was decent, and quiet, and who had some genuine feeling for me.'

'Oh.' She considered that statement, for a moment. 'I thought that, well, you seemed almost defiant when you made the introduction…'

'Yes, well, once again I'd married without presenting my bride to her before tying the knot. And I wasn't sure if she'd be angry with me. If I'd completely destroyed any chance of a reconciliation. But later, she said she could see the way you looked at me made up for any other faults she may be able to find.'

'Oh.' So he'd taken rather a big gamble on her, hadn't he?

And all that tension, simmering between mother and son, had at least as much to do with past history, as with her sudden appearance at his side.

'I think,' he said in a voice that sounded as though he'd swallowed a razor blade, 'that Mother had seen how…shallow Sarah truly was. That all she cared about was frippery things. Pleasure.' He paused, as though gathering his strength. 'She was the kind of girl, in short, who was prepared to go through with her duty by presenting her husband with an heir, but who expected the freedom to take lovers, after that.'

'You mean,' she said, when it didn't look as though he was willing to spell it out, 'that she was unfaithful to you?'

'It didn't progress that far,' he said bitterly. Then lowered his eyes. Flicked a small speck of fluff from his trouser leg. 'Were you aware that I have two brothers?'

'No.' She gulped. His brothers? Could he possibly mean what she thought he meant? 'I did not know you had *any* brothers.'

'Well, I do,' he said bleakly. 'Both younger than me. Obviously, since I bear the title. But that is beside the point. Marcus, he is the older of the two, is in the army. Cuts a dashing figure, in his regimentals,' he said bitterly. 'Well, he couldn't make it to my wedding, but he came to pay his respects to my bride when he did eventually get some leave. And...' He paused, clasping his hands between his thighs, his head lowered. 'One day, Sarah came to me, in tears, saying that he'd...attempted to, um, make love to her. That when she'd rebuffed him, he'd become violent. She showed me some marks on her shoulders. Front and back. I was furious. I went straight to Marcus's room and told him to get out of my house. He asked, calmly, if I wouldn't like to hear his version of events, too. The mere suggestion that Sarah could have been lying infuriated me so much that I threatened to call him out. Brother or no brother. He said that he would spare me the bother, gave me a look of...such contempt...mingled with pity, which was the worst of all…' He shook his head again. 'Then he just turned and began packing his things. And walked away. And I've never seen or spoken to him again.'

'So…you think, now, that it was a lie? That she lied about what happened?'

'Oh, yes,' he said bitterly. 'Because not long after, my youngest brother, Benjamin, told me that she'd been a bit…forward with him, when I wasn't round. I didn't believe him, either, not at first. But then, one day…' Abruptly, he got to his feet and walked over to the tea table by the window and stood with his back to her. 'Long story short,' he said, 'I found them in bed together. Actually in bed. She was naked. Totally naked.'

She raised her hands to her throat, against a tide of nausea. 'Your own brother?'

He nodded, resolutely keeping his back to her.

'What…what happened? What did you do?'

He turned round to her, then, a sardonic smile twisting his mouth.

'I shot him,' he said.

Chapter Seventeen

He *had* to look her straight in the face as he confessed this bit of the sordid events surrounding the end of his first marriage. He had to know how she felt about marrying a man who could shoot his own brother.

Her eyes were wide. But she didn't look disgusted. If anything, she looked a bit confused.

'But,' she said, 'you are still at liberty. So…you could not have killed him…'

'No. Wounded him, merely. It was just a bit of bad luck that I'd been at Manton's trying out some new pistols when I received the note from Benjamin begging me to go to his rooms quickly, that it was an emergency, or I would probably have just thrashed him.'

'But…' she looked more confused than ever. 'You said that Benjamin, that is your brother, wrote asking you to go to his rooms? Where you found him in bed with…' She shook her head. 'What was he thinking?'

'He was trying, I believe, to show me what Sarah was like. He'd said right from the start of the rift with Marcus that he couldn't believe he'd behave so shabbily. Nay, violently to a woman. That the bruises must have been caused in some other way. She…she was a consummate actress,' he said, hoping Mary would see, if not immediately, then in time, why that profession, above all others, was anathema to him.

'But at the time,' he continued, 'I wasn't capable of thinking clearly. I was too shocked. Too angry. And I just turned round, opened the case, and seized the pistols. Then I stalked back into the bedroom and fired. My hand was shaking so much, it was a wonder I hit anything.'

'You did hit something then? You…wounded your brother?'

'Yes. I succeeded in blowing off a portion of Benjamin's ear. And terrifying Sarah. There was blood everywhere, and she was screaming fit to bring the house down.' Saying it out loud was every bit as bad as he'd suspected it would be. He could smell the pistol smoke, and the blood, and the scorched material of the pillow where Benjamin's head had been. He had to gulp back a wave of nausea, before he was able to continue. 'She fell to her knees, at my feet, gibbering all sorts of excuses.' His voice sounded hoarse to his ears. So she must have a good idea of how difficult it was for him to be telling her all this. 'But mostly, how it was my fault for not having got her with child by then. How she'd been prepared to *do her duty* as she put it, until she'd presented me with an heir and a spare but how after that…' He paused, watching Mary's face to see if the implication had sunk in, without having to spell out the fact that his first wife had wanted what many termed a fashionable marriage, where each indulged in numerous affairs.

'And she claimed,' he continued, 'that she was just trying to speed up the process by using my brothers. So that at least the child she bore would be genuinely related to me. I had only discharged one pistol at that point. I had the other one in my hand. The temptation to shoot her, right then, at point-blank range...' He faltered to a halt, reliving the rage that had consumed him, the despair. The humiliation. 'Heaven alone knows how I stopped myself. I have a damnable temper, Mary. I say things...and do things, in the heat of the moment...'

'Hold on a moment,' said Mary, who looked thoroughly confused. 'What was all that about having trouble getting an heir? I mean, you got me with child almost as soon as we married.'

'Yes. It only goes to show that she was grasping for a plausible excuse for her behaviour, doesn't it? Anything, rather than own up to her sins.' It had only been much later that he'd realized just how flimsy her excuses really had been. For they'd only been married a few months when she'd staged that scene with Marcus.

'But at the time...well,' he continued, knowing he needed to get back to the matter which had the most importance to Mary, 'I wondered if I really couldn't father children. And after that, I couldn't...' He felt the blood drain from his face as he prepared to tell her his worst, most humiliating secret. He took a deep breath. 'Whenever I looked at her I pictured her naked in bed with Benjamin, and saying it was because I couldn't father children. And I couldn't… That is, I lost the ability to…'

Sweat broke out on his forehead as he grappled for words to explain his inability to function as a man. To say it, out loud…

She mercifully spared him the necessity of saying anything at all by getting up, flying across the room to him, and flinging her arms round his waist. 'You have been through such an awful, awful time,' she said. 'I am so sorry.'

He clung to her. Buried his face in her soft, fragrant hair. '*You* have nothing to be sorry for,' he grated out. 'You brought me back to life. Made a man of me again. Until I met you, I thought I would never be able to look at a woman with desire again. Every time a woman smiled at me, it felt as though something inside me shrivelled up and recoiled. But you…' He pulled back a touch so that he could look down at her, and frame her face with his hands. 'You were so different. As unlike Sarah as night is from day. Shy, self-effacing, kind. You never lost your temper with that besom you worked for, no matter how unreasonable she was. You were so timid, so lacking in confidence you flinched every time so much as a shadow fell across your lap. Except when you saw me. And then your face lit up.' He gazed down at her serious expression, recalling the stars she'd had in her eyes in those days, and mourning their loss. He'd blotted them out, with his selfish, suspicious behaviour. And he had nobody to blame but himself. Not even Sarah. He'd known Mary was nothing like her. Wasn't that why he'd taken a chance on love, again?

'The way you looked at me back then, made me feel...' He took a deep breath. 'As though there was goodness in the world. As though there could be light again, in the darkness. I didn't propose because I hoped to father an heir. Or even believe that might be possible. I just wanted *you* in my life. I wanted to see you looking at me like that, as though I was something grand. When I offered for you, I imagined long years of placid contentment.' He sighed. 'That makes me very selfish, doesn't it?'

'No,' she said vehemently. 'No, I totally understand why you would need someone to love you, unconditionally, even with a touch of worship thrown in, after the way she humiliated you.'

That was so typical of her. She was so generous. So compassionate. 'Thank you. Thank you for your generosity,' he said. And then, because having her in his arms like this was having a predictable effect upon his body, the effect she always had, even, amazingly, after talking about the impotence he'd suffered in the dying stages of his marriage to Sarah, he took another step back. 'I think we had better go and sit down, so that I can tell you the rest.'

Her eyes widened. 'You mean, there's more?'

'Yes,' he said, leading her to the sofa that she'd taken him to, not so many minutes before. When they were settled comfortably, side by side, he took her hands in his, turning the upper half of his body to her so that he would be able to see exactly what she was thinking, when he told her what he'd just discovered that morning.

'When you began to suspect you were increasing, I could hardly believe it,' he began. Then paused, feeling the need to choose his next words very carefully. 'You had, within a few weeks of our marriage, overthrown everything Sarah had made me suspect about myself. You restored me. Healed me. And I...' He lowered his head then, looking at where their fingers intertwined on her lap. 'For a while, I loved you so much. If you thought you had idolized me, it was nothing compared to how I felt about you. You seemed like...a miracle.'

'But you never said anything,' she said, looking bewildered. 'If anything, once the doctor confirmed I was, indeed, carrying your child, you seemed to go right off me.

'Well, I didn't deserve a miracle, did I, after the appalling way I'd treated both my brothers? And, well, it made me go into a sort of...spiral of black memories. I couldn't stop going over all the accusations she'd flung at me, in the light of this new information. So that instead of just being able to rejoice in a normal, healthy way, I went back to a place I thought I'd left behind. Besides, I was alarmed by how strongly I felt about you,' he admitted. 'You were too perfect. Too good to be true. I'd been so wrong about Sarah, you see, that I became...gripped by the fear that I might have been wrong about you, too.'

'But...'

'I know, I know. You still gazed at me with worship in your eyes. But, that core of darkness inside me hadn't gone away. Sarah had made me feel that I couldn't trust my judgement. How could I, when I'd been so deceived by her? When I'd believed her, over my brothers whom I'd known all my life? I found it hard to believe that any woman could really love such a...failure.' He paused. Forced himself to continue. 'Last night,' he managed to get out, 'when you said I was nothing but a facsimile of a man, covered by the gilding of rank and wealth, you spoke only the truth. For years, that is what I was. How I felt about myself. Apart from a few, blissful weeks, after we married...'

'Oh, Anthony,' she said, shaking her head. 'No wonder you jumped to the wrong conclusion, when I disappeared. You were so full of jealousy, and fear of history repeating itself... It sounds as if you were almost braced for something to go wrong between us.'

'Yes! That's exactly how it was. And also, to be frank, you'd become a threat, I suppose, for want of a better word.'

'A threat?' She looked appalled. 'I would never have hurt you in any way.'

'But you had come really close to shattering my... facade. The pretence I'd kept up, right through my first marriage, and after it ended, that I was impervious to the kind of emotions that affected...lesser mortals.' He offered her a wry smile. 'If I was talking about someone else, I would describe him as panicking over how hard I was falling for you, and how swiftly.

'But,' he continued, 'however you wish to describe the state I was experiencing, I… I wanted—no I felt I *needed*—to put some space between us. To gain some sort of perspective. To regain some balance, I don't know. It is hard to explain. But when I saw you start to find the travelling, and the duties as countess, too taxing, I leaped on the excuse that you were in a delicate condition, to stash you away in Blanchetts. It was unfair of me, I know…'

'Oh, no, not completely,' she put in soothingly. 'Because I *was* glad not to have to do all that travelling and face all those people telling me I'd never fill Sarah's shoes. And the heat *did* make me feel awful, some days. And I was sick, often, too. So I was grateful to you, though at the same time…' She gave him a look he couldn't interpret. 'I felt such a failure. I used to lie there thinking that Sarah would never have been so feeble as to need to lie on her bed half the day. That Sarah would have known how to cope with those…catty women…'

'Well, Sarah was probably the sharpest clawed of all the cats, so yes, she would have shredded the others, with ease,' he said wryly. 'Although I rarely glimpsed that side of her. Especially to start with, when she showed me only what she wanted me to see. But you were in no way a failure. For one thing, you quickened with life.' He tugged his hand free from hers, and laid it on her belly. Now flat, and empty.

Her eyes filled with tears. 'But I couldn't hold on to it. I lost it, Anthony. I lost it!' And then she began to sob.

Tears spilled from his own eyes as he gathered her to his chest and held her while she wept. 'I can't…' he gasped. 'To hell with it!' He abandoned the attempt to stem this particular expression of emotion. 'There is nothing wrong with a man mourning the loss of his child, is there? Particularly not when the conception of that child had been such a wonderful, unexpected, undeserved gift. Though at least I didn't lose *you*,' he breathed into the crown of her head. 'At least you came back.'

She raised her head then, and gave him a searching look. 'You are glad then? You want me to be your wife? Still?'

'Always,' he swore. 'I know that it cannot be as it was. That you no longer regard me as some sort of demigod,' he said ruefully. 'I may strut round pretending to be above the concerns that afflict mere mortals. But inside, I am frequently a seething cauldron of emotions. Some of them so torrid that they have even caused me to shoot one brother and alienate the other. And you know that, now. But do you think that one day, perhaps…'

Instead of flinging her arms round his neck, and sobbing out, *Yes, yes Anthony, you are my world*, which was, he had to admit, far too much to hope for, she carried on looking at him with that same expression on her face. It wasn't exactly confusion, it wasn't exactly wary, but neither was there much evidence of joy.

'What,' she said, after chewing on the inside of her lower lip for what felt like an eternity, 'made you change your mind? I mean, when I first stumbled into this house again, you were furious. You weren't ready to listen to any explanations…'

His insides turned over. It felt as if he was about to take a blind leap, into what he suspected would be a bottomless abyss.

So he gripped her hands tight. For it was the only sure way he had of holding on to her.

'That visitor I had this morning…' he began. 'He was an investigator I sent up to Blanchetts to dig about a bit.'

'I see,' she said, her face closing up. 'So you only began to believe in my version of events after somebody else proved that what I'd said was all true.' She tore her hands from his and got up. Took a few steps away from the sofa.

He decided it would be wise to get up as well. And take up a strategic position by the door, in case she felt like running out on him again. And he was not going to let her do that. This time he was going to stand and fight for her. 'I know you must be angry with me for not being able to take your word for it,' he said, 'but I hoped, that after hearing how Sarah destroyed my ability to trust in anyone, or anything, particularly my own judgement, that you might be able to understand…'

'Oh, yes, I understand all right,' she said, pressing one hand to her forehead. 'I paid the price for Sarah's sins!'

He wanted to make some objection, but in all honesty, what could he say? She was right.

'You weren't the slightest bit pleased to see me

again, either, were you?' she flung at him. 'You shouted at me!'

He wondered, fleetingly, if he could admit that one bit of him had been exceedingly pleased to see her again. Especially naked, in the bath. And that his lustful response to the sight of her magnificent body had made him angrier than he'd had any right to be. Because it made him feel the way Sarah had made him feel. As if he was a slave to his lusts.

'I can only apologize,' he said. 'But please, try to imagine how I felt. For all those months, I'd thought that my worst fears had come to pass. That you weren't the angel I'd believed you to be. That you'd behaved just like she used to. And then you came back, with some wild story about brigands, and losing your memory, and perhaps worst of all, you didn't show the slightest hint that you were sorry.'

'Sorry? Why should I have felt sorry? I hadn't,' she said marching up to him, her chin jutting out, 'done anything wrong!'

'No, but the girl I'd married would have begged for forgiveness for so much as causing me to frown. Don't you see? You came back utterly changed. As though you'd become someone else. And I didn't know who she was, or how I ought to feel about her.'

The fury left her face as abruptly as a snuffed candle flame.

It made his heart twist with dread.

'Yes, yes, I see,' she said, her shoulders drooping. 'I have felt it, too. That I… I *did* become someone else, during those weeks of not knowing who I ought to be. Jack gave her a name. Perdita. And though now

I do remember that I used to be Mary, a girl who fell head over heels in love with a man who was far, far above her in station...' She stopped, raised her hands to her head, and twined her fingers in her hair. 'Oh, oh, I don't know how to explain this. But it is as if... Well, I don't think she exists anymore. Mary. I think she died in the canal, or perhaps it was in the narrow boat, along with her baby...' She turned away, wrapping her arms round her stomach, as though to console herself. Or perhaps to have her arms filled with the baby that was no longer there.

'I expect,' she said tremulously, 'I sound as though I've lost my mind. Indeed I wouldn't blame you if you had me locked up somewhere,' she finished despondently.

'No, no, Mary,' he said, striding over to her and putting his arms round her. 'I don't want to do that. Never! You are as sane as anyone else!'

'But I just told you, it is as if there are two of me now. Sometimes I'm timid Mary, but then Perdita, the woman I learned to be when I'd forgotten all about Mary, rears up and pushes her aside.'

He held her tightly, though she remained stiff in his embrace, her back resolutely turned to him.

'I don't care,' he swore. 'You are *you*. The woman I married.'

'But you cannot possibly love the me I am now, the way you loved Mary.'

For a moment or two he felt as if he was teetering on the edge of that abyss again. If he made one wrong move he could lose her again. This time, perhaps, forever.

There was no option, he saw, but to cut through all the pretence, all the protective, face-saving excuses he'd ever made, and tell her the bald truth.

'I didn't love Mary the way I should have,' he admitted. 'So I don't want to love you that way anymore. To be blunt, I have no intention of loving you in such a...niggardly, restrained manner. I thought only of myself back then. Not how my words, or my actions, could affect you. And, surely, you cannot possibly still love the Anthony you thought you'd married? He never really existed at all, did he, the golden demigod you built up in your imagination?'

He could feel her taking that in. Turning it over in her mind. He didn't know *how* he could feel it, only that he did. It was perhaps something about the way her breathing changed. The way her muscles relaxed, even though she didn't turn round and return his embrace.

'What then,' she said, after a while, in a voice so quiet he could barely hear it, 'are we to do?'

Chapter Eighteen

She felt him sigh into the nape of her neck, the warmth sliding down her spine, distracting her from what they'd been talking about and replacing thought for longings of *doing* things together again.

Did she have the courage, now, to suggest that they go up to her room, and renew their marriage that way? The last time she'd tried to get through to him in the only way she'd ever felt truly connected to him, he'd called a halt before it could get very far.

'What I want to do, more than anything,' he said, making her heart pound. Oh, if only he was to suggest what *she* wanted, more than anything! He turned her in his arms. Gazed down into her face with an expression half hopeful, half braced for rebuff. 'Is to kiss you,' he said.

Then he lowered his mouth to hers. Slowly. Agonizingly slowly. As though he half expected her to push him away.

Naturally she did no such thing. This was a promising step in the right direction.

And he kissed her. Gently. Hesitantly.

But she didn't want hesitant or gentle. So she flung her arms round his neck and kissed him back. Twined her fingers into his hair and pulled his head closer.

It was all the encouragement he needed. His kiss turned greedy.

'I want you so much,' he panted, burying his face in her neck, his big hands kneading at her bottom.

He'd never shown his desire for her like this before. He'd always been decorous about it. Polite. And had always restricted this sort of activity to her bedroom. *Her* bedroom, not his. Never his. She'd felt as though he'd wanted to keep his own room as a sanctuary and had never dared venture in.

And he had never made any sort of advances to her in broad daylight. During the day he had always been too busy, she'd thought.

He groaned, then, as if in pain.

He really, really wanted her. She could feel the evidence of how much, pressing into her stomach. There was no hiding it, even if he'd tried to hide it, which he wasn't doing. Not at all.

It was exhilarating to feel the effect she was having on him, coming as it did almost directly after his confession about the trouble he'd had in that department. To know that no other woman could do this to him.

That no other woman had this…power over him. Why, even last night, in the study, he'd been aroused. Even though he'd fought it. Would he fight it again, today? Because they weren't in what he considered an appropriate location?

She rained desperate, urgent kisses on his cheek, his brow, any part of his face that she could get at, and, keeping her arms about his neck, she began to move her legs, pushing him into movement, pushing him in the direction of the sofa. She suspected he would rather go up to her room, and get into bed, but she was afraid that if she suggested it, and if they started discussing it, the moment would be lost.

Was it even possible on a sofa? Well, she was about to find out.

Stumbling a bit, because neither was willing to let go of the other, they dropped onto the cushions with their arms still locked round each other.

Next to each other.

He began to kiss her again, feverishly, his hands roaming all over her, as though desperate to re-acquaint himself with her shape. Or as though he couldn't believe she was really there, without physical proof.

It was wonderful. But there was no way that they could join with each other whilst sitting side by side. Somehow they had to get face-to-face. Now. Now! She was too impatient to wait for him to take charge.

Some instinct had her pushing him back onto the cushions, which was remarkably easy, considering how much bigger than her he was, and how much stronger.

But then this was what he wanted, too. Finally. She knew, beyond any doubt, that he was ready to take another chance on her when, as she clambered on top of him, he helped her by hitching her skirts up out of the way, so that she could straddle him more easily.

Their kisses became frantic now that they were in this position. Now that she could feel his body, all along the length of hers. And his hips, flexing upward as she ground down onto him, his hands roving all over her back, her bottom, her upper thighs.

It wasn't enough. She needed…

Oh, why wouldn't he…

Well, if *he* wouldn't, then she'd have to.

She delved between them, to feel the outline of him, thrusting urgently against the confines of his breeches.

And tore open the buttons, freeing him. Removing the last barrier of clothing between them

She looked down into his face. His eyes were half closed. Sweat beaded his brow.

It looked very much as if he was that close, that were she not to do something drastic, he was going to finish on his own.

She wasn't having that!

She needed fulfilment as much as him.

She took him in hand, wriggled about until she could feel him just where she needed him the most, and guided him there.

He gave a strangled sound, halfway between a groan and a sigh as he glided into her, and then, for a few seconds, it was a blur of frantic activity.

Until she exploded with rapture.

And with a hoarse cry, so did he, his fingers digging into her bottom as though he was trying to wring every last ounce of pleasure from the moment.

She fell forward, burying her face in his neck. They were both panting. Both slick with sweat.

And she was thirsty.

Would it be inappropriate to ring for tea, she suddenly wondered? Then had a sudden urge to giggle. Tea! Of all things to be thinking about at a time like this!

'What is it?' Anthony began struggling to sit up, sounding alarmed. 'You are not crying again, are you?'

She shifted position so she could look him in the face. 'No. Far from it. It is just that… I cannot believe we just did that. I am never going to be able to look at this sofa the same way again. How on earth am I going to be able to entertain the likes of Lady Dalrymple in here, without wishing to burst into fits of giggles?'

'Giggles,' he repeated. She felt the tension ease from his taut body. 'At least that is better than having a fit of remorse.'

She stroked the fine arch of his right eyebrow. 'I don't regret this, not one bit,' she vowed.

His brows drew down. 'But you used to be so shy of…intimacy. I always felt I had to be careful not to frighten you.'

'Oh. That's strange. Because I always wondered if I was a bit disappointing, in that regard.'

'No!' He cupped her face. 'How can you think that after what I confessed about…about…?'

'Oh, not now,' she said, interrupting before he had the chance to use words to describe what he must have thought of as a failure. 'Not any longer. But…

before…well, I was so inexperienced. I knew nothing of what should happen between a man and woman in bed. But I just had a feeling that we shouldn't be so…polite about it.'

He made a move to sit up. 'About that,' he began.

She sighed. For his move marked the end of this delicious period of intimacy. They were going to start talking again.

There followed a few awkward moments while they disentangled, straightened clothing, and resumed decorous positions, side by side on the sofa.

But at least they were holding hands, now. The way, she felt, that lovers should.

'The thing is,' he said, rather sorrowfully, 'that although this has been wonderful…'

Her heart sank. He was going to say something she wasn't going to like…she was sure of it.

'Well, as I said last night, giving way to physical urges never really solves anything.' He hung his head for a moment, before looking back up at her with renewed resolve. 'Sarah was adept at distracting me from the real issue, whenever we had an argument, by seducing me into bed. It only ever shelved things, rather than properly solving them. And this, you and me, it is too important that we get things right, after all that has gone wrong.' And then he added, ruefully, 'Isn't it?'

She went almost giddy with relief. She didn't know what she'd feared he might say, but hearing that he wanted to solve things properly, rather than improperly…

She suddenly felt another inappropriate urge to

giggle. Which would not do at all. Not when he was trying to take their future so seriously. It was just… she was happy, that was all. Happier than she'd ever felt in her life.

So far as she could recall.

'I know I have no right to ask you,' he said, his face, and voice, grim. 'Or to blame you, if, after everything you went through, and not remembering you had a husband, you…'

'But you *want* to ask me. Even though you fear what I might have to confess.'

He nodded, looking drawn, uncertain. And he was sitting bolt upright now, as though trying to brace himself against what she might have to say.

Her happiness dimmed. How could he go on expecting the worst from her? After what they'd just done? Hadn't that meant anything?

Although, from what he'd just said, it sounded as though that hateful Sarah had tainted even that. His first wife had taught Anthony that coming together could be no more than a slaking of desire. Or a way to exert control over someone. When she'd felt as if she'd come home, at last, by choice, and not just because her toes were tired of being cold.

'I will tell you,' she said, resolutely, 'everything. Otherwise I suspect you are going to torment yourself imagining all sorts of things I might have done while I was wandering the countryside, with no idea of who I was, aren't you?'

He looked a bit sick. But nodded. His jaw muscles clenched as though he was gritting his teeth.

'Oh, Anthony,' she said, shaking her head. 'You

do find it hard to trust anyone, don't you? I mean I suppose I can understand why you had to hire that investigator, to check my story, now that you've told me about Sarah, but...' A sudden shaft of anxiety pierced her.

'Can you even trust me to be completely honest, now? Will you be able to believe me, in future?'

'Yes,' he said.

'But how can you?'

'Because I almost did, right from the moment you came back. Or at least I wanted to. That was what scared me the most, you know. That you could have been telling me a pack of lies, yet I wanted to believe that...oh, not that you'd been through such an ordeal, but that you hadn't run off with another man. You know that must be true. Or else why didn't I throw you out of this house at once? Or pack you off to one of my far-flung estates and set a jailor over you? I could have done it. I'd fantasized often enough about doing it to Sarah, so it wouldn't have taken me five minutes to set it all in train.'

His perfect wife? The one that everyone had told her she couldn't hold a candle to? He'd fantasized about locking her up and throwing away the key? Well, this *was* a day for revelations.

All of a sudden, she felt much better. 'I... I hadn't thought about that aspect of it. You *did* let me stay here, didn't you? And you didn't hamper my movements. Much...'

'I didn't hamper them at all,' he protested.

'Apart from setting your servants to report back on all my movements. Or how else would you have found out about me going to visit Jack? Or that trip to the theatre?'

He gripped her hands more tightly.

'I didn't,' he said vehemently. 'I mean, I didn't order them to report on your movements. It is just that after Sarah, I wouldn't hire any staff who weren't completely loyal to me. She had a maid, and a couple of footmen and a groom who... Well, never mind,' he said darkly. 'But the thing is, I think that, having seen the state I descended into when you vanished, they probably...'

She squeezed his hands back. 'I see. I think I'm beginning to see a lot more clearly now. That dreadful woman at Blanchetts, for instance, who did act like a jailor. Was she round when you were married before?'

He nodded. 'I am sorry for that. I should have made sure you had someone who could have been a bit...kinder, more considerate of your condition. But from what Baxter told me, earlier on, all the staff in that place were so unnaturally loyal that he couldn't persuade a single one of them to speak out of turn. And, and I'm sorry,' he said, bowing over her hands and kissing them with a kind of reverence, 'for ever suspecting you might have run off.'

'Well,' she said, a swell of emotion bringing tears to her eyes at this sign of remorse, 'it looks to me as though you've been punished enough for that. I mean, you went through months of torment, imagining the worst.'

'Instead of searching for you and bringing you home,' he said sorrowfully.

She ran one hand over the crown of his luxuriantly thick, glossy hair. She knew he was sorry. She understood his reasons for acting the way he had. And yet it still *hurt*.

'This Baxter,' she said, after coming up with, and discarding several responses to his humble apology, none of which would grant him full absolution, and deciding it might be better to change the subject, 'is he the man you hired to find out if I'd told you the truth?'

'He's the man,' he said, raising his head and gazing at her earnestly, 'I hired to prove your innocence.'

To his own satisfaction, yes, she could believe that.

'So what else,' she said, 'did he discover?' She needed to know how much he'd learned so she'd know where to take up the tale. She didn't want to leave anything out. Because, seeing how hard it was for him to trust anyone, if he later discovered that she'd inadvertently left something out, it could plunge him back into that maelstrom of dark, suspicious thoughts he'd told her about. And ruin everything.

'Apart from telling me that he couldn't get much out of the staff at Blanchetts, or one good word from the locals about my first wife,' he said, his mouth flattening into a grim line, 'he reported that it didn't take him long to find that family of Methodists who took you in and nursed you back to health. And from them it was but a short step to tracing the canal bargees who pulled you out of the water.'

It felt as if the sun had gone behind a dark cloud.

And it wasn't primarily from casting her mind back to those terrible days when she'd lost everything. It was hearing how easy it had been for Mr Baxter to retrace her movements. How easy it would have been for Anthony to have found her, had he tried to search.

No. She must not allow bitterness to ruin what had been feeling like the beginnings of a reconciliation. Anthony had explained why he'd assumed the worst. That Sarah had put him through such torment that it had been hard for him to trust anyone.

And he was gripping her hands, which he held on his lap, and looking at her intently, as though what he was saying was important to him.

It was just a pity that he hadn't thought she was important enough, back then, to have bothered...

No! She must *not* give in to such thoughts. Or they would never get anywhere.

'The Hapcotts told Baxter,' he continued, 'that they entrusted you to the care of a minister who was being sent to another area, a sort of parish, though that wasn't the term they used. A Mr Jacob Pendle.'

She couldn't help grimacing.

'What happened? They told Baxter that...' He hesitated. 'That Pendle reported back that you were an incorrigible sinner and reverted to your ways in spite of all his exhortations to repent and reform.'

'My *ways*? Oh, the...the cheek of the man! No wonder you looked so sick when I offered to tell you everything. You must have already been imagining... dreading...' She made as if to stand up.

He grabbed her hand, preventing her from moving so much as an inch away. 'I cannot deny it,' he said.

'But I have already vowed, have I not, that I will not blame you, or chide you, for *whatever* you may have done while you were away. Only, this time, I would rather hear it all from your own lips, than ask a third party to delve into our private business.'

Oh, Anthony. He was trying so hard to trust her. And at least this time, having heard something bad about her behaviour, he was asking for her side of things. And looked prepared to try to believe whatever she said. On his terms, she supposed he was paying her a very great compliment.

'Thank you,' she therefore said, 'for being willing to hear my side of things. Because there is always more than one side to any story, isn't there?'

A frown flitted across his brow, as though he wasn't wholly convinced by that. He probably thought that things fell into two categories. Truth, or lies.

'I think the Hapcotts probably believed they were telling the truth, as they saw it,' she mused. 'But the trouble was that right from the start, they'd put two and two together and made five. The canal barge people didn't have time to stop and give much of an explanation, I don't think. Because when I came out of the fever, my mind a total blank, the Hapcotts had decided that I was a fallen woman, who'd tried to take her own life. That didn't feel right to me. But they insisted it was so. And they kept on urging me, if it wasn't true, to own up to who I really was, and where I'd come from. They didn't believe I couldn't remember a thing before waking up in their home. They believed I was trying to cover up my misdeeds by telling lies. They told me that they knew I was lying because the people who'd pulled me from the water had said I'd mentioned coming from a place called Epping.'

'But you couldn't have done. I mean because you don't come from Epping. That must have been,' he said, looking extremely upset, 'when you were calling for me, mustn't it, when you were in a fever? But…did nobody think of making a connection to me, and getting in touch?'

She felt sorry for him. She did, truly, even though she still felt hurt and angry about the effect his actions, or lack of them, had had on her. And it was all she could do to bite back the tart retort that it was no use blaming everyone else for not trying to find him, when he'd done all he could to hush up the fact she'd gone missing at all.

'Blanchetts,' she pointed out, as kindly as she could, all things considered, 'was only one of your lesser properties, wasn't it? You hardly ever went there. You didn't have much to do with the folk of whatever town it was the canal went through.' She couldn't recall its name. Perhaps she'd never heard it.

'But anyway,' she continued, pushing aside that particular gap in either her knowledge, or her memory, for the irrelevance it was, 'they had it fixed in their heads that I had been speaking of a place, to those canal people. I don't know how they got that idea. Much of that part of things is still a bit…fuzzy. But then I did have a fever, and the woman kept giving me this stuff to drink, to take away the pain, and the fever.' And to this day, she'd resisted delving too long into that particular, nightmarish set of memories. It was too hard. Even when they flared up, unbidden, she preferred to push them away. 'And speaking of pain, do you think you could let go of my fingers? You are crushing them.'

'Forgive me,' he said, not letting go, but raising them to his lips and kissing them, again, before replacing her hands on his lap. 'I won't squeeze so hard. I promise.'

'Hmm.' How different he seemed, today. When they'd first been married, he'd seemed so aloof. So proud, and distant.

But then she'd learned since then how afraid he was of getting hurt again, the way he'd been hurt in his first marriage. That he did have emotions. And feelings. So many that he had to suppress them, for fear of what might happen if he gave them free rein.

So she squeezed his hands, and gave him a chance to prove that he could be gentle with her, no matter how worked up he might be feeling, by letting him keep holding hers.

'The Hapcotts,' she said, taking up the thread as near as she could to where she'd dropped it, 'got pretty cross with me when I kept on saying that so far as I knew, I'd never been to Epping. And they got that preacher, Mr Pendle, to agree to take me there, as it was not far from where he was going to take up a new post. They believed that once they got me there, I would no longer be able to keep up the pretence I'd lost my memory, that I'd give myself away somehow, by being able to find my way round, or...or that some-one who knew me was bound to be able to identify me, and expose my sins for what they were. I didn't bother arguing about it, because, so far as I knew, a trip to a place called Epping would be no worse than sitting about listening to people accusing me of all sorts of things I had no recollection of having done.

'I even wondered if they might be right. And if Epping was a clue, then it would be a good thing to follow it up, and find out who I was. Because, I have to tell you, not knowing a thing about oneself is extremely...' She shook her head, words failing her.

'It must be,' he said. 'I cannot begin to imagine it.'

'But I was wrong,' she said with a shudder. 'It was *much* worse. The Hapcotts, you see, were genuinely kindly souls, and only really exhorted me to repent because I think they truly cared about the state of my eternal soul. But that preacher—' she paused as she remembered the zealous, almost fevered look he sometimes had in his eyes '—well, he was so sure I was a fallen woman, that I wouldn't have put it past him to call me Jezebel to my face. Sometimes I wasn't sure how he stopped himself doing so. But, you know, the more he went on about what a terrible person I was, the crosser I got. Because I was *not* lying about not having any memory of who I was. After a bit I started wondering if it was the Hapcotts who had been lying about me. I mean, how did they know what sins I'd committed before they met me? Or even if I had committed any? And I was so sick of him preaching, and refusing to believe a word I said, that by the time we reached Epping I was ready to push him off his horse into the nearest pond.

'Oh,' she said, sitting up straight and gazing straight ahead. 'Saying all that, out loud, has just made me realize that Perdita hadn't been entirely Jack's invention after all. He'd only given her a name. Perdita had been steadily emerging all the way to Epping. I had a lot of time to think, you see, while Mr Pendle rode on ahead, studying his Bible, thinking he was punishing me by refusing to speak unless I repented of sins I was growing steadily more certain I hadn't committed. Steadily more sure that I wasn't the person people kept telling me I was. I didn't know who I was, or rather, who I had been, but I simply couldn't believe that I would throw myself into a canal, out of desperation. There was always, I'd been sure, some practical method of dealing with any problem. And trying to drown oneself in a busy waterway was the very opposite of practical. If I ever *had* been desperate enough to wish to kill myself, which I hadn't been able to imagine, or scarcely bear to think about, I was sure I would have come up with a far more practical, reliable way of doing it.'

She turned back to Anthony, who was watching her with that same wary, yet determined expression on his face.

'Well, anyway,' she said, pulling herself back to the more important task of finally telling Anthony about how she'd met Jack, 'as soon as we reached the town, we saw it was market day. And he went all poker-faced about the amount of beer people had clearly been consuming, and started ranting about the evils of carousing in the streets, and decided to climb up onto the market cross and preach them all a hellfire sermon. Not that many people took much notice, because, on the other side of the square, Chloe

was singing a comic song, and Jack was doing acro-
batics and Toby was copying him, the way he does,
which was so funny…and I felt as if I hadn't laughed
in such a long time,' she sighed. 'And I couldn't help
going over to get a better look.'

She felt Anthony's fingers tense up over hers. She
knew how he felt about actors, now, but at last she
had the chance to explain to him how very much he
owed them. Jack in particular.

'I'm not sure how long I stood there watching
them, but eventually I noticed a sort of…brawl going
on over on the other side of the square. Some of the
people in the market day crowd had clearly taken
exception to Mr Pendle's sermon, and had started
throwing stuff at him. Rotten fruit that had been
accidentally underfoot to begin with, so I believe.
But Mr Pendle, far from turning the other cheek,
began throwing things back. And so the crowd re-
taliated with cabbages, and even, eventually, tankards of beer. Finally, somebody tried to drag him
down from the thing he'd been standing on, and it
turned out that Mr Pendle could have made a living as a prizefighter. I heard people laying wagers
on who would win, those trying to drag him off his
pulpit, or him. Of course, he was outnumbered, so
the outcome was inevitable. Except that there was a
sort of marshal whose job it was to keep the peace
on market days, and he decided that the entire brawl
was Mr Pendle's fault, and hauled him off to jail. I
would wager he never reported *that* to the Hapcotts,
or admitted that was the reason he lost sight of me,
did he?' She didn't bother to wait for Anthony's an-

swer. It had only been a rhetorical question. 'Oh,' she said, smiling as she recalled the look of outrage on the preacher's face as he was dragged away, still throwing punches in all directions. 'That was the absolute best moment of my life.'

Anthony stirred. Frowned.

'You look,' she said rather tartly, 'as if you are thinking that was not a very tactful thing to say. That I should feel as if the time you proposed was the best moment of my life, or perhaps when you slid your ring onto my finger.'

'Well...'

'Yes, but I didn't remember any of that, did I? All I'd known was the Hapcotts, and the road with the preacher.'

'Yes.' He subsided at once. 'Stupid of me to feel offended...'

'And typically self-centred,' she couldn't help saying, rather irritably. 'Honestly, Anthony...'

'I know, I know,' he said, kneading at her knuckles. 'I am trying...'

'Yes, you are,' she conceded. 'And I can see how hard this all is for you. But honestly, it would be much better for you if you could just sit still and listen. Without interrupting. So I can get it all out in the open, in my own way, as quickly as possible.'

'Like lancing a boil?'

'If that is the way you choose to think of it,' she said, exasperated by the way he still kept expecting the worst, 'then yes.'

Chapter Nineteen

Anthony found it hard to credit that she could speak to him in that tone.

But then hadn't he already noted the contrast between her behaviour before, when she'd been too shy to raise her head in company, compared to the woman she'd become since she'd had to fend for herself, out there in the world, without him on hand to protect her? She'd felt it, too, though, hadn't she? Wasn't that what she'd meant about feeling as if she was two distinct people?

'I will try to just listen,' he vowed. 'Though you cannot expect me not to *feel* anything, when I hear what you went through. When I cannot help knowing that much of it was my own stupid fault. My pride…'

He wanted to hang his head. Or walk out of the room so that he wouldn't have to see the anger and hurt that kept flashing from her eyes whenever she related some particularly unpleasant experience.

But he owed her the courtesy of facing her scorn.

Her contempt. Her anger. If they were ever to restore even a fraction of what they'd once had together, he had to take it all on the chin.

She lifted hers. Then gave him a wry smile.

'Well, thank you for saying you will *try* to keep a still tongue in your head. That cannot be easy for a man who is used to everyone treating everything he says as pearls of wisdom.'

People did do that, he realized. He always said that he despised toad-eaters, but was he so used to people being deferential that he took it as his due?

'You don't pull your punches, do you?'

'Not anymore. And what,' she added, with a very pointed look, 'happened to trying not to keep interrupting me?'

He was about to argue that he hadn't been interrupting, only responding to her observation. But then she might argue that doing so was almost as bad.

So, then, he'd just tell her that from now on, he really would not say another word.

Except, that would mean saying several more. So he just pulled his lips tightly shut, and waited for her to continue.

She looked at him.

He said nothing.

She kept on looking.

So he maintained what he hoped was a dignified silence.

And to his relief, he saw the ghost of a smile play about her lips.

'Hmm,' she eventually said. 'Right, where was I?' She looked up at the ceiling as if trying to locate something. Then at him, as though waiting for a prompt.

He was about to remind her about the preacher being carted off to prison, when he noticed the challenging look in her eyes.

She was testing him.

Testing his resolve to keep his word.

A phrase sprang to mind, one that came from the Bible, about he who was faithful in little was also faithful in much. And though she was only, apparently, testing him to see if he could stick to his word about not interrupting her, he couldn't help feeling that if he didn't prove to her that he could be faithful about this one little thing, she would never find it easy to trust him with more important things, in future.

And he did need to prove that she would be able to trust him, from now on. That he was determined not to make the same mistakes again.

So he pressed his lips even more tightly shut, and waited for her to speak.

'Ah, yes,' she said. 'I'd just told you how I felt about watching Pendle being dragged away, hadn't I?' Could he detect a gleam of admiration in her eyes when he stayed resolutely silent, even when she'd been trying to tempt him into speaking?

Or was he clutching at straws?

'Well, the crowd was starting to disperse,' she continued. 'It was growing dark by then. And I was wondering what on earth I was going to do that night. Mr Pendle had, obviously, been the one to arrange our board on the road, usually with sober, earnest families of the Methodist persuasion.'

He was glad she'd stayed with families of that sort. They may be beneath him, socially, and so far as he knew he'd never had much to do with any of them, but they had a reputation for being decent, in their own unconventional way. And at least she hadn't travelled with someone who'd exposed her to the indignities of wayside inns.

'And I had no money in my pocket,' she continued. 'I was just starting to feel a bit anxious, when this lady came up to me. Very motherly, she looked, if rather gaudily attired. And she told me that she'd noticed I was alone, and wondered if she could help me. And that was the moment when Jack sauntered over, and told her, rather rudely I thought, that I was most definitely not alone. That I was a member of his band of actors. While I was trying to puzzle out why this stranger should be claiming I worked for him, the woman...' She frowned, and gave her head a little shake. 'Well, I don't know how to describe it, but it was as if she...changed. All of a sudden she no longer looked motherly, but, well, downright vulgar. It was the way she scoffed at Jack,' she mused, as though working it out in her own head, as much as telling him about it. 'The way she demanded to know why I'd been standing there watching, in that case, rather than performing. The way she declared that she knew an actress when she saw one, and I *wasn't*.'

A fond smile played about her lips, for a second. 'Quick as a flash,' she said, in an admiring tone, 'Jack said that was because I was the one who had trained the dog and stood in the crowd to give him the signals to perform his tricks.'

He supposed she wanted him to be as impressed by the fellow's quick wits as she'd evidently been. Never had he been so glad he'd promised to say nothing.

'Well, you can imagine,' she continued, apparently unaware of the resentment that flared up every time she mentioned that man's name, 'how confused I was by all this. For days everyone had been treating me as though I was a thorn in their side. Then, all of a sudden, two lots of strangers were arguing over me like stray dogs over a bone. And then, while Jack and the motherly, yet vulgar woman were going at it hammer and tongs, Chloe sidled up to me, and told me that unless I wanted to end up working as a prostitute, I'd better agree with Jack that the dog was mine. And somehow, the dog was sitting at my feet, looking up at me as though waiting for a command. And before I'd even decided to throw in my lot with the actors, the woman I'd mistakenly thought was motherly stalked off in apparent high dudgeon.'

His blood ran cold. The woman had been an abbess? He couldn't bear to imagine what would have happened if that Jack person hadn't intervened.

The shock must have shown on his face, because Mary nodded.

'Yes, that's it. I must have looked like a…pigeon for the plucking,' she said, darting him a look as though wondering if he'd object to her using the kind of cant she could only have picked up from those travelling actors.

'Jack told me,' she continued, 'once he'd seen her off, that he'd seen women like her loitering round coaching yards, on the lookout for innocent maids fresh up from the country, many a time. And never done anything about it before. Only, that there was something about me that made him decide he could not just stand back any longer.'

He just bet there was. It was all he could do to refrain from curling his hands into fists. Or saying something pithy about the fellow's motives.

Only, he'd *promised* her...

'It was the way he described me as innocent, that made me...disposed to like him, I think, as much as his attempt to rescue me. Because he was the first person I'd met who spoke of me the way I felt...inside.' She pressed one hand to her heart. He hoped to God she was only referring to her certainty she'd been innocent, rather than indicating her heart had become involved, at that first meeting.

'And Chloe—' she smiled in a rueful sort of way '—well, she tried to stand up for me, too. But against Jack, if you can believe it!'

Yes, he could. If the Chloe woman was in any kind of relationship with the actor, then naturally she would try to keep rivals at bay.

'She warned me to watch out, because he was planning to take advantage of me, every bit as much as the abbess would have done.'

There! It was just as he'd feared!

'The troupe,' she carried on, blithely unaware of what torments she was putting him through, 'were one actress short since someone called Pippa had just gone back to the apothecary who'd been her childhood sweetheart. And she warned me that Jack would be hoping that I could replace her.'

As an actress. Just as an actress, he said to himself, in a vain attempt at consoling himself against the worst that he could so easily imagine.

'Jack retorted that he wasn't a charity, and that of course I'd have to work to earn my keep. But defended himself by saying that he thought I looked as if I needed a job. Then he said that if he'd been mistaken, and if I didn't need rescuing, and if I'd prefer not to take to the stage, then I was welcome to tell him to, er, go away. Only of course,' she added, her cheeks flushing, 'he didn't use such polite terms.'

He supposed he ought to be grateful that she hadn't fallen into the habit of using all the impolite terms she must have heard from that fellow.

And he *was* grateful to him for keeping her out of that abbess's clutches, to be honest.

His poor Mary. He couldn't bear to think of her being…abused in that way. Or at the *risk* of being abused.

Why in heaven's name hadn't *he* been there to rescue her?

'Jack also said I ought not to take any notice of Chloe's warnings, because they stemmed largely from fear that I might turn out to be better than her, and she hated anyone trying to upstage her. Then, and only then, did he ask me what my story was. And, do you know,' she said, her eyes shining, 'when I told him what had happened, well, all that I could remember, up to that point, he just—' she shrugged

'—accepted it. And so did Chloe. And Fenella. Oh, Fenella, I should explain,' she added, 'is the girl I shared a room with when we came to London. I didn't get on with her particularly well, to be honest, but Chloe insisted on having a room to herself. But anyway...'

He could scarcely believe she'd tossed in that most significant piece of information as though it was a mere trifle. Had she no idea how...relieved he must be, to learn that she'd shared a room with another female, rather than that Jack, who she seemed to idolize?

He watched her, as she carried on with her tale, without showing the slightest inkling that she'd just revealed something so momentous.

She really was, at heart, he marvelled, still remarkably innocent.

He could have caught her up in his arms and...

But no. He needed to let her tell him *everything* she considered significant. He'd *promised* he would.

'And Jack said,' she was saying, 'that there was no better occupation for me, than to be an actor, because it didn't matter that I didn't know who I was, because actors spend all their time pretending to be different people depending on what play they are performing anyway. That I could be whoever I wanted to pretend to be. And he solved the problem of me not knowing even so much as my own name, by suggesting I take the name Perdita, as my stage name. Because it means lost. And I had looked lost.

'And then Chloe said her name hadn't been Chloe when she'd first taken to the stage, and that Jack's real surname wasn't Nimble, either. And all of a sudden, I felt…at home with them. Because they were willing to accept me as I was. They didn't disapprove of me, on principle,' she said, with a trace of bitterness. 'Didn't treat me as though I was a nuisance. Instead, they encouraged me to…find out who I was. Who I am.' She leaned forward, an intent expression on her face.

'Do you understand what I mean? Can you understand how…novel it was, for the people round me to let me be…me? Even though I didn't know who… *me* was supposed to be?'

He could see that in his own way, Jack had been kind to Mary. Which didn't alter his firm belief that Jack was a rude, vulgar fellow.

She leaned back, looking exasperated. 'Oh, it must sound so…strange, and foolish to you. From the moment of your birth you've had a secure station in life. A position to uphold. But, now that I remember *all* my life, I can appreciate the gift that Jack and Chloe and the rest of them gave me, even more. Before…even before I met you, I had spent all my life trying to earn my place. Trying to please everyone round me, so that I could have a home, and food. And nothing was secure. Lady Marchmont could have dismissed me at any moment. At any moment I could have become homeless, and penniless. It was like…living on the verge of a precipice, overlooking a chasm of want, the whole time. I had to…shut my eyes to the dizzying drop, pretend it wasn't there, or I would not have been able to sleep at night. For years, and years…ever since I was a child, I had known that I could lose everything I thought I had, in the blink of an eye.'

She paused, a thoughtful expression on her face. 'I wonder if that was why I managed, so success-fully, to slam the door shut on my bad memories? Because I had been doing something of the sort for most of my life…'

She sat there, looking lost in thought, for some time.

And he could not remain silent any longer.

'Mary,' he said, gently. 'I know I said I would not interrupt, but…when do you think you might be ready to answer a few questions?'

The dreamy look faded from her eyes. She was back in the room with him again, he could see.

'What,' she said, a little uneasily, he thought, 'would you like to know?'

He swallowed. So many things. Only they were what *he* wanted to know. And that was not going to be good enough, not today. He needed to ask her what she wanted to tell him.

'What happened next?'

She blinked, in apparent confusion.

'After,' he explained, 'you met Jack and Chloe, and decided to have a go at becoming an actress.'

'Oh,' she said with a smile. 'Oh, *that*. Yes, well, as it turned out, I was hopeless at it. And it wasn't just because I am naturally shy, and don't like peo-ple staring at me. That much, Mary and Perdita both share,' she said, as though she was two different people.

'Also, there is a sort of…awareness,' she said,

'that actors have, of where they need to be on a stage, in relation to everyone else, which I simply don't have. So that although Jack gave me every opportunity to appear in his productions, I was an unmitigated disaster. Which, ironically, meant that I gained great favour with Chloe.'

'Did you,' he asked, deciding it was time to grasp the nettle, 'try to act in many productions?'

'A fair few,' she said, twisting her lips into a grimace of disgust. And then she looked at him. And seemed to understand his concern. 'You need not worry that anyone who knows you will ever recognize me as having performed in the market square of Brentwood, or Copdock, or anywhere of the sort. Because right from the start, as I said before, Chloe flatly refused to let me do anything that might take attention away from her. I was always covered in the most unflattering masks or costumes they had with them. But mostly, they stuck me inside the goose costume. Well, you saw what Jack made of it, at the theatre the other night. I must have sidled into the scene looking as though I wished I was anywhere but there. And, because it was very hard to see out of the eye holes, and because I had no sense of where I was, I was always bumping into people, and knocking over props, or tripping over things. At first, I used to feel mortified at how…awful I was. But do you know what? Jack didn't mind a bit. Because the audience, every single audience, thought I was hilarious. The clumsier I was, the more they laughed. Which was why he decided to bring the clumsy goose to London, and make her a feature of the pantomime.'

She gave him a challenging look. 'I daresay you don't like the notion of your wife becoming a figure of fun.'

'Only a few days ago,' he admitted, 'I would have hated it, yes. But when I consider all the things you went through, all the perils you faced, I can only be grateful that you were earning your keep in a manner that, if not completely respectable, was at least not downright dangerous. That Jack and his associates kept you from having to sell your body, just to stay alive.'

'And that I did so in such a way that nobody will ever know what I did, too, I suspect,' she said shrewdly.

'Yes. That was fortunate,' he admitted. 'But,' he added, 'even if you had been obliged to…even if that woman, or someone like her had…' He swallowed as his stomach churned at the mere thought of what Mary might have had to do.

'I don't think, actually, that you would have coped with that,' she said, rather coldly. 'You were angry enough with me, when I first came back, as it was. Before you even knew…' She broke off, biting down at her lower lip.

'I would have tried to, though. Because, even when I was at my most furious, even when I suspected you had played me false, I never stopped wanting you. The night you came home, I had walked back from that meeting, planning all the things I was going to say, how utterly I was going to cut you down to size, before throwing you back out onto the street, but then I saw you, naked in that bath, and instantly I was… on fire for you. The words I'd planned, the steps I

was going to take, they all flew out of the window
before the hurricane of…lust that almost knocked
me to my knees.'

She looked down at their hands, fingers intertwined, on her lap. Darted him a look. Blushed.

'You looked like the living embodiment of a thunderstorm when you strode into my room,' she said.
'So angry. Speaking such unjust words. And yet, all
I could think was how handsome you were. What a
beautiful mouth you had. How I had kissed those
lips…'

She reached up with one hand and ran one finger
along the seam of his mouth.

He'd promised he wouldn't interrupt her by speaking.

And he'd pretty much kept to that, until she'd
asked him what he wanted to know.

But this, the way she was touching him, was more
than flesh and blood could stand.

'Mary,' he grated. 'Unless you are willing that I
take you, right now, right here on this sofa, again,
you are going to have to stop doing that.'

Chapter Twenty

'Again?'

She couldn't believe he was suggesting such a thing. Or warning her it was possible, anyway. Once, in the drawing room, had been surprising enough. But if he went on like this it would almost become commonplace.

'Much as I would enjoy, er...' She felt her cheeks heating. No matter how far she'd come since Mary had tumbled into that canal, it seemed that she hadn't gone away altogether. She still couldn't bring herself to use the words she knew referred to the act which Anthony was suggesting they share, on this very sofa. Even though she'd learned an awful lot of ways to speak of it, thanks to her time on the road, and hanging round the theatres of London.

'The thing is,' she said, regretfully ceasing her study of his mouth, and pulling her finger away from his lips, 'that although it would be...wonderful...'

'Would it?' His voice sounded as though he really,

really needed to know. 'I mean, just now, it was all over before it had begun. And I wasn't sure…'

'It was wonderful,' she reassured him. 'But, as you yourself pointed out, it doesn't always solve everything, does it?'

He sighed. 'Yes. I did say that, didn't I?' He looked as though he wished he hadn't, though.

'And, well, the thing is, there are still a couple of things I need to…well, confess, I suppose, before we…'

He drew in a short, sharp breath, as though she'd punched him.

'Confess? Are you afraid I'm going to be very angry?' His face worked as though he was striving to control his expression. 'I promise, I will stay in control. Although…'

'So long as you don't march straight out and shoot Jack, I shall be happy.'

'I won't shoot Jack, no matter what you have to confess about him,' he said manfully. And then added, with a wry twist to his mouth, 'I only shoot members of my own family.'

She couldn't help admiring him for making a jest, at a moment like this, in order to put her mind at rest, when his own was clearly in some turmoil.

'Well, it isn't anything very bad, really,' she hastily reassured him. 'At least…' She felt herself worrying at her lower lip. 'The thing is, I soon found out that actors are rather like…children in some ways. Or at least, all the ones I've met have been. In that they love to dress up and play out a part. And it seems to me that the more talented they are, the more they care about their craft, as they call it, the less grip they have on practical things. Like paying the bills. And making sure that there is food on the table, and coals for the fire. Even on the road, I soon realized that if I didn't keep a firm hold on the takings, they'd be likely to fritter it on things like, oh, rounds of drink in the taverns, or bolts of pretty material that would probably come in handy for costumes, even though not for a specific part they had in mind to play. And before long, they began to let me deal with all of what they called the tedious business of staying in credit, rather than just skipping a town when they'd run up debts all over the place they couldn't pay. They scoffed at what they called my strait-laced ways. Yet they came to rely on me.

'When we reached London, and we took lodgings for the winter season, Jack, er, asked me to marry him.'

She darted him a look to see how he would take that news.

'I can hardly blame him,' he said, rather stiffly. 'After all, *I* asked you to marry me, didn't I? The fellow clearly has good taste.'

He was annoyed, she could tell. And manfully keeping a lid on his annoyance.

'Yes, well, of course I didn't accept him. I never felt…that way about him, for one thing,' she said, 'no matter how kind he'd been, and how much I felt I owed him. But I didn't want to tell him that. He might have been hurt. So I just said that I ought not, in case it turned out that I had a husband already.'

She hung her head, afraid of what she might see

in his eyes. 'I didn't ever flirt with him, I promise you. Nor did I encourage him. Or at least, I never intended to. The first time he asked me to marry him, it took me totally by surprise. I mean, he was the one who insisted that when we found lodgings, it must be on two different floors. At the top, was rooms for the girls, as he called us. And below, the boys and Toby.' She flicked him a glance. And then, because she'd vowed to tell him everything, so that he would never think she'd tried to hide even the most trivial thing, she added, 'Oh, except Chloe, who took the poky little room at the front, on his landing, over the parlour which had the only fireplace in the building.'

Anthony was frowning. She braced herself for recriminations.

'Did he ever attempt to kiss you? Did he, at any time, tell you that he loved you?'

'No.'

'Does that not strike you as odd?'

'I am not sure what you mean. *You* never tried to kiss me before you proposed. And you never said you loved me, even after we were married.'

'That was remiss of me,' he said, bitterly. 'Had I done so, you would have felt more secure. You might have coped better. All this might never have happened.'

He got up, suddenly, and paced away from her. Then turned back, looking rather fierce.

'I did love you, Mary. So much that it scared me. I began to fear you might have the power to make a fool of me, the way Sarah had done. And I…'

It was as if the scales fell from her eyes.

'You panicked!' she said. After all, he'd said as much. 'That is why you left me at Blanchetts. You ran away from what you thought was a dangerous woman!'

'No. It was *not* panic,' he retorted hotly. 'At least...' He shifted from one foot to the other.

'Very well, let us refer to it as a tactical withdrawal,' she said, deciding not to make him feel worse about his errors than he already did. Because it wasn't going to do any good, in the long run, to touch on what she was coming to discover was a very sensitive form of pride. And anyway, she rather liked the idea that he'd found her dangerous. It was in such contrast to the way she'd felt about herself. As if she was the weak, dependent one. And he was the one who had all the power.

'And as for that Jack fellow,' he continued, placing his hands on his hips and glaring down on her. 'From what you told me it sounds as if he was trying to keep you on, in his life, in any way he could. He could tell you had no love for theatricals, the way he did. But he was coming to rely on your common sense. I would wager it would have saved him a packet if he could have married you, rather than paying you a wage. He did pay you a wage, I take it?'

'Oh. Yes, he did,' she said, as a few things suddenly fell into place. 'Oh, what a rogue he is,' she said, with a fond smile. 'And there was I, trying not to hurt his feelings, when all the time...'

She shot Anthony a glance. 'How come you got the measure of him, after seeing him for only five minutes, when I didn't see through him after living so closely with him for months?'

He looked thoughtful. And then shrugged. 'I don't know. At one time, I thought I was a keen judge of character. My belief in that part of my abilities died away, almost entirely, after the fiasco with Sarah. Yet I only had to take one look at Jack, to know what he was. Well,' he said, with a frown, 'at least I thought I did. But what you have told me since, has made me alter my opinion of him, somewhat.'

'Oh, no, you are quite right about him. He *is* a rogue. And a chancer. Though he could also be very kind. And understanding of one's faults and failings.'

'Do you know something,' he said, rather irritably. 'I am heartily sick of talking about Jack. I am grateful to him, of course, but do you think we could now talk about *us*?'

'I beg your pardon,' she said meekly, as he sat down beside her on the sofa again.

'Have you,' he said, taking hold of her hands again, 'told me everything you feel you need to tell me?'

'Yes, I think so. Except...' She lifted her chin and looked at him squarely. 'Well, I know you don't approve of actors and the like. But I want to continue supporting my friends, if you are going to allow me to stay with you in London. And I want to be able to go and watch more of their performances. You see, Jack has this notion of doing something slightly different at every performance, so the audience won't grow bored. What we saw was just one of the routines he thought up for the goose, but he has plenty more. In one, which is absolutely charming, he pretends to leave Toby on the stage after an altercation between the goose and the stage manager, and Toby decides to join the ballet. He mimics all the movements of the dancers in a most comical fashion...'

He wasn't looking the slightest bit interested in what had been her whole life, until a few days ago.

'What is the matter? I thought you wanted to talk about our future? I'd thought you might want to know of my plans and hopes, but clearly...'

'Yes, you are right. I should be interested in your, er, outside interests.' He sat there, looking across the room in the direction of the window, but she was pretty sure it wasn't the window he was seeing, not really. At length, he looked back at her, again.

'Most society ladies have hobbies. Interests, as you call them. Some of them love horses. Some devote themselves to becoming leaders of fashion. I see no reason why you might not become known for your love of the theatre. Although,' he said and paused, briefly, 'you will need to take care that the fact you spent some time acting, for a living, remains a secret.'

'I know that, Anthony. I'm not an idiot.'

'Yes, but have you considered...? I beg your pardon, I know you say they are your friends, but is it at all possible that they may take advantage of your... situation?'

'I am quite sure,' she said tartly, 'that they will take as much advantage of my peculiar circumstance as possible. But I am also sure,' she added, 'that they are sensible enough to know not to bite the hands that they hope will feed them. And also that you are wealthy enough to afford them. They certainly won't cost you as much as a carriage and horses.'

'I can see what Jack meant,' he responded, drily, 'about you being exceedingly practical.'

'Well, I've always had to be, haven't I? I've always had to earn my keep. Oh, I didn't mean when I married you. I thought that was going to be an escape from drudgery. But...'

'Are you saying that life with me was dreary? Hard work?'

'No. Oh, no. It was...' She struggled to find the right words. 'It was that I never felt I measured up. That I wasn't good enough. That I didn't *belong* with you, somehow.'

'I bear much of the blame for that, myself,' he said grimly. 'I should have taken greater pains to make you feel you did belong, and that you were good enough, rather than worrying about getting hurt myself. I wasn't much of a husband, was I?'

'Anthony,' she protested. 'You are talking as if we are no longer married. But you are still my husband. And, since I've returned from my wanderings in the wilderness, you have been...'

'Suspicious. Angry. Insensitive. Jealous.'

'Well, yes,' she admitted. 'But you have also set about laying your suspicions to rest, by looking for the truth. And you were only angry because you thought I'd played you false. And after what you have told me about Sarah, it is hardly surprising, is it? And, yes, you have been insensitive at times but now you are trying to see my point of view. And as for the jealousy…well, when it came to Jack, you did have reason, I suppose. If my memory hadn't returned, I might have considered marrying him.'

He flinched.

'I would never have loved him, the way I loved you, though,' she added wistfully. 'He might have come to my rescue, but I never thought of him as my hero, the way I did you.'

'Loved,' he said. 'You say you loved me. In the past tense. Don't you…' He broke off, looking troubled.

'You spoke of the way you *had* loved me, too, just now,' she reminded him. 'And, to be honest, we have also spoken of the fact that we are no longer the same people as we were at the start of summer. You have had to learn some salutary lessons about your addiction to pride, and so forth. And I have walked in the shoes of another woman. And I am not at all sure that the woman I was will ever allow Mary to take up the reins of my life again. Her life.' She shook her head as confusion sprang up, the way it so often did when she tried to work out who she was, now. 'I am also,' she confessed, 'rather worried that I must sound rather odd, talking about myself as if I am two separate people, living in one body.'

'No. It is not strange at all. Well, actually, yes, it is, rather,' he added with a rueful grimace. 'Except for the fact that I can see how you might feel that way. But you know,' he said earnestly, 'when you didn't know your name, or anything about your past, it sounds to me as though you just let your deepest nature take over. And in your depths, you are a bit shy, very practical, honest, trustworthy, and loyal. That hasn't changed. And although circumstances and hardship made you fear speaking your mind in days gone by, now you no longer fear saying exactly what you think. In fact Perdita sounds to me like a grown-up, more confident version of Mary.'

'Is that a good thing, though, Anthony? You liked the way I was, all timid, and adoring, didn't you?'

He looked thoughtful. 'I did adore my shy, rather puritanical wife. I felt that she was a safe woman to marry. A wife I could, one day, hopefully, start to trust. When you could barely cope with me undressing you fully, in the bedroom, with just one candle flickering away in the corner...' He glanced at the sofa, with a rather wicked gleam in his eye. 'You would have fainted dead away at the thought of making love during the hours of daylight. So... I have to say that there are definite advantages to your newfound confidence. I like the way you go after what you want, with such determination.'

'Oh.' She felt her cheeks heat. And it was a bit of a struggle to continue. But she had to. 'Still, it was the thought that I might worship at your feet that made you want to marry me, wasn't it?'

'You make me sound like a coxcomb!' He let go of her hands, then.

She grabbed hold of them again.

'You were wounded. Unsure of yourself. You needed to feel that in your second marriage, you would be in complete control. I understand all that,' she insisted. 'But what worries me is that you might not like the way I keep losing my temper. And shouting at you. That isn't being meek and adoring, is it?'

'Didn't I just touch upon that? Didn't I say how it was circumstances and hardship that made you fear speaking your mind in days gone by, but that now you no longer fear saying exactly what you think? Isn't that a step forward?'

'Is it?' She considered what he'd said. 'You know, I *do* remember getting cross about things, and having to...rein in my temper because I didn't dare let it off the leash. And people did keep telling me I was useless and a burden so often that I believed that was all I was. But when I forgot about all that...'

'Precisely! And in future, nobody will tell you that you are worthless, or a burden, so your confidence will continue to increase.'

'But you cannot possibly want to live with a woman who is always shouting at you,' she pointed out. 'Getting cross over the slightest little thing...'

'You don't get cross over the slightest little thing, though, do you? Believe me, I know the difference between the behaviour of a wife who is permanently irritable, and one who only loses her temper when her idiot husband fully deserves a dressing-down.'

Then he sighed. 'To be honest, I find it hard to see how you are ever going to be able to forgive me for the appalling way I've treated you. And get back to what we had. You are generous, and have been very understanding and sympathetic, and we have discovered that it is easy enough to rekindle the passion we once shared, but...'

'But what?' She felt a flare of icy cold panic clutch

at her insides. 'Are you worried about what it might be like to take on a woman who loses her temper at the slightest provocation? And who isn't…well, normal. I mean people don't usually forget who they are, do they? Or invent new personalities for themselves? Or act as though they are one person in certain situations, and someone else in another?'

He made a sort of snorting noise. 'Well, I do! You just said as much. I put on a…front, so that nobody can see the real me, cowering behind my ramparts!'

'You don't *cower*…'

'And as for being normal,' he said, with a curl to his lip, 'who is qualified to say what that is? I mean, take the Dowager Lady Benbury, for example. She lets a troop of monkeys dressed in scarlet jackets roam freely throughout her house. Or Lady Duckshot, who dresses like a man, swears like a trooper, and drinks like a fish. When you go to visit either of them, you just have to accept that is the way they are. Everyone just says they are eccentric.'

'Yes…' she said hesitantly, understanding that people could get away with bizarre behaviour if they were wealthy enough and of high enough rank. 'But would you want to live with one of them?'

'It would be a nightmare,' he said emphatically. 'But didn't you hear me saying that the very worst that I might expect from you is that from time to time you might call me to account if I step out of line? Which would no doubt do me good. Or you might become a little…lost. Unsure of who you are. But from what you've told me, both Perdita and Mary are women I can embrace wholeheartedly. Perdita is a little more bold than Mary,' he said, flicking a glance in the direction of the sofa. 'But she is basically loyal, and kind, and pure of heart. Just like Mary. But look,' he said, squeezing her hands a bit harder for a moment. 'If you ever did have another lapse of memory, and forgot your name, or your way home, you can be damned sure that next time I will chase after you and drag you back by the hair, which was what I wanted to do last time, but talked myself out of doing, because I was too proud to risk making a spectacle of myself.'

Ooh… She rather liked the sound of that. Not literal dragging by the hair, of course. Anthony would never do anything that might hurt her, physically. It was hearing him wanting her so desperately that touched her, deep inside, where she'd never felt as though she had any real value.

'And when I brought you back,' he continued, staunchly, 'I would remind you, every day, that you are my wife. The woman I love, no matter what your name is. That I will keep you safe, even though you have no idea who I am.'

Something inside her melted.

'Oh, Anthony,' she sighed. 'I don't know how I could forget you. Why, I only had to take one look at you, this time, to be certain that I belonged to you. Even though you were shouting, when I looked at your mouth, as I told you, I knew you had kissed me with it…'

'Yes. I felt that, too! The same stirring of attraction that I felt for you the first time I saw you. It was overwhelming. I couldn't fight it this time any more than I could that first time you slammed into me and knocked all the breath from my lungs.'

He gazed at her with all the longing she could feel stirring within her own heart. For a few moments she was convinced he was going to kiss her again. Push her down among the cushions and renew their union in the most symbolic way that any two people could demonstrate that they were one flesh.

But then, abruptly, he pulled back.

'I don't want to go back to the way things were.'

'What?'

'I want to start again. And get it *right* this time. I want us to get to know each other in a way we never did before. With you just being yourself, whoever you happen to feel like at any given moment. And with me…stepping out from behind my defensive walls and just being…myself, too. Whoever that is.' He gave a short bark of laughter. 'To be honest, I'm not even sure who that is. I've spent so long acting a part…'

'You?'

'Yes, me.' He gave her a long, searching look. And then he surged to his feet, pulling her up to a standing position, too.

Then he let go of her hands, went over to the door, turned, and made her a courtly bow.

'Good day,' he said. 'Allow me to introduce myself. I am Anthony Radcliffe. A widower. A lonely widower, in search of a woman with whom I can share the rest of my life. I am really hoping that woman will be you.'

'Oh,' she said, seeing what he was doing. He was

acting out the scenario of them meeting for the first time. Acting! When he'd made no secret of the way he felt about the profession.

He was doing it for her. Laying his pride aside. Showing how far he was prepared to humble himself. Why, even in the way he'd introduced himself he'd said nothing of his title, or the gilding which she'd once told him she despised. He'd introduced himself as the man beneath all that. The lonely, bruised soul who was looking for someone who would love him as he was.

Just as he'd promised to love her exactly as she was.

Her heart leaped for joy. She made a curtesy in response to his bow.

'It is a pleasure to meet you, Anthony,' she said. And then paused, wondering how to introduce herself. She was no longer Mary, the timid, poverty-stricken orphan who was afraid of her own shadow. But could she claim to be Perdita? The woman with no past, who'd discovered through trial and error that she couldn't act, but was a dab hand at keeping the dibs in tune. She had been both. But now...now she was neither of those women, not completely. They had merged, somehow, when this man had persuaded her that he loved them both.

They had formed a new, whole person. The woman he'd married. His Countess.

'I am,' she said, feeling suddenly reborn as the beloved wife of this broken, valiant, adorable man, 'the Countess of Epping.'

'Are you,' he said softly, his eyes brimming with tears, 'sure?'

'More sure,' she said, walking across the room to him, 'than I have ever been, of anything, in my life. In either of my lives,' she said, with determination.

They moved together in unison, so that neither of them would be able to tell, later, which had been the one to start kissing the other. Nor did she have to push him in the direction of the sofa this time, either. They made for it together, as though they were of one mind.

And, as they tumbled back down among the cushions, she knew, beyond all doubt, that she really would *never* be able to regard this sofa as merely a piece of furniture, ever again.

Epilogue

One year later...

As the vicar splashed icy cold water over the crown of his head, the Honourable James Percival Radcliffe let out a lusty protest.

Anthony shot his wife a glance which she understood as a plea to do something to restore the peace and happiness of their precious son. He couldn't bear to see the boy crying. Mary, on the other hand, felt as if she would never grow tired of hearing him exercising what was a prodigiously healthy set of lungs. She had been anxious all through her second pregnancy, fearing it might end in tragedy, after the trauma she'd experienced during her first, but the sound of his first cry as he'd made his way into the world had made her heart leap for joy.

Silently thanking God for the miracle that she'd borne a son healthy enough to set the rafters ringing, she reached across the font, took little James from the arms of the vicar, draped him over her shoulder, and rocked him.

'Thank God for that,' muttered Benjamin, her brother-in-law, and godfather to his nephew, as soon as the bawls of outrage turned to whimpers of protest. 'I was beginning to think that getting me here to listen to all that racket was part of some devilish plot to ruin the hearing of the one good ear I have left.'

Mary flinched. It was hard to look at the ragged remains of Benjamin's left ear, and not recall that it was her husband who had caused the injury. Though to claim that he couldn't hear out of that side was decidedly untrue. The damage was all external, and minor, in spite of what Anthony had told her about it bleeding so much.

But Anthony, to her surprise, was grinning at his youngest brother. Mary wondered if she'd ever grow accustomed to the way the three Radcliffe brothers treated each other. It had shocked her when the first thing Benjamin had done, on arriving at Radley Court for Christmas, had been to march straight up to Anthony and punch him. She'd been terrified that what she'd hoped would be a wonderful reunion would end up being the beginning of a second feud. She'd turned to the Dowager Countess of Epping, who had been sitting calmly sipping a glass of mulled wine, and begged her to do something.

'They are never happier than when fighting,' she'd explained with what Mary had thought was a shocking lack of motherly concern. 'They used to roll about like puppies in the stable yard, snarling and kicking, and came in with jackets torn, covered in mud and bruises.' She sighed as though recalling fond memories.

And then, as though to confirm it, Anthony had flung his arms round Benjamin, and they'd hugged each other fiercely.

'You see?' The Dowager Countess had smiled knowingly. 'Anthony wouldn't have believed Benjamin had really forgiven him if he'd been all polite and formal. A good scrap is the only way to show that normal relations have resumed.'

That scene had at least had the benefit of making it easier for her to cope when Marcus had arrived, late on Christmas Eve, long after they'd given up hope that he would also accept the olive branch Anthony had extended, and punched him, too.

Mary still couldn't understand it, but she'd had to believe it when Anthony had declared that he'd never enjoyed a Christmas more, even though he'd sported a black eye and a swollen jaw for a week. It really had looked as though the brothers had restored peace and harmony with each other by calling her husband a buffoon and a bonehead, and knocking him down.

And they'd gone much further than that, in the months since, to prove their loyalty to him. Anthony had taken them into his confidence, over the matter of Franklin's murder, and what he'd discovered about the gang who'd waylaid her at the bridge.

'There is nobody better,' he'd told her, after he'd done so, 'to help me bring those villains to justice, than my brothers. I cannot,' he'd said, taking her hands between his, 'let them get away scot-free. But nor could I bear for you to have to stand up in court and tell strangers what they did to you.'

It had been too late for her to make any objections. By the time Anthony had told her about it, Marcus and Benjamin had already set out in pursuit of the criminals.

She eyed Marcus warily over the top of her infant son's head. He unnerved her far more than the ragged-eared and therefore rather villainous-looking Benjamin. Because he so rarely said anything at all. His habit was to just stand there, glaring indiscriminately round the room. Benjamin had quipped that it was his stern front that made him such a success in the army, because all his subordinates were far more afraid of him than of the enemy. Marcus had just shrugged, and replied that since he had the Radcliffe eyebrows, he might as well make the best use of them.

He'd unnerved her even more when he had drawn her to one side, not long after arriving for the christening of her wonderful, healthy, vocal son, and informed her that he'd dispensed justice on behalf of young Franklin.

'None of those men,' he'd added, darkly, 'will trouble innocent travellers, ever again.'

He hadn't told her how he'd found them, or what he'd done, but she suspected that it was something very final.

'Franklin,' he'd added, confirming her suspicions, 'has been avenged.'

Poor Franklin. Poor, brave, heroic boy. He'd given his life to save her. She still couldn't think of him without tears coming to her eyes. If he hadn't happened to be walking down that particular path, when she was seeking some air, if he hadn't been trying to impress her by showing her that he was trusted to take that little cart out whenever he wished...

'Tears, sweetheart?' Anthony came up to her and put his arm round her shoulder. Even though they were still in the chapel, and surrounded by so many well-wishers, and various family members. 'Thinking of our first little miracle baby?'

'Oh, no.' Although she did, often. She didn't suppose she would ever completely forget the loss of her first baby. 'I was thinking about Franklin.'

Anthony kissed her cheek, then the crown of their son's head.

'I have been thinking about him recently, as well,' he said. 'And I was wondering how you'd feel about doing something more than just putting up that memorial for him, at the bridge.'

'What were you thinking of?'

'Well, you know how he didn't have any family. How he grew up in various institutions.'

'Yes.' The investigator, Baxter, had tried to find out if there was any family to whom Anthony could offer compensation, and had instead uncovered a tragic history of poverty and hardship. A tale that had made her heart bleed for him all over again, when she heard it, though sadly a tale that was all too common. But knowing what the boy had gone through, before ending up working in the stables at Blanchetts, she was amazed that he'd become such a thoughtful and brave young man.

'I was wondering,' Anthony continued as they began to make their way down the aisle, 'how you would feel about setting up some kind of foundling home, in his name. Or perhaps a school for older foundlings, to teach them a trade.'

'Could you afford to do both?'

He smiled at her. 'I could certainly become a sponsor for such a charitable institution. Without people asking too many questions that might make you uncomfortable.'

He could. Since returning to his life, she'd discovered a lot about Anthony that she hadn't known before. That he was well known for acts of philanthropy, for example. All those meetings that he'd had to go to, which she'd thought were just some dreary, lordly business, had been of far more importance than she could have guessed. Important to the poor and needy of the land, at any rate.

She beamed up at him. Life couldn't get any better than this, could it? She had a wonderful husband, who adored her so much that he no longer thought twice about showing his affection for her in public. Brothers-in-law she could trust with her life, and her secrets. Godfathers for her son who would not permit anyone or anything to stand in the way of his progress.

What more could she want?

For herself, nothing.

But for little James Percival, perhaps a couple of brothers like the ones Anthony had. Ones who'd be loyal enough to warn him should he make the mistake of marrying a woman who wasn't worthy of

him. Who'd scour the length and breadth of the land
to avenge the sister-in-law they credited with reunit-
ing the whole family. And who'd knock him into the
mud should he get too full of himself!

* * * * *

*If you enjoyed this story,
why not check out one of
Annie Burrows's other great reads?*

His Accidental Countess
A Scandal at Midnight
How to Catch a Viscount
"Invitation to a Wedding"
in Regency Christmas Parties
Wooing His Convenient Wife